Murder

COMES TO THE

Vineyard

THE FOURTH
Snoopypuss
MYSTERY

Georgann Prochaska

outskirts
press

Murder Comes To The Vineyard
The Fourth Snoopypuss Mystery
All Rights Reserved.
Copyright © 2018 Georgann Prochaska
v3.0

Cover Photo © 2018 thinkstockphotos.com. All rights reserved - used with permission.

Outskirts Press, Inc.
http://www.outskirtspress.com

Paperback ISBN: 978-1-4787-9852-1
Hardback ISBN: 978-1-4787-9913-9

Library of Congress Control Number: 2018903964

Outskirts Press and the "OP" logo are trademarks belonging to Outskirts Press, Inc.

PRINTED IN THE UNITED STATES OF AMERICA

For Pat Moffitt
Handler, Owner, Trainer of Bloodhounds
And Sadie, who touched my heart

List of Characters

Residents from the Midwest
  Alice Tricklebank and Audrey, the bloodhound
  Lena Vincenti and Julian Mueller, Alice's best friends

Residents of the Mitten area, California
  Guthrie Musgrave Huff, married O'Dare Huff
  Cade Huff, son
  Eleanora Whipkey Huff, Guthrie's mother-in-law
  Officers Marci Breakiron, McNally, Garcia
  Detective Joshua Galati
  Elka, house manager
  Jess and Drew Okazaki, Henry and Juliana, Alice's family
  Roddy Merritt, lawyer
  Nimble Cipriani, vineyard manager
  Rayne Musgrave
  Xavier Nettle
  Sunny
  Steve from the Hungry Fool
  Gaius Eyestone and his son Austin

Chapter 1

Time: Monday, May 19, 2014, 1:58 a.m.

"Firecracker? Cherry bomb?"

Alice Tricklebank awoke in the dark to the uncertainty of hearing gunfire. Her heart hammered as she looked at her bloodhound Audrey. The black-and-tan dog stood up at the foot of the bed with a low rumble in her throat and stared at the door of the vineyard cottage as if any minute someone would enter.

"You heard it too?" whispered Alice. She checked her watch.

Without turning on a light, she struggled to pull on sweatpants and shirt over her pajamas and tripped over her shoes. At least the dog's backpack was an easy find. She fumbled, retrieving her phone and weapon-size flashlight. Carefully, she harnessed Audrey who wiggled like mad to explore.

"Hold still. This isn't our fenced backyard. No way I'm letting you run free if someone has a gun."

Seeing her owner open the door, Audrey jolted Alice forward.

Outside the cottage, Alice scoped the dark stillness of the yard and sky before taking measured steps toward the main house. The dry, cool California air of May carried the fragrance of roses planted at the end of rows of grapes.

Three rapid, additional shots blasted from inside the main house.

Startled, Alice stopped and listened for any movement. Her hands trembled.

"Audrey, is someone out there?" asked Alice in a hushed voice. "Are we in danger?" A low rumbly growl came from her dog. "Shhh, have to be quiet."

The bloodhound moved to a spot off the gravel foot path and squatted for a quick pee near a cement saucer filled with flowers.

"Seriously?"

Even though she was six feet tall, Alice was also in her sixties, unarmed except for her flashlight, and with a dog more prone to slobbering on new people than attacking bad guys. Alice knew both she and her dog were easy targets for someone with a big, nasty gun, but she couldn't let snooping slide. Friends described her as inquisitive. Acquaintances chuckled at her full-throated prying. But in a crisis, the residents of her hometown—Limekiln—welcomed her problem-solving meddling.

Slowly, she walked up the path in the dark with Audrey and weighed what her next move should be if she stumbled onto a prowler. With each step, gravel crunched underfoot. On full alert, Alice listened for any rustle or scrape near them.

Again, she held her dog back and eyed the outbuildings set apart from the main house, utilitarian buildings built with barn wood and rusted roofing. Was there any movement there? Near the hunched Quonset-like structure? Did someone slip behind a tree? Audrey's nose twitched, and she stared into the dark but showed no desire to explore. The dog's head turned toward the house.

Tall trees crowded near flower beds and crackled softly in the dark, evening breeze. Otherwise, shadows held the night still. Too still?

For a moment, Alice felt foolish. What if the gunfire had been only warning shots? Perhaps meant to prevent a mountain lion from coming onto the vineyard property? Maybe the danger was no danger at all, some poor animal taking a shortcut in search of food or water.

All the lamps seemed to be on in the house, but the blinds and curtains were drawn, blocking Alice's ability to see activity inside. Twenty feet from the porch, Alice heard a car speed away, down the long, snaking driveway to the road. She flicked on the flashlight and increased their pace.

Alice couldn't help but feel murder had followed her to California when all she wanted was to see her grandson graduate from high school.

"Well girl, what do you smell?"

She and Audrey walked up the three wooden steps to the porch that encircled the house and into a small, yellow pool of light provided by one lonely outdoor bulb the size of a Christmas tree light. As in her Midwest hometown, the backdoor into the house was unlocked. Alice felt a chill and took a deep breath.

"Guthrie?" called Alice from the kitchen doorway. "Is everything all right?"

The house stood silent except for the ticking of a clock. Audrey's nose twitched in the air at some lingering scent. After a moment, Alice also picked up the pungent odor of gun powder.

"Guthrie? It's Alice. Are you okay? I heard a loud noise?"

The previous night Guthrie had welcomed Alice to her vineyard home for dinner on the porch off the kitchen and allowed her to stay with her dog in the guest cottage near rows of young grapes. Guthrie was a yoga friend of Alice's daughter Jess—the guest cottage the only place Jess could find to accommodate Alice and the muscular, one-hundred-pound, slobbery bloodhound.

Alice stood with a lump in her throat and tremors in her knees as she looked at the inside of the house for the first time. The kitchen was big enough for a restaurant. A pair of swinging doors led to the rest of the house. Alice pushed one door open—slowly—with dread.

"Guthrie?"

With a series of baritone barks, Audrey shot forward dragging

Alice to a parlor near the front door. There was Guthrie's body lying on her back, her head twisted to the side, blood covering her torso.

"Oh, dear," whispered Alice. "No, no, no—"

Swallowing hard and biting her lip, Alice looped the dog leash onto the front door handle to prevent her bloodhound from disturbing the scene of a crime. She knelt next to Guthrie and carefully put her trembling fingers on Guthrie's neck. No pulse. She fought tears and grabbed Audrey's leash. Still dark outside, Alice flicked a nearby switch, and all the outdoor lights came on. She took her dog out the front door to call 911. Somehow, she managed to stammer out the tragedy.

Together Alice and Audrey sat on the porch glider to wait for the police. Alice pushed on the hound's hips to convince her to settle, but Audrey's nose still twitched, sniffing the air. The bloodhound was restless, wiggling free of Alice's arms and jumping to the floor.

It's the blood, thought Alice. *She's caught up with the smell of Guthrie's blood in the house.*

"Quiet, girl. I know you want to go back to investigate." Alice used her sweatshirt sleeve to wipe Audrey's mouth of a cord of slobber. "We are all washable."

She rubbed her thigh with the heel of her hand to keep tears at bay, but her knee continued to dance with fright. Her thoughts tumbled. Should she go back to sit with Guthrie?

"No," said Alice pulling her hound close. "Who knows what the police may think? Please sit with me. You can't go back inside. Not a good idea to be with the body or to have you contaminate the crime scene."

Audrey insisted they leave the porch. As she muscled against the leash and harness, wrinkles bunched up around her jowls.

"Come on. I need you quiet," said Alice. "Do you have to go? Right now? You made a pitstop moments ago."

This ratty behavior wasn't like her hound at all, but then in the past there had been a time or two when fresh blood made Audrey rambunctious. A wrestling match followed with Alice trying to contain Audrey on the porch, the dog wanting to explore the yard. Alice feared how the police might react to seeing a stranger flee around the side of the house as they pulled up. She concluded Audrey needed to wait. The hound's paw struck down her left arm as she attempted to hold the dog back, but Alice was ready and grabbed the harness with her right hand.

"I'm onto you," said Alice. "Just give me a couple more minutes. Please."

Audrey snorted, clearly frustrated with being confined.

"Well, we're involved in a murder again," said Alice, hoping conversation would act to calm her hound. "This time we're on our own. Our friends Lena and Julian left yesterday for Silicon Valley, and we don't know the local police here in Mitten. I can't rely on Jess to help. She's mildly okay with our searches but hates it when we get involved in a murder. Although I don't know what she was thinking when she accepted Guthrie's offer."

At dinner Guthrie had explained why she needed Alice. Her twenty-year-old son was missing. After hiring a private investigator who found no evidence of Cade on social media, Guthrie's thoughts turned dark. Perhaps her son hadn't run off as her husband, O'Dare, claimed. Her fear, loneliness, and depression concocted an ugly story of murder. On the last night Guthrie saw her son, Cade and O'Dare had screamed venom at each other and continued the argument outside. Guthrie listened at the window as the yelling moved into the distance.

"Am I losing my mind to think O'Dare killed our son?" Guthrie had asked Alice. "With all the vineyard acreage, a body could be buried without anyone knowing."

In their conversation after a yoga class, Guthrie had listened to Jess tell of her mother's escapades with Audrey—once finding the graves of missing boys. Guthrie wrote to Alice and offered the guest cottage for her visit to California, for as long as she wanted—*if* Alice agreed to walk the vineyard with her dog and maybe find Cade's grave.

The colorful, pulsing lights of an ambulance and two police cars twisted up the long vineyard driveway.

"Audrey, what are the chances that a son disappears, and months later his mother is shot dead?"

As the cars stopped and the bloodhound tried to wrench her way off the porch, Alice said, "Here we go . . . again."

Two police officers and two paramedics left their vehicles and approached the house. Alice started talking using her fire-drill, teacher voice, hoping her volume didn't crack.

"I called 911. I'm Alice Tricklebank. No one else is here, but I haven't been upstairs. The body of Guthrie Huff is through the door and to the left in the parlor. My dog is a bloodhound and not an attack dog."

With that said by her owner, Audrey gave a determined lunge, not with her usual interest in crotches but wanting to be off the porch. She headed for grass.

"I think my dog has to pee," called Alice, a little embarrassed as she watched her dog tap dance in front of her before thrashing wildly toward the side of the house.

But, Alice noted her dog's nose wasn't on the ground searching for a relief spot. Audrey's attention was in the air as she bellowed a baritone woof. Dread again hit Alice. She flicked on the flashlight.

Without time for introductions, the two officers went into active crime scene mode. The male officer, his gun in hand, ordered, "Wait! I'll take the house."

The paramedics stood aside to allow the officer to enter the front door.

"I got her," said the female officer. One hand held a gun; the other turned on a bright flashlight that looked to Alice like a fountain pen.

"This behavior isn't for a squat-down," said Alice over her shoulder to the officer. "I was mistaken."

The policewoman waved the light well ahead of them, focusing on another set of stairs leading to the wrap-around porch.

Although Alice tried to restrain Audrey, the hound bounded toward the stairs. Her face and nose swept across a step. As Alice pulled her back, she and the policewoman saw red on the steps and on the dog's muzzle.

"Looks like blood," said the policewoman.

Alice pulled a tissue from her pocket and wiped Audrey's face before the dog's tongue could lick away evidence. When Audrey looked up at her with an agitated expression in her eyes, Alice held the tissue in front of her dog's nose and gave the command, "Find!"

Audrey bolted toward the rows of grapevines, nose still in the air.

Someone's close, concluded Alice, aware that Audrey's nose didn't have to go to the ground to pick up the scent of sweat or skin cells. The scent of blood was in the air.

About seventy feet down a row of grapes, the dog's bark demanded attention. Both flashlights panned up to reveal a man's body. Alice pulled her dog back to let the officer move forward.

"Who's this?" demanded the officer. "I thought you said no one else was in the house."

"Don't know. Never saw anyone else." Alice's words staggered out. "Last night Guthrie didn't say she expected anyone. Is . . . is he badly hurt?"

Foolish. Foolish woman, thought Alice looking at the neck wound. *Of course, he's hurt.*

The officer didn't answer Alice but patted the body for identification. Her search was futile. His pockets, empty.

"McNally?" called the officer to her partner, holding what Alice knew was a miniature walkie-talkie.

Before the female officer continued, McNally said, "We've got additional blood splatter in another room."

"And we got another body out here," said the policewoman. "Dressed in black. No ID. No weapon."

Audrey turned and placed her paws on Alice's shoulders, awaiting her customary hug for mission complete. Alice felt cold as a tremble of fear shook her body. Not knowing how to help the police, Alice walked Audrey back to the porch stairs and sat. The dog's face nuzzled forward, jowl to owner's cheek. Grateful her sweats had pockets, Alice reached for more tissues to wipe away wetness.

"Yes, you're a good girl," whispered Alice into her dog's ear. "We're officially tangled in an investigation, so you'll have to wait for a reward. Not every one of my pockets holds your special dog treats. Murders always come as a surprise."

Chapter 2

Time: Monday, 2:17 a.m.

Efficiency spread out as two more police cars raced to a stop in the driveway, and red and blue lights flashed emergency. One of the new officers moved into the vineyard to stand over the body outside, releasing the female officer to hustle Alice and the bloodhound back to their cottage. One officer trailed behind. The investigation continued in the main house with Officer McNally and the paramedics.

Before Alice entered the cottage, the male officer pushed past them into the dwelling. He turned the lights on and came out with a nod.

"Looks okay. Why were your lights off?"

"We were asleep when we heard shots," said Alice. I didn't want to draw the shooter's attention to the cottage. We're maybe sixty feet from the kitchen door."

"Smart."

"I'm Breakiron," said the female officer at last, keeping Alice outside. "This is Officer Garcia. We'd like you to wait in the cottage until we're ready for questions. You said your name is Alice Tricklebank?"

Alice nodded and pointed to her dog. "And Audrey."

The officer gave her a tolerant smile that signaled the additional information wasn't useful. In the flashlight shadows, an authoritative look crossed Breakiron's face as she moved to stand directly in front of Alice. She was short, sturdy, and maybe thirty-five. Her face was round and sunburned, her dark hair wound into a bun at the back of her head, cheekbones, prominent.

"Officer Garcia will stay outside . . . to keep you safe," said Breakiron. But Alice knew the police regarded her as an unknown and questioned her role in the murders.

"Thanks," said Alice. She had been involved in police investigations back home in Limekiln. First, the police officers at the scene would gather what they knew. Second, they would determine exactly who she was and what she was doing on the property. These officers would ask for details to brief the detective assigned to the case. He'd then ask her questions. And more questions. Her dinner conversation with Guthrie the night before would all come out. Probably, they'd question Guthrie's state of mind.

Alice wondered what the police knew about Cade, the missing son.

Alice and Audrey walked into the cottage, and Garcia, his broad back turned to the door, took up his post outside. The first order of business for Alice was inspecting her dog's fur, muzzle, and paws.

"I should have listened to you when we sat on the porch," said Alice as she wiped away dirt caught in a smear of red. "You have always been smarter than I am when it comes to investigations. I guess I'm still groggy from the trip and having only three hours' sleep last night."

After a routine foot massage with Alice also wiping the webbing between each of Audrey's toes, the bloodhound jumped onto the bed and tucked her long legs under her.

Still feeling fidgety and undressed with no underclothing, Alice searched for her bra. A quick scan proved it wasn't in the usual spots.

"Did you hide my bra?" asked Alice. Audrey's head rose off the bed and fell back onto the comfy lump of bedding. "Look, I'm sorry I forgot your sock toy in the dryer." The dog paid no attention. Alice remembered the toy's surface discolored and stiff with dried slobber. "It needed to be washed."

The hound made a growly discontented sound, and Alice continued to search, finding her bra wedged behind the small couch.

"This has to go into the laundry. Are we even now?"

She forced down her desire to peek out the window every ten seconds. Instead she dressed for the long day ahead: blue jeans, gray pullover, and a sweatshirt with a logo of a steaming coffee cup. Still as she crawled back into bed, Alice felt cold and wrapped herself in the covers. A shiver came as she closed her eyes. Audrey curled next to her owner, sharing her furnace heat.

"I won't sleep," she said to her dog, "but I better get some rest. Maybe just close my eyes. You and I have a big day." The hound's breathing, punctuated by quiet snoring, became hypnotic. Alice's thinking faded into disjointed dreams.

She awoke to a knock at the door and rubbed her eyes to hide the fact she had fallen asleep after discovering two murders.

Audrey stood at the ready to collect crotch information with a good sniff, her own investigative style. Alice's caution held her dog back until the two officers settled. Breakiron entered along with Officer McNally, a tall, young police officer. Dawn was breaking in the distant rolling hills, and the rosy reds and fiery oranges sent highlights into McNally's red hair. Before she closed the door, Alice admired the colors framing the morning.

"You're Alice Tricklebank," said Officer Breakiron, not as a question but more like a time-filler. She sat on a wooden chair at the small, kitchen table and took out a notebook. Alice nodded at her question and sat across from the officer. McNally perched on the edge of an overstuffed pink chair. Apparently spotting an easy mark, Audrey stood at attention in front of him. McNally's hands automatically scratched Audrey's ears and jowls. Breakiron continued. "We need to verify information. Dispatch said you reported hearing gun shots and found the body of Guthrie Huff."

"Yes, I called 911. The first shot woke me. I wasn't sure what I'd heard, but my dog also reacted to the sound. I arrived yesterday afternoon, and I'm staying here in the cottage," said Alice trying to stick to the facts. So far, she had held it together, but her jittery kneecaps jumped and belied her control. "When I heard the first shot, I got up and layered on sweats, attached Audrey's harness, and as we opened the cottage door, I heard three more shots in the main house."

"How much time elapsed between the first shot and the next three?" asked Breakiron.

"Minutes. Only long enough for me to dress and ready Audrey." Alice's hand rose to tug at the collar of her pajamas, but she remembered she had dressed. *What's the matter with me? Where's my head?* She took a breath and said, "Maybe five minutes, but I think less."

Both officers nodded.

"As you can see, I'm older and not armed, so Audrey and I moved carefully, at first. The gravel path to the main house makes noise. I wasn't sure if someone inside could hear us walking. About half way there, I heard a car speed away. That's when we hurried into the house and found Guthrie in the parlor. I entered the house through the French doors to the kitchen. I called to Guthrie. No answer. Audrey pulled me through the swinging doors to the parlor. I obviously touched doors in the house and particularly when I looped my dog's leash around the front door handle. Felt Guthrie's neck. No pulse. We left through the front door and sat on the porch, where I called 911."

"What's your relationship to the deceased?" asked Breakiron.

"She's a friend of my daughter, Jess Okazaki." Breakiron wrote down the name. "Guthrie generously allowed us to use the cottage," continued Alice, suddenly feeling tears forming. "You see, my grandson is graduating from high school on Sunday, and Jess's house is too small for all the relatives coming to visit, not to mention a bloodhound. And the motels and hotels in the area have a size restriction on dogs of sixty-five pounds, and Audrey is a hundred. There's simply no place for us. And I so want to see my grandson graduate. He's our oldest. And has such ambitions. And I had to . . ." Alice stopped the run-away train of words.

Audrey's head turned as her throat gurgled and a paw reached for Alice's knee. Breakiron's hand covered Alice's.

"We'll need your daughter's contact information," said McNally.

"Of course."

Breakiron slid a piece of paper and pen to her.

"You said there was no one in the house." McNally's tone revealed his doubt. "Guthrie lives alone?"

"No one else was here as far as I know, but Guthrie lived with her mother-in-law, Eleanora Huff. I understand Eleanora is visiting out east," Alice quickly clarified, "not China, but Pennsylvania or New York." Alice's hand twirled in the air as if the motion were helpful. "I can't remember exactly what Guthrie told me."

"You only met Guthrie yesterday?" asked McNally.

"Yes."

Alice's kneecaps jumped again in their own little dance. Audrey leaned heavily against Alice's leg.

"The body of the man in the vineyard—who's he?" asked Breakiron.

"No idea. Guthrie and I were alone last night, and she never mentioned she expected anyone."

Looking at his phone, McNally said, "The detective's still a half hour out." He turned to Alice. "He's with the county police force. When he arrives, he'll have questions for you."

Alice nodded.

The two officers looked at each other, and the tone changed, becoming less stern.

"You said your grandson's graduating from high school?" asked Breakiron, her dark eyes taking on warmth.

"Yes." Alice welcomed changing the subject away from murder. "It was difficult traveling to California from the Midwest because Audrey and I can't fly. Audrey has issues with crates. They make her a little crazy."

"Then how'd you get here?" asked McNally as if flying were the only mode of transportation.

"I put friendship on the line," said Alice. "Two very dear friends drove us here."

The two officers received a call, nodded at Alice and left. Alice stood at the window, watching them hightail it toward the main house as a flood of uncomfortable memories returned. So generous of her best friends to volunteer transportation, but with a bloodhound, the trip soured friendship.

"We're alone in this one, Audrey. Our pals are gone. Lena always says we have a posse of friends to help with a murder case, but not this time. Just you and me, kid. No Lieutenant Unzicker. No Gary the historian. No lawyer. No Julian. No Lena. No one to watch our backs. We got nothing."

Chapter 3

"Wait 'til you hear," giggled Lena, her face full of surprise. "Julian's a genius." She grasped her hands together in front of her mouth. Lena was in her sixties, her marshmallow body, animated. Long, blonde curled hair added to her glamour. "Tell her."

Alice didn't understand the merriment.

Julian rolled his shoulders and straightened taller. He was also in his sixties, hair thin and covered with a bandana, his body stiff from years of hard work. "I got a ride for all of us to travel to California for your grandson's graduation. You don't have to leave Audrey behind."

Alice's nose tingled as she fought tears. Her main worry had been boarding Audrey with their trainer and a passel of other bloodhounds. Not that her hound didn't enjoy running, jostling, and piling together with seven bloodhounds, but she did draw the line if she didn't see Alice. After a year of being with Alice, Audrey still had severe separation anxiety. No amount of training with Jimmy curbed Audrey's heavy breathing and wild-eyed panic. The offer of taking Audrey to California was a gift worthy enough of Alice's tears.

"In Silicon Valley," said Julian, "living space is at a premium, and a guy I know has set up a sweet rental business for himself. Uses old motor homes as apartments. He needs us to transport an RV for rehab. The beast is big enough for the three of us and the big girl."

"I hope you were referring to the dog," said Lena with a naughty smirk.

"I can't thank you enough," said Alice, her voice husky with emotion. "But you know Audrey can be demanding."

"We know all about Audrey. Doesn't like crates. Doesn't like being alone," said Lena. "Alice, we can do this. It's all planned. Julian and I will drop you off at Jess's house, deliver the RV, and tour California. I've never been to Los Angeles or San Francisco." She turned to Julian, grasping his arm and resting her head against it. "Ol' Love Monkey promises to be my tour guide."

Both of her friends' eyes were bright as if they had pulled off a fast one on Alice. She swallowed her concerns. Maybe they were right. A big motor home might be just the transportation they needed.

"Well then, okay, but only if you allow me to buy your flight home," said Alice.

Lena started to protest, but Julian said, "Won't say no."

"Your offer is generous, but I'll understand if you decide to back out," said Alice.

"We can roll with anything Audrey throws at us," Julian bragged with a dismissive laugh. He was a retired truck driver who had hauled dangerous loads including livestock. "How difficult can it be to escort one bloodhound? The RV's large enough not to distress Audrey. She sleeps most of the time. Right?"

"Provided she has the right amount of exercise," warned Alice.

Nothing Alice said about the dog's demands registered with her friends. As they saw the plan, Julian would drive the bus-size RV during the day, and at night Julian and Lena would sleep in the big bed at the back. Alice and her dog had their own private space on the bunk beds in a curtained-off alcove, resembling old-fashioned train berths. If Audrey needed pitstops now and then, well so what?

"We have plenty of time," Julian said.

But Julian soon learned that driving a big rig wasn't the same as encouraging an old, belchy RV containing a very demanding dog.

Time: May, 2014

Before dawn on a Wednesday in May, Lena, Julian, Alice and Audrey loaded suitcases and Audrey's gear into the RV for the journey to California. It was in rougher shape than Julian had thought. The motor home truly needed to be gutted and refitted before any renter considered it for everyday living space. Lena hustled about, packing the kitchen with baked goodies.

"What's the weather? I packed my raincoat just in case," said Lena as she slipped a crunchy treat to the dog.

"Magpie," Julian scowled, "It's California. It doesn't rain."

The first snafu came minutes after entering the motor home. When Julian took the wheel, Audrey insisted on sitting in the bucket passenger seat. Stressed by the shape of the seat not conducive to stretching out or gazing through a window, Audrey's brow furrowed as she twisted and plopped into new positions. Before Alice could act, Lena pulled the dog away from riding shotgun.

"Honey, this is my seat," explained Alice's dear friend. "I'm the navigator, not you. You belong in the back. Look, there's a nice big couch for you."

After nudging Lena's elbow and trying to crawl into her lap, the hound wasn't happy with this whole arrangement. Plopping on the floor behind Lena, the dog bided her time in the battle for power and jumped into the seat every time Lena left it.

The second discontent came at bedtime. Sleeping on the lower bunk without Alice's foot for her pillow wasn't acceptable to the dog, and Audrey's baritone bark let them know it. First Alice squeezed into the top bunk and dangled her arm over the edge to let Audrey know she was there. Audrey licked her hand and then barked again as if demanding Alice to come down.

"Sorry." Alice called to Lena and Julian. "I guess we'll pull out the hide-a-bed."

Encouraging noises came from the two in the back room. Alice pulled, yanked, jiggled, and bumped the smelly couch, but no effort released the mattress. Julian came out in his pajamas, and together they tried to pry open the couch. It made grinding noises but didn't open.

"They'll junk this piece of garbage, for sure," he concluded as he walked back to bed.

Grabbing blankets from the bunk beds, Alice assured him the couch seat would be fine. She angled her six-foot height onto the couch by turning on her side and dangling her feet. Audrey instantly joined her owner, pushing Alice's legs off the couch to make room for a snuggle-down with butt to butt.

Half sitting, half reclining, Alice thought the problem settled until her hound wiggled, stood up on the couch, and barked a series of deep woofs.

No amount of Alice's coaxing convinced Audrey to sleep on the leather couch. The dog eyed the open accordion door to the back bedroom, lunged for the big bed, and landed on Julian.

"What the hell, Audrey?" He promptly pushed her off the bed.

Audrey barked at the bottom of the bed until Alice redirected her toward the couch. When Julian closed the door to the bedroom, locking her out, Audrey threw her shoulder at the door, causing it to rattle. Alice made attempts to pull her dog back. Muscling herself away from Alice, Audrey scratched at the door. Finally, Alice sat on the floor and secured the dog in her arms, whispering in Audrey's ear to calm her wiggling and thrashing.

"Oh, for Pete's sake," said Lena. "I can hear you talking to your dog. You can't stay up all night holding her. Julian open the *damn* door."

Julian grumbled and got out of bed. "I have to hit the head anyway. But she better not be in bed when I get back. We're not sleeping with a dog."

With Julian out of bed, Audrey ripped away from Alice's arms and pounced for Julian's place next to Lena, stretching out and claiming territory.

"Goodness! Alice, take the bed with your dog," said Lena as she threw back the covers. "Julian needs his sleep if he's going to drive tomorrow. We'll take the bunk beds for *one* night. It won't kill us."

Alice apologized for Audrey's behavior and tried to explain again about the stress of being in a new place.

Lena crawled into the lower bunk bed and complained how cramped she felt. "No wonder the dog didn't want to sleep here. It's like a small coffin."

When Julian came out to the new arrangements, he checked out the upper bunk. "No way in hell am I going up there."

"I can't," said Lena. "Unless you want to hoist me up."

"I'll take the couch," said Julian. "You're free to join me."

After one more struggle session to release the sofa bed, Lena returned to the lower bunk, and Julian buried himself in covers on the couch.

"Tomorrow will be different," called Julian.

Alice bit her cheek. With her two best friends settled, Alice knew her dog's victory would be repeated the next night and then the next until the trip ended.

In the morning, Julian complained about not making time on the road because Audrey was restless and needed one of her customary long walks. She couldn't find the right spot for a morning squat-down and interest in unfamiliar smells delayed her return to the RV. Convincing the one-hundred-pound dog to re-enter the RV became a challenge, with Alice talking sweetly to her hound while Lena gently pushed on Audrey's rear.

"She's strong," grunted Lena.

"We'll never get there," said Julian, giving Alice an evil eye and wiping his hand over his head.

They arrived at Jess's door after five days of miserable driving and long stretches of quiet grumbling.

"We're never telling anyone how long this trip took," said Julian, one eye closed, the other squinting.

"You'll be okay?" asked Lena. "Her home looks small and the houses tight."

"We can't be her guests because the other grandparents are already here, but Jess has found us a cottage with lots of room for Audrey. We'll be fine."

"And you're all set for traveling home?"

"Yes. Remember Henry's spending the summer with me. We'll all drive back in his car." Alice gritted her teeth. After difficulties in the RV, was travel in a car even possible?

"Let's go," demanded Julian.

Not even waiting to see if Jess or Alice's grandchildren were home to greet her, the couple hopped back into the RV and drove off.

Knocking at the door, Alice's gaze followed her two friends as the RV blasted away with a puff or two of nasty, black smoke coming from the exhaust.

Well, who can blame them, thought Alice. *It wasn't an easy trip from the Midwest for three adults and a self-absorbed bloodhound, in a wreck of a motor home.*

"I tried to warn them that you are a dog in need of creature comforts," said Alice feeling strangely alone. She knocked again at her daughter's door.

Eventually, Alice's grandson Henry opened the door with smiles and hugs, picked up her bags sitting on the sidewalk, and rushed everything into his small car. She barely had time to see shoes piled inside the entrance.

Alice studied Audrey's size before glancing back at the car.

"I'll take you to the car rental," said Henry, "but then I have to go to work." Henry looked shocked. "Boy, she's big."

At eighteen Henry looked every bit a man. He stood taller than Alice's six feet. He hadn't shaved for a day or two, and his brown hair fell tousled to his collar. The small scar under his right eye made him look older, his eyes serious. To Alice, he looked like someone who could move mountains. With his arm around her shoulders, he explained how his parents and Okazaki grandparents were watching his sister's performance in a play, and again apologized. He couldn't take time to visit with her. He was late for work.

"Then let's move," said Alice. "I'll drive and you sit in the back seat." Alice hustled toward the driver's side.

"Gram, I'm eighteen. I can drive. The car rental's four blocks from here."

"Here's the thing. Audrey isn't used to a back seat." Alice looked at the car, *much* smaller than her neighbor's Taurus. "It's probably not going to work to have her sit in the front seat with the two of us. So, you in back, Audrey in passenger, I drive."

Henry looked unhappy but complied. Angling his legs across the seat and clicking the seat belt in place, he said, "All your stuff pretty much takes up my trunk."

"Is this the car you planned to drive to Limekiln?" Alice felt a thread of panic.

"Yep. This is my car." Alice blinked at her grandson and knew he was aware of the impossibility of adding his suitcases to the trunk or of her driving the whole way across the country.

"We'll work something out when the time comes," said Alice, pushing the problem away.

Once in the passenger seat without her tether, Audrey smeared the front and side windows. Barked at strangers on the sidewalk. Whipped Alice with her tail. Hung over the seat to sniff Henry. Generally thrashed about. Alice felt Henry's anxiety when her dog climbed into her lap to look out the driver's window.

At last they arrived at the car rental, and Henry gave Alice a map to the small town of Mitten along with directions to Eleanora's Vineyard. He again apologized for everyone's commitments. Alice apologized for the goo left on the windows of his car.

"We expected you Friday, Gram. We'll see you tomorrow?"

"Yes, tomorrow. Very sorry. We got . . . delayed," Alice said and gave Henry one more hug. "Off you go to work. I got this. Love you."

"Love you too, Gram." His soft eyes belonged to his grandfather, Baer. Alice blinked back tears.

Into the trunk of the rental she loaded her dog's duffel bag, another bag of cleaning supplies and towels, a bag of dog food and bottled water, a backpack, and one small bag of Alice's own clothing. Using the car's GPS, guidance from her phone, and Henry's instructions, Alice welcomed the moment when traffic in rural California turned out to be slow and spare, much like that of rural Limekiln. She took a deep breath at last, feeling more at home. The surrounding vineyards were, after all, farms much like the Midwest cornfields. The landscape filled with barns and houses, corner stores, and acres of rolling vineyards. As far as she could tell, Limekiln was just flatter with rows of crops. The beauty of wine country was in the symmetry of thousands of rows of vines, rising on hills against a blue sky.

Guthrie sat on the wrap-around porch as Alice and Audrey walked up to the house. She was a tall, slender, stunning woman in her forties. Her honey-colored hair was long and curled about her shoulders. But it was her blue eyes that caught Alice's attention, full of fear. She welcomed Alice, showing her the guest cottage behind the main house. The cottage had a delicate, ruffled feminine sitting area, a table and chairs, and a bedroom with flowered wallpaper in light taupe and pink. Kitchen appliances hid behind wide closet doors. Rugs covered wood floors. Alice started to apologize for Audrey's slobber, but Guthrie held up her hand.

"My son likes things simple. *When* he gets home," Guthrie's voice cracked, "we plan to redecorate the cottage and set it up anyway he likes. If he comes home——" Guthrie hung her head and whispered, "No. I meant to say when he comes home. I'm trying to be positive. I just need to know Cade hasn't been harmed." Alice saw her clench her fist and hold it near her chest before she added with more confidence, "Your dog can't hurt anything."

Another gut and refit, thought Alice. She looked at the furniture and fabrics. Neither her son nor grandson liked girly chintz curtains. Still it seemed a shame to destroy something lovely. Alice had questions for Guthrie, but quickly shut down her buttinski-mode. She was a guest and knew details would spill out in time.

"Two weeks of peace," said Alice, once she and her dog were alone. "Just think: We can get up early and walk, visit Jess and the family when we want, and I don't have to nag you about not teasing Julian. Outside is beautiful. Weather great. And Guthrie has asked us to dinner on the porch. Her invitation asked us to do one tiny search of the vineyard. But so unlikely to find a grave here. Clear sailing for us babe. Henry's graduation ahead. What can possibly go wrong?"

Chapter 4

Time: Monday, 5:57 a.m.

A woozy Alice opened the door to Officer Breakiron and blinked at the bright light of morning. Officer Garcia nodded to her before leaving for the main house.

"Alice," said Breakiron, "Detective Galati arrived from the county police force and asked to speak with you."

"I'll have to bring my dog," said Alice with a what-can-I-do face. "She has separation anxiety."

"So you said," answered the officer. "We have briefed the detective on our conversation, and he thinks it's best if you meet outside on the porch at the back of the house. The forensic team is inside."

Alice was relieved. Outside on the porch, Audrey had a chance to show her quiet, obedient side. Inside the house, Audrey's curiosity might be snared by an enticing smell of blood.

The bloodhound moved like a kid going to a party, her paws barely skimmed the ground, her ha-ha-ha face ready to greet a new odor.

Half way to the house, Alice said, "Oh! Let me go back and grab some dog treats to keep her occupied."

"No need," said Breakiron with a cool smile. Her voice suggested a future surprise. "Elka's here." Breakiron rolled her eyes. No explanation followed for Elka's identity.

Detective Galati sat at a table on the porch, drinking coffee. He was probably in his fifties with rounded shoulders and carried a few extra pounds around his middle. His hairline receded, and he'd pulled his long, peppered hair back into a ponytail at the base of his neck. Recently, he had spent time in the sun. His face and neck almost glowed a reddish brown.

"Sit, sit," ordered Galati. "Breakiron has already told you, I'm Joshua Galati. Sit and eat breakfast with me."

Alice was taken aback. This house was a crime scene. But she sat and looked at his plate. "Thank you, but I'm not sure I can eat."

"With Elka in charge, that's not an option. The woman came in extra early to make us breakfast." Galati sipped his coffee. "Elka makes an excellent lemon ricotta pancake. You top it off with maple syrup with a squeeze of lemon, or lemon curd if you prefer, you got yourself a mouthful of heaven."

"Who's Elka?" asked Alice.

"You didn't meet Elka last night?" Galati filled his mouth with a big cutting of pancake.

"No. I'm sure no one else was here." Alice felt uneasy. Back home, she had seen how detectives sometimes conducted questioning, a ping-pong game of slipping between topics, first to comfort then trap.

"But you had dinner, yes?" asked Galati. He pointed to the blackberries with his fork and hummed.

"Yes. Guthrie and I had dinner."

"Elka leaves around two in the afternoon to pick up her children from school. She also tells me she is the house manager at Eleanora's Vineyard." Galati leaned forward as if telling a secret and lowered his voice. "Made the mistake of asking her if she was the cook." He leaned back with a grin. "When did you arrive yesterday?"

"Maybe four," answered Alice.

"There you have it," said Galati with a nod to Breakiron who then wrote in her notebook. "Do you know what a house manager does?"

"Afraid not," said Alice.

"Me either." Galati faced Breakiron. "Does she clean up?"

"Carmelita cleans and does laundry on Tuesdays and Thursdays," answered the officer.

"Ah. Thank you," he said. "Elka told us she arrives in the morning, normally at eight, to make breakfast for the Huff family, one o'clock is lunch, and she leaves a cold dinner for the evening unless the family has plans to be away. Sounds like a cook to me." Galati grinned

"I met only Guthrie last night at dinner," volunteered Alice.

"A wine-marinated tenderloin with blackberries." Galati's eyes crinkled with amusement. "Elka apparently keeps a menu for the week posted in the kitchen. Last night was tenderloin, and a frisee salad with bacon and deviled eggs. Breakiron, frisee that lacy lettuce?"

"More-or-less."

"Treated you pretty good," said Galati, his voice lowering to a level of suspicion.

Alice stuck to facts about the previous evening. She and Guthrie had dinner on the porch at seven. Yes, it was tenderloin. Guthrie poured a syrah, and after small talk, she made a request. Her son, Cade, a quiet boy of twenty, had been missing for nearly eight months.

"First we take care of dog." The interruption came from a woman in her thirties with a severe haircut, blonde including a swath of blue. She stood bolt straight with wide square shoulders, dressed in a yellow T-shirt and an overly long white apron, cropped pants visible as she turned. On her feet were heavy socks and chunky clogs. She carried a stainless-steel mixing bowl of water and a plate of something chopped. Audrey took instant interest and stood with her brow furrowed as if this lovely smell might *not* be for her. Her face went to the plate before the woman could put it down.

"What kind of meat is it? Does it have beans?" asked Alice a little fearful of what people sometimes fed dogs.

"Don't worry. Elka know dogs," said the younger woman. "Is mashed chicken, no grains. Very healthy. Tomorrow the same?"

"No reason to bother. I brought Audrey's dog food."

"Okay, tomorrow mashed chicken," said Elka.

Alice was about to protest, but she was a guest, and Audrey might relish a meal or two of chicken.

"You sit," Elka said to Breakiron although the officer was already seated at the next table. "I bring breakfast."

"I don't need breakfast. Really," said the officer. Elka raised her chin and eyebrow and gave Breakiron a stern look. "Thank you, Elka, a *small* morning snack will be lovely," conceded Breakiron.

Turning back to Alice, Elka said, "Now, I bring you breakfast, Mrs. Alice. My homemade yogurt, blackberries, and lemon pancakes." She went back into the house.

"Learned a long time ago," said Galati with a smile, "not to argue with a woman who intends to feed you."

As he finished his sentence, Elka returned with the prepared tray for Alice and another of equal portions for Breakiron. An additional pot of coffee dangled from three fingers of her right hand.

"You like my coffee?" she asked Galati. Elka's chin lifted.

Not one to be ignored by authority figures, concluded Alice. She liked the young house manager.

"Strong and hot. I like it very much." Galati grinned.

Elka's chin came down in affirmation, and she went back into the house. Alice heard Breakiron take a deep breath as if overwhelmed by pancakes.

"Officer Breakiron briefed me on your statement," said the detective. "But I like to have witnesses go over the story again because in the heat of the moment, details get lost . . . even from someone who is a detective."

At hearing him mention *detective,* Alice felt queasy. People might grant access privileges to a registered private eye, but not everyone welcomed a snoop. "Why did you say *detective?*"

"Isn't that what you are?" Galati had a smug expression, a *gotcha* face.

"No. I'm not a private detective," said Alice.

"But your dog is certified in search-and-rescue."

"No, she isn't," said Alice, puzzled by the police detective. *Where is he going with these questions?*

"Why isn't she certified?" asked Galati, sipping more coffee.

Alice knew even embarrassing truth is best told in a police investigation. "She has separation anxiety and an aversion to crates. Something happened to her as a puppy. Don't know what. She came to my back door as a stray. Never found her previous owner. Her trainer said she's good enough to work with the FBI, but I'm afraid we might be asked to go somewhere that demands we fly, and like I said, she's not good with a crate or being alone. We've never gone through certification."

"She has found people though." Galati waved for Breakiron's notebook. "An old man. Graves. A kidnapped guy." Galati looked up at Alice, waiting for an explanation. He took a bun from a basket of pastries and bit into it, turning it to show her. "Almond paste. Quite good."

Not sure how Galati knew of her past, Alice launched into her experiences.

"I live in a small Midwest town. Up to a few years ago, I was a teacher. Now I'm retired and a widow. Audrey and I train for searches, mostly to give her challenges and a routine. Sometimes we've been asked to find people, but most days we play with neighborhood kids. They hide. Audrey seeks. I don't know where you got your idea I'm a detective, but I'm not an official one. Audrey is amazing at finding people, but she has issues." Alice left off her last thought about not feeling smart enough to help her dog heal from separation anxiety.

"You called your dog amazing on your website," said Galati. His expression reminded Alice of a former student, who'd gloried in citing little-known facts to prove how smart he was. *Mrs. T., did you know in*

1900 a leading cause of death was diphtheria? Today with a smart-phone, she'd check if he were correct. Back then, she mustered a tolerant smile.

"What website?" stammered Alice.

Galati waved his hand, and Breakiron turned her tablet toward Alice to show the "Alice Tricklebank Investigates" website.

"Before we discuss the murders last night," said Galati with serious authority, "I want to know who you are, Alice."

Gone was the easy, laid-back tone.

Alice took the tablet and swiped through pictures. Many she had seen before, like the pictures of her and the female police officer when an elderly man had wandered off, or the one taken with Lena when they'd sought information about a little girl. Other photos were new to her, such as the picture of Crystal Butterman and Audrey when they'd looked for Crystal's West Highland Terrier.

Who created the website? Alice's mind raced through possible designers. Her best friend? Maybe. Next-door neighbor? Not really. The dog trainer? Maybe. But he had a website of his own. A former student? Another probably not. When she saw a picture of herself dressed as the Statue of Liberty, another possibility hit her: the Limekiln historian. She had dressed up to play the part of Lady Liberty when the historian gave a lesson on immigration to young children.

"I don't know where this came from. This site isn't mine. Who's doing it?"

"Have you never Googled yourself?" asked Galati.

"I'm not . . . I usually . . . I guess I haven't for a long time. My close friend Lena does research, and I rely on her."

Galati drew the tablet back. "Then let's review how you know Guthrie Huff." He read off the details she'd told Breakiron and McNally. "Did she really think your dog could find her son's grave in the vineyard?" His face held heavy doubt.

Alice turned to study rows of vines curling around guide wires, holding young clusters of grapes. The rolling hillside appeared to be raked into a spacious, pattern of precision. But eight months ago, the foliage of the vineyard would have been lush, heavy with fruit adding to the density of rows. Alice doubted Guthrie's story. How could a man dig a grave if he were crowded by big leaves and grapes?

"Guthrie hoped her fears were wrong."

"You told Officer Breakiron your daughter arranged for your accommodations. That right?"

"Guthrie and my daughter Jess were in the same yoga class."

"Did Guthrie give any indication last night that she felt endangered?" asked Galati.

"No. She said eight months ago her husband, O'Dare argued with his son. Both left the house, but only O'Dare came back. She worried their argument away from the house got out of hand. Two weeks later, O'Dare died." Seeing their eyebrows go up, Alice added, "Mr. Huff apparently knew he had an aneurysm and chose not to treat it. When Cade didn't return for his father's funeral, the family filed a missing person's report on her son."

"Scary stuff for a mother," said Galati. He rubbed his hand over his forehead. "But the kid was twenty. Right?"

"Still terrifying," said Alice, forcing herself to meet Galati's eyes.

"Had to be a bad scene."

Alice realized she'd twisted her napkin into knots as they spoke and stopped to take a breath before continuing. "After O'Dare passed away, his mother, Eleanora Huff, hired a private detective to search for her grandson Cade."

"Not his mother?" For the first time in the interview, he looked confused.

"I don't know. Guthrie said Eleanora hired the private eye."

"Interesting." Galati gave a signal to Breakiron that Alice couldn't interpret.

"Well, worry will cause a mother to have dark thoughts," he said, turning his attention to the rows of grapes. He closed his eyes as if enjoying the cool breeze and the warm morning sun, only to open them to the soft sound of wild turkeys making their way across the yard to the shelter of the vines. "You think it's a coincidence the son is missing, grandma's out east, the mother's murdered?"

"I never trust events as happenstance," said Alice.

"Neither do I," said Galati with a smile. "Eat. I don't want to explain to Elka why food is still on your plate."

Alice picked up a blackberry and forked a piece of thin, folded pancake. Audrey shifted her position but continued to stare at the French doors where the chicken-giver had disappeared.

Alice's fear matched her dog's alertness. *Was the nice lady coming out with more chicken?*

"Guthrie say if her husband's death was a surprise?"

"Apparently, he had been ill for a couple of years. She never described the aneurysm other than saying he had severe headaches and that influenced mood swings. He could be . . . brutal."

Galati's fingers invited something from Breakiron, who provided a brochure. He gave it a glance and pushed it toward Alice.

"My wife always envies people who go on yacht weekends. You ever been on a yacht?"

"No."

"Setting up a getaway on other people's yachts was O'Dare's business. Ever hear about it?"

"Sorry." Alice's fork was busy stabbing a berry and scooping an overly large piece of pancake. Despite the circumstances, Alice wanted to call Lena and tell her of these habit-forming ricotta pancakes with lemon.

"So yesterday, did you walk your dog in the vineyard?"

"No, not yet. I worry about Audrey's feet and any chemicals that might be used in the field."

"Feet?" asked Galati as he frowned at Audrey.

"Do they use weed killer in the vineyard? Audrey licks her paws," said Alice like a protective mother.

"Understood. I can't help you there."

"Guthrie thought walking is safe because the men are in the field most every day. She told me to talk to Nimble Cipriani. He manages the vineyard."

"Ah, another manager," said Galati.

"The Huff family only owns the land," interjected Breakiron. "The crop gets trucked out to a winemaker with a contract."

"I have to ask," said Alice, "the young man we found, could he be Guthrie's son?"

"No. According to the pictures in the house, the body isn't Cade, but we don't have identity yet."

"No identification was found on the body?"

"Makes you wonder what kind of no-good he was up to, doesn't it?" Galati's eyes narrowed, "Who visits without anything in his pockets?"

Alice shook her head.

"Now about last night, you told Breakiron you woke to a single gunshot."

Alice explained her activity after hearing the first shot and the cautious walk to the house. Breakiron sat looking at her notebook, and Alice assumed the officer was comparing her answers to the first statement.

"The three shots you heard later, were they rapid? Like from an ordinary handgun or an automatic?"

"I think a handgun, but I'm really no judge."

"But you didn't call 911. You went to the house to investigate."

"I've visited my family in California before this. I've heard stories of wild boar and mountain lions, even bear, coming onto a property looking for water or food."

"Ah, willing to take on a bear, are you?" The detective's grin wasn't friendly.

Alice didn't like Galati's tone. "I figure wild animals are more afraid of us than we are of them. Yes, I heard gunfire, but those of us from the Midwest don't like to waste someone's time with nonsense. If I had called 911, the dispatcher would have asked the nature of the call. Information I didn't have."

"You walked to the house to check it out. After all, you got a big dog."

"Audrey's not an attack dog. Not a protector like a German shepherd. We took a careful walk toward the house."

"Breakiron said you had a flashlight." Alice nodded. "See anyone outside? Hear anyone?"

It was curious he should ask. Alice thought she'd heard movement crackle outside near her side of the house, not the other side where they'd found the body. But night fills with sounds, even imaginary rustling as if someone were lurking, maybe spying.

"There was a slight wind. I'm not sure I heard anything."

"I got a list here of what you touched in the house," said Galati. His voice was back to being friendly and casual as if her answer were unimportant. "French doors into the house, swinging doors, a doorknob, front door, porch swing."

"It was a glider." Alice felt peeved. If the police detective could be picky with detail, so could she.

"Glider," said Galati as he looked at Breakiron. "Alice, you never mentioned the blood splatter against the opposite wall from where we found Guthrie."

"I never noticed it. I was concerned about her."

"You never saw the motorcycle tire iron apparently left behind in the room? What's it called, Breakiron?"

"A spoon iron, I think."

"Does it look like a car tire iron?" asked Alice.

"Has a spoon at the end, but just as hard as a car iron."

"Did the intruder strike Guthrie?" Alice's heart pounded at the thought.

"We'll know better when the lab is finished."

Alice interpreted, *No.* No bruise visible, so maybe the intruder used the weapon to threaten.

"You never toured the house? Even when you arrived the day before?"

"No. Guthrie took me to the cottage behind the house to unpack, but she returned to the main house, and I walked my dog down the road toward the town of Mitten. I didn't see Guthrie again until dinner. I wasn't invited inside."

"Huh?" Galati's brows drew closer together. He took a healthy chomp of the almond pastry and with his mouth full, said, "Breakiron will take your fingerprints unless you object."

"No objection." Alice almost told him her fingerprints were on file with the Limekiln police but decided not to confuse the detective with too much information. What line of questioning might Galati pursue if he knew even the FBI had her fingerprints on file?

"You never saw Elka?"

Alice shook her head. They had already established Elka wasn't at the house. She felt weary with not knowing what the police detective was after. Did he suspect the house manager?

"May I ask you a question?" Alice leaned toward the detective and took a deep breath. "When I saw Guthrie, her wound was . . . I'm guessing Guthrie was shot three times. If that's true, the young man was the first to be shot." Galati's eyes narrowed as he eyed her over a sip of coffee.

"So, you're *guessing* the young man was shot first, and Guthrie minutes later," said Galati.

Alice felt intruding into the investigation didn't please the detective. "It's just that her wounds had a lot of blood." Quickly she diverted to her question. "Did you find a gun?"

"No, but we're searching," said Galati. "Maybe the driver of the car you heard took it? Forensics will tell us what we're looking for . . . one weapon or two."

Elka came out of the backdoor, and Audrey rose to attention. "You not letting Mrs. Alice finish." Her hands went to her hips. "What I do with pancakes leftover?"

From behind her back, Elka produced a bone as large as a man's fist. Audrey politely accepted the treat and flopped belly down to concentrate.

Audrey's new-found love said, "Is deer bone. Good for dog. Now you?" She pointed at the detective. "Let her eat."

Galati smiled, then explained, "We got talking. Sorry."

"You talk *too* much. You say let you know when Mr. Roddy Merritt here. *You* talk inside," said Elka to Galati, tilting her head toward the house.

"Yes, ma'am."

"Who's Roddy Merritt?" asked Alice, unable to stop herself.

Before Galati could answer, Elka said, "Lawyer. Good lawyer. *Big* lawyer." She pointed her finger again at Galati as if ready to scold, then turned and walked back into the house.

"I've been told," said Galati, his forehead wrinkled. "Breakiron, the house manager is like one of those German clocks, don't you think? Where the little people go in and out?"

Breakiron kept her eyes averted.

"I'll go talk to the *big* lawyer, but I'd like you to stick around, Alice. I guess the lawyer'll tell me if you can call the cottage home for the next few days. Otherwise, it might be a good idea to call your family and let them know what's happened. I'll be calling your daughter in an hour or so. Want to talk to her about her friendship with Guthrie." He rose stiffly from the chair but continued to poke at the almond paste with his finger and swipe it across his tongue. "Too good to leave behind." He smiled in a knowing way that gave Alice a chill. "Being a free-lance *detective* yourself, you know not to get in my way? I wouldn't want to arrest you for obstructing an investigation or stalking our residents."

"I understand." Alice nodded, keeping her focus on Galati. He liked control, a conductor of the orchestra, she concluded, willing to give up a smattering of details but more than likely shielding what he knew. Alice guessed he talked to Elka when she arrived and dismissed her as a suspect. But something he said put the house manager's nose out of joint.

"You and I will talk again when your daughter arrives. Probably tomorrow," said the detective.

Jess! How was she to explain two murders to her daughter who hated every minute Alice was out searching with Audrey. Alice gritted her teeth. The detective wanted to talk to Jess, involve her in a murder case. But, she reminded herself, it was logical. Jess was a friend to Guthrie. Enough of a friend to listen to and trust Jess's stories of Alice and offer housing to both owner and bloodhound.

What to do? Where would she stay if evicted from the cottage? Audrey wasn't exactly spoiled, but her fears were real. Jess's three-bedroom house was smaller than Lena's, her children's beds, too narrow to accommodate both Alice and her dog. The RV bed fiasco flashed through Alice's mind. No way could she ask Jess or Drew to give up their bed to a dog. And there were the other grandparents from Hawaii, unpacked at the house. Hotels and motels were a possibility, but many had limits on the size of dog they'd accept. Lena and Julian were handing the RV over to a new owner. Where was she to go with a big, slobbery bloodhound?

"My dog will need her long, morning walk," said Alice to the detective as he approached the French doors of the house. "I need to leave the property."

"Breakiron will join you on the walk," said Galati, motioning with his hand for the officer to finish eating and follow. "After all, Alice, you're our only witness." He paused at the doors. "I meant to tell you. I called Limekiln. Your Lieutenant Unzicker, understanding guy, didn't sound surprised when I told him about you discovering the murders. He said I can trust you even if you are a pain-in-the-ass. Said to say, *Hi*."

Chapter 5

Postponing the fingerprinting until Audrey had her customary long walk, Alice and her dog left the main house with Officer Breakiron. She hoped for a chance to collect her thoughts of what to say to Jess, who saw herself as a shield against the world but turned prickly when a loved one's life became complicated. In Jess's mind, a mother who finds dead bodies is in danger and in need of a good talking to.

At first Audrey's face looked worried as she glanced back at the cottage where Alice stowed her deer bone.

Breakiron reminded Alice that she was their only witness and trailed behind owner and dog as they walked down the narrow two-lane road toward the town of Mitten.

"Why are you taking a backpack?" asked Breakiron.

"Habit, caution, and clean up. Audrey's a big eater so———"

"Got it."

"Galati called Limekiln and checked me out with Lieutenant Unzicker?" asked Alice as Audrey sniffed the side of the road. Alice knew her dog's walk would be particularly long. Without sidewalks, the grading sloped sharply toward the ditch. The bloodhound looked disappointed as Alice held her back from exploring the depth.

"Galati's thorough," said Breakiron, "but doesn't always want people to know that right off. Didn't mention your lieutenant at first because he likes to take the measure of people."

"How am I doing?"

"He's working on your brand. The detective website threw him. It's not squaring with the details you shared about who you are."

"Ah."

"Might help if you name the keeper of the website."

Alice nodded. "Wish I could. I just hope the keeper thinks he or she is helping me, not giving me a shot to the knees. Have you lived in Mitten long?"

"Over nine years or so. We moved here when my oldest son was a baby. You have children besides your daughter?"

"A son. He and his wife own a bed-and-breakfast in Vermont," said Alice. "If you need to be off to do something, this walk may take my girl here a little while. Mitten looks like a safe town."

"Says the woman who found two dead bodies this morning," Breakiron raised an eyebrow and gave a sly grin. "No, I'm on duty to get you back to the vineyard cottage. Preferably in one piece. Then I can go home. It's been a long night."

"As vineyard's go, is Eleanora's a large one?"

"I'm guessing it's maybe forty acres. Makes it smaller than most. Why?"

"Just curious," said Alice.

The countryside outside of Mitten was lovely with vineyards covering rolling hills, mostly in full sun, and houses nestled down in the middle of tall shade trees. After a mile walk with no results from Audrey, Breakiron asked, "Did you go into Mitten yesterday when you took a walk?"

"No. Just to the edge," said Alice. "Many tourists drove into town on Sunday. I didn't want to rattle Audrey with the commotion."

"Cute town, but you're right. Weekends are busy. Traffic heavy."

The houses on the outskirts of town had front yards with groomed orange or walnut trees. It seemed to Alice people landscaped every inch of California with food. Warm air carried the perfume of flowers and rosemary. But Alice licked her lips with the dryness in the air, and Audrey sneezed after inhaling the roadside.

The three walked down a steep incline toward the town. Vineyards gave way to small colorful houses clustered together. A few houses had large cowbells labeled with address numbers, hanging at their front doors.

"This is the first time I've seen bells as address markers."

"Not authentic bells," said Breakiron. "Downtown Mitten is written up in tourist books for its German architecture. I'm told Main Street looks like the town of Mittenwald in Germany. Don't know. I've never been." She shook her head and directed Alice to look ahead at the town of colors. Three-story buildings in yellow or pink had the same dark green shutters on all the windows. The blue buildings didn't have shutters, but below their sparkly windows, hung flower boxes with colorful blooms.

"It's charming," said Alice as she and Audrey stopped. "Officer, what's your first name? I don't think you ever said."

"Marci. The guys on the force tend to tease me and call me *Mercy*." Breakiron grasped her hands together as if begging. "They don't mean anything by it. You get the picture?"

"I do," said Alice.

"I'm currently the only woman on the force," said Breakiron, her voice expressing weariness. "Lots of teasing."

They walked to a beer garden in the center of town. Breakiron invited Alice to sit at one of the outdoor tables.

"The restaurant's not open yet, but no one will mind if Audrey's here. Residents of Mitten like dogs. I swear the beer garden was built for dog walkers." Breakiron cleared her throat. "We're a small town, and I see a woman who might have questions about the incident at the vineyard. News travels fast."

"The same is true of my hometown," said Alice. "Mitten's colorful. I find myself smiling despite everything that's happened."

Audrey's head turned, and her tail wagged. An older woman approached. Her hair was covered with a scarf tied in back, and she wore baggy blue shorts with a flowing top under a navy cardigan. She pushed a stroller.

"Got Brenda's daughter today," said the woman who immediately fussed with the child's light blanket.

Alice and Breakiron talked to the child who continued to play with her giraffe and ignored them. Audrey's nose went to the child's bare feet, and the girl pulled her toes away. The dog's tongue, however, made the child giggle and her feet to dance with tickles.

"Say, I heard about Guthrie Huff. Do you know who did it?" asked the woman.

"Not yet, Mrs. Rotolo. Detective Galati from the county is on the case."

"Oh, he's good," responded the woman, and her shoulders relaxed. "I've been on the lookout for Sunny. Do you think someone should do a wellness check on her. I worry this will frighten her. If you see her, please tell her I have packages of hand wipes."

"I will. And don't worry about Sunny's safety. The detective will sort things out."

Alice was about to comment on the number of dogs she saw walking through town, when a man with an apron and broom threw two big doors open and exited the beer hall. "Marci, you bringin' your family to the Knack and Kraut Friday night?" His hand shielded his eyes against the bright sun before he began to sweep.

"Sure thing, Mitchell. Band gonna be there?"

"You know it." He continued his sweeping and stopped only to water flowers in the window boxes. The windows looked old world with wavy glass. With the doors open, Alice glanced inside. Wide cedar planks covered the floor. Orange covered the upper half of the walls. Dark green, the bottom half. A rhythmic squeak came from the ceiling fan.

"Years ago," said Breakiron, "German immigrants came to California from Pennsylvania. That's why we have so much German architecture." She took a moment to look up and down the street, and Alice followed her gaze. "We still have German families in the area, but you're more likely to see a Mexican or Italian restaurant in a building with German murals painted on the exterior. Our population is now quite a collection—from Thai to Norwegian. Of course, German-quaint brings in tourists, and wine production provides most of the jobs."

Life-size murals were everywhere, mostly of men and women drinking beer from steins. Alice remembered a woman back home who painted flowers on the side of her house. Perhaps her behavior wasn't so odd after all.

Unable to keep her curiosity buried, Alice asked, "Who's Sunny."

In a quiet voice Breakiron said, "She's a homeless woman who started one of Mitten's quirky traditions. If you lose anything, check the nonfiction department in the library."

"Library?"

"Before I joined the force, Sunny found a bicycle and was afraid to turn it over to the police. She's very smart, but careful to keep in the shadows and away from trouble. Anyway, she took it to Mrs. Rotolo at the library. Her reasoning was that the bicycle is real and nonfiction is also real, so the bike should go to the library. Since then the town's lost items have been catalogued with nonfiction."

"I like it," said Alice with a grin. "Might have to suggest it when I return home. Mitten feels like a community of friends."

"It is that. People go out of their way to help."

Audrey stood in front of Alice as if expecting an order. "Marci, Audrey and I may need a place to sleep, particularly if Galati wants me close-by and if the Huff family has objections to us occupying the cottage."

"See the last blue building on this block?" said Breakiron. "I know the owner, Anthony." Her face gave a naughty grin as she explained, "He has unpaid parking tickets. I'll talk to him about his campground. Not as posh as your cottage, maybe too rough for your taste, but the cabins have wall units for air conditioning and he allows pets."

"Thanks. Time to head back," said Alice, as an insistent wiggle came into Audrey's hips. "Don't want Audrey to be indelicate."

"I hear ya," said Breakiron.

The two women rose, and Audrey pulled forward.

"Does Mitten have much crime?"

"In my years as an officer, this is our first murder. The most memorable event we had was when a truck with a load of appliances tried to make a U-turn on one of the hill roads. Really narrow up there. The road wasn't even paved, and you won't find guard rails. No idea what he was thinking. It sure didn't save him any time when he tried to turn around. He attracted quite a crowd. Most of the audience had opinions about what he should do. The driver panicked. It took two huge tow-trucks to rescue the appliance truck before it tumbled down the hill. We all had racing hearts. Other than that, our officers work traffic control, illegal parking, you know. Watch for tourists who overindulge."

Audrey stopped to investigate a tree. Breakiron smiled as if expecting results, but the sniff was only to collect odors.

"Do you know the Huff family?" asked Alice.

Breakiron shook her head. "Not really. I hadn't even heard their son was still missing. When the notice first came through to be on the lookout, we all shrugged. I mean, a nineteen-year-old kid goes missing and no one thinks to report it for over two weeks? Odd. The older Mrs. Huff keeps to herself even though she's something of a celebrity. One rumor has it that in her younger years, she sued someone to be on television. Everyone says she was once on *Gunsmoke*. Do you know it?" Alice nodded.

"Last night, Guthrie didn't talk much about her mother-in-law. Never mentioned her acting."

"Don't get me wrong," said Breakiron. "Eleanora's a charming woman when she has an audience but she's a character. Our Mitten museum has a small display of head shots that she furnished. No actual footage from television shows. I've never met anyone who remembers her as an upcoming starlet. Still, hearsay has it she earned enough when her son was a baby to retire to the vineyard. Lawsuit must've paid off."

At that moment, in a very public spot in town, Audrey twisted her head around and found the perfect grass for a leisurely poop. Alice was ready to preserve the cleanliness of Mitten. She reached into her backpack and pulled out appropriate supplies.

On the walk back, about a hundred feet before Eleanora's driveway, a motorcycle raced toward them. Suddenly, the rider—dressed in black with a black helmet—geared down, slowing as he passed the entrance.

"Everything is so peaceful," said Alice. "Seems out of place to have a loud motorcycle. Do you think he slowed down because he saw an old lady with a bloodhound walking along the road?"

"Nah. He was over the speed limit and saw my uniform. Probably thought I'd call ahead and have him ticketed."

They both laughed. Yet, Alice noted that when the biker slowed, his helmet was turned toward the driveway, not in the direction of the two women and dog. As they walked to the main house, Alice saw a white disaster clean-up truck parked near the front door.

"They'll be scoping the extent of work," said Breakiron. "May start small clean-up today and finish the parlor tomorrow after forensics finishes their collection of samples."

The only police cars were Breakiron's and the one parked on the grass near the road. Galati's car was gone.

"One of us will be posted all night for the first night," said the officer, "just in case an intruder wants to come back to see what he can take."

Alice nodded, feeling grateful.

"We'll take your fingerprints tomorrow. This is me off to my three sons, two beagles, and a hamster." Breakiron's nose wrinkled. "We said no to the baby snake."

After reminding Alice that another interview was scheduled with Detective Galati, Breakiron left. Alice returned to the cottage, no longer able to delay the call to Jess. Behind the house near the four-car garage were her rental, a small Toyota, and a big, black BMW.

"Which one do you think is Elka's," asked Alice of her dog. The hound snorted. "Yup, that's what I think too. Let's sit outside."

Alice retrieved the deer bone from the cottage and a happy Audrey found a shady spot for intense gnawing. Nearly toppling a planter of petunias, Alice sat in one chair outside the cottage door. "Well, here goes," she said. Tapping her foot rapidly and rubbing her palm on her jeans, Alice took a breath and pulled her phone from her pocket. "I almost hope she's not home. Is it terrible of me?"

Chapter 6

Time: Monday, 9:24 a.m.

"Jess," said Alice, keeping her eyes closed. "I've run into a bit of trouble. Something unexpected."

"Did you fall? Car trouble? Is it your *dog*?" Jess sounded peeved.

"No. No. And no." Alice swallowed hard. "Last night Guthrie and I had dinner, and she told me about her missing son. I went to bed about ten, but somewhere between one and two o'clock I heard gunfire—"

"Are you *hurt*?" Jess's voice notched up. "Is Guthrie okay?"

"I'm fine, but Guthrie was . . . shot." Alice paused picturing the parlor. An obvious scuffle had taken place—not a flat-out brawl with chairs overturned, but a struggle. Nothing broken but furniture sat at peculiar angles as if pushed, the couch askew, a few papers stepped on and wrinkled. She hadn't mentioned it to the police because the skirmish was obvious. Surely, Detective Galati had noticed.

"My God, Mom. Is she okay?"

"No, Jess, she's gone." Alice heard her daughter gasp. "I called 911. The police are investigating. Detective Galati wants to talk to you."

"Me? Why me?" Her voice sounded stunned with the news of her friend's death and investigation.

"You knew Guthrie. Right now, they seem to be looking for a conflict that might have resulted in her being shot."

"It wasn't a bad break-in? Mom, Guthrie and I took yoga classes. I haven't even known her a year," said Jess. "Sometimes we stopped for tea. She was a nice person, but I didn't know her that well. Why involve me?"

"She trusted you enough for her to allow me and Audrey to lodge at the cottage. And you knew her when her son disappeared, and her husband died."

"I guess. Is Eleanora back? How is she taking it?" asked Jess. Her voice held irritation.

"She's not back yet."

"I've never met her," said Jess, "but I understand she's a hard nut."

"Last night Guthrie said her mother-in-law invents stories," said Alice choosing to be careful with language.

"She told me Eleanora's a born liar and a master manipulator." Jess apparently caught her snarl and segued to her training as an understanding therapist. "But not in a mean way."

"I imagine the lawyer who is here might be representing her." Then Alice couldn't help herself, "Jess, was Guthrie seeing a younger man?"

"What do you mean? Her husband died not even a year ago."

"Well, I wondered because the body of a younger man was found between rows of grapes."

"A second dead body!" Rather than shock, Jess's voice reflected criticism as if her next words might be *such bad form to have two murders at one vineyard.*

"Afraid so."

"Mom! You've been here less than a day, and you're taking on a murder?" Jess's voice pivoted and gained control with heightened anger. "I'm sorry. You're just not taking on a case."

"I'm only walking Audrey through the vineyard."

"No matter what, Henry's graduation is Sunday. One o'clock. The school has security, so we are in our seats at twelve-thirty on the dot. After that they lock the gates. I'll never forgive you if murder takes priority and you miss Henry's graduation."

Alice squirmed, not because of the scolding, but for the worry. Would the school accept a dog at graduation? Henry had said he had a plan for Audrey to be at the school. But how could a school cope when people had allergies or feared big, sloppy dogs? A shiver shook her shoulders.

"Jess, I'll be there. Sunday, twelve-thirty. My bottom parked on the bleachers. Got it."

Alice heard sounds from Jess's end of the line. Whispers at first and then full voices as her two grandchildren moved within range of the phone and prodded for more information.

"Are the children there and not in school?" asked Alice.

"Today's a late start," said Jess. "You were supposed to be here for breakfast, remember?"

"I texted a message." Even Alice thought of her own voice sounded whiney and weak.

"I received it. 'Have to miss breakfast,' Very detailed, Mother."

Alice didn't respond to Jess's criticism.

"I know this will sound crazy," said Alice, "but Guthrie asked me to walk the vineyard to make sure her son wasn't buried on the property, and that's exactly what I plan to do if the family doesn't ask me to leave." Alice closed her eyes and waited for Jess's explosion.

"You *can't* be serious."

"From what I saw yesterday, there are plenty of workers around in the field during the daytime. I'm guessing any burial would attract their attention. Anyway, searching with Audrey will be a way for me to earn my keep."

Jess made sounds of frustration. "You know I'd have you here, but our house is too small. Drew's parents arrived last week from Hawaii. Juliana and Henry are taking turns bunking at friends' homes. Maybe if Eleanora kicks you out, we can manage . . . but a futon in the dining room? That won't work either. We're getting ready for the party . . . Mom, I'm sorry, the best I can do is the living room couch."

"Drew has pet allergies. Jess, it's okay," said Alice remembering the RV's couch and Audrey's disapproval. "Today I walked into Mitten, cute town, and saw a possible cabin." Alice took a deep breath with her fib. "Don't worry about me. I know how hard you've looked for an appropriate place for Audrey, but now that I'm in California, I'll handle whatever comes up."

"People were very nice," continued Jess, defending her failure, "until I mentioned Audrey's one hundred pounds and that she is a bloodhound. People are under the impression bloodhounds stink."

"Not if the owner keeps them clean," asserted Alice. "Audrey has a spit-and-polish clean-up every night. I wipe her ears and eye wrinkles, brush her teeth, and give her a foot massage. Playing with a dog's toes is good practice for cutting toenails. Less stress."

"Mom, we don't have room." Alice heard the defeat of Jess the General.

"I know. It's okay."

Alice's fingers patted the top of Audrey's head. She understood the reluctance of having a bloodhound as a house guest. Audrey's whip-like tail could send a lamp crashing to the floor, and one of her power shakes often slung cords of slobber to crown molding. Alice pictured Drew's swollen, weepy eyes from one trip to the San Diego Zoo when the children were small. He hadn't even touched fur when walking up a steep hill with shady trees triggered his wheezing, sneezing, and coughing.

"Mom, I gotta go. A call's coming in from the police."

Jess hung up, and Alice felt alone as she watched the workers among the rows of grapevines. The day was warm, yet the workers wore shirts that covered their arms. Scarves draped from wide-brimmed hats covered their necks and protected their faces. Alice couldn't tell one worker from another.

"Huh? The rows are far apart. Not a bit like the tightness of corn plants in the Midwest. Vines not so tall either. Should be easy for someone to see a man slinging soil out there. So why did Guthrie think her son could be buried without anyone noticing?"

Audrey's head came up as if her attention were needed. Her eyes held glassy delight, the ground below her wet with slobbery bedeviling of the bone.

"Just thinking, sweetie. Protective gear is a good way to hide a person's identity. Not that it matters. The young man, found dead, wore black and came in the middle of the night."

Audrey's face dropped back to the bone, and Alice took the time to sit and remember.

Last night Guthrie had talked about her marriage. She, her husband, and son arrived at the vineyard a year ago when it became obvious O'Dare's headaches had turned into a nasty challenge. According to Guthrie, O'Dare's temperament was dangerous. One minute he laughed and freely gave away money, the next he shouted threats to neighbors and friends. But he saved his real venom for Cade.

Chapter 7

Sunday dinner with Guthrie

"It was his aneurysm," said Guthrie. "After O'Dare was diagnosed four years ago, he delayed going back to the doctors for the next three years." Guthrie hung her head. "His headaches became worse. He became emotional. Unpredictable."

"Why didn't he go back?" asked Alice.

"He believed in mind over matter. Health through positive thinking. No doctors. No insurance of any kind. But I think he feared the brain operation." Guthrie offered to pour another glass of wine for Alice.

"No, thank you. I'm afraid one is my limit."

Guthrie splashed a generous pour into her own glass.

"In the last four years, everything began to slide. The tourist business of parties on yachts fell off. Our money disappeared, not that we had any great wealth like Eleanora. She reluctantly took us in."

"Cade was in college?"

"Yes and no. After he graduated high school, O'Dare insisted he go into the tourist business. Forced him into hospitality classes. I thought Cade and his father would finally bond. It was time for Cade to take some pressure off his dad. But the tension only became worse when Cade found errors in O'Dare's bookkeeping. Both were furious. Cade accused O'Dare of keeping two sets of books. O'Dare fired him." Guthrie's chin dropped. "To me, Cade hinted at other women."

Alice reached down to pet Audrey. She had no comforting word for Guthrie.

"Cade wanted to study winemaking. O'Dare called it a waste of time and money. Any son of his needed to make real money. Cade switched to accounting classes. He told me he wanted to catch his father in his lies."

"Living at a vineyard seems like a practical place to learn about wine," said Alice.

"Cade caught the bug when he was ten." Guthrie looked toward the grapevines. "I sent him to Eleanora every summer to protect him from O'Dare's . . . anger."

"Forgive me, but you said O'Dare was diagnosed four years ago."

"True. But the two had this running skirmish from the time Cade was little. The aneurysm made the situation worse." Guthrie avoided making eye contact. "Cade's a quiet boy, and Eleanora took to his gentle side. After we moved here, he escaped to the fields when his father wasn't around." Her eyes filled with tears. "He gathered grape information the way other boys might collect baseball cards."

"You asked me to walk the vineyard. Do you really think O'Dare had something to do with Cade's disappearance?" Guthrie nodded, keeping her face lowered. "What happened the last time you saw Cade?"

"An argument between them. A lot of name-calling. With the last confrontation, Cade fought back. The argument continued outside, away from me. Particularly away from Eleanora."

"Why do you say particularly away from Eleanora?"

"She protected Cade. If she had seen O'Dare being vile to him, she might have chucked both of us out and kept Cade. Eleanora holds the purse strings. I didn't know that at first. All these years of marriage, we've been living on an allowance she paid O'Dare. Maybe that's the discrepancy Cade discovered. I don't know." Guthrie's face came up in a plea for understanding. "I thought O'Dare made good money in his party business. But if he did, where did it all go? He didn't particularly drink to excess. Didn't gamble."

Guthrie poured herself another glass of syrah and slugged down two gulps as if the taste no longer mattered. Alice concluded Guthrie wanted numbness.

"The night of the fight," asked Alice, "how would you describe their moods when they both came back to the house?"

"That's just it. They were gone for a long time. A couple of hours, maybe three. O'Dare returned fiery angry. He particularly didn't want to talk to me. Wouldn't let me go look for Cade. I think his headache must have been bad. I had bruises on my wrists for a couple weeks."

Alice knew women who accepted abuse as discipline. Her jaw set.

"Cade came back to the house. Right?"

"I . . . don't know," said Guthrie pulling back a sob. "I never heard sounds from his room. In the morning, he was gone."

"Did O'Dare have an explanation?"

"Only that it was a good time for him to strike out and work. He said there was nothing like poverty to make a man of him. Even Eleanora suggested Cade should cool his heels."

Guthrie's face changed as if she'd made a colossal mistake.

"When I first met him, O'Dare was a charmer. But what I took for charm was an act. It took me a while before I realized I'd married a child who relied on his mother to bail him out."

As their meal together ended, the bottle of syrah mostly consumed by Guthrie, she admitted regrets. "If only I had forced my way past O'Dare to check on my son. At first, I didn't believe O'Dare would actually do something wicked."

"So, you waited for Cade to calm down and return, but he never made contact even after his father passed away?"

"No. He never came home for the funeral. That's when Eleanora finally became worried." Guthrie's eyebrows drew together as if she were in pain. "I must know that Cade wasn't killed in a field somewhere because of O'Dare's rage. I must know it wasn't my fault."

Chapter 8

Alice stood at the cottage door torn by her memories of Guthrie. *What am I to do next?* she wondered. She wanted to call her best friend Lena and share the events, but the lawyer's car was still parked nearby, and Alice had questions. Did she need to scout out a new place to bunk?

"Best to find out our fate," said Alice to her hound, and together they walked toward the main house.

Out of the corner of her eye, Alice spotted a woman carrying a package close to her chest. She ducked between rows of grapevines. She wore a long, dark purple coat, her gray hair hung in dreadlocks down her back, past her waist. Audrey stopped dead and turned to watch the woman but showed no interest in investigating who she was, only stared.

Elka came out of the main house through the French doors and cranked the porch umbrella open over one of the three tables.

"I begin to worry, Mrs. Alice. Mr. Merritt wants to talk to you. He call Mrs. Eleanora. I make lunch now. Twenty minutes on porch. In meantime, talk to lawyer."

"I saw a woman walk into the vineyard," said Alice turning in the direction of the vines.

Without making eye contact, Elka said, "She nobody," and walked into the house.

Audrey's head tilted as she wedged herself under the table and curled up in the shade.

"I know you missed your beauty sleep last night," said Alice. "Me too. Let's see if we can sleep here tonight. Maybe I'll have to make calls later while you nap."

"Detective Galati left." Roddy Merritt introduced himself and shook Alice's hand. "We talked about your situation and the needs of the Huff family."

Merritt was a tall, thin man in his late forties. His black hair was slicked back, his face tanned like leather. He wore a dark blue suit but no tie, black loafers but no socks. His hands were soft, nails manicured to pink and white perfection. Alice thought his polite smile signaled sugary superiority.

"Please, when Elka brings your lunch, eat." He took a seat across from Alice. With a sharp sparkle in his eye, he added, "She's promised me a package of strudel to take home. Now, Mrs. Tricklebank—"

"Alice, please."

"Alice, I've talked to Eleanora Huff and broke the news about her daughter-in-law." Merritt's voice disturbed Alice as it switched to funeral-eze with a somber intonation like that of Mr. Heatherwick, the funeral director of the Limekiln Funeral Home. "She is understandably upset." His voice rose, feigning concern. "She plans to return tomorrow." His voice became grave. "But, a flight could be difficult." His tone was positively in the dark basement.

Alice worked at concentrating on his meaning and not his weighty vocal delivery.

"This is most distressing to the family . . . to Eleanora," said Merritt. "She may not have always gotten along with Guthrie, but she wants the murderer found."

"Detective Galati seems very capable of finding the murderer," said Alice.

"He is that, but Eleanora wants you to continue with the work Guthrie proposed, if that is acceptable to you. She has requested you finish the search of the vineyard with your dog." His chin rose with challenge. "She does not believe her grandson is dead as his mother feared, but it doesn't hurt to verify he is *not* on the property. Gossip, you understand. Do you agree to continue?"

"I'm happy to follow through. I can't promise Audrey is one-hundred percent accurate, but she is good. Almost intuitive about finding people."

"Good. Eleanora has read your website. She is up to speed."

Alice cringed. *The website! Who's keeping a website of Audrey's activities?*

"While you are here," continued Merritt, "she asks that you search Cade's room. It's almost the same as it was the day he left. The only changes, Elka dusts, Carmelita vacuums."

"There is one difficulty with searching his room. I can't leave Audrey in a strange cottage by herself. She can become unruly or panic if she can't see me."

"Bring her into the house," said Merritt. "Eleanora can't mind. She once owned two Standard poodles. Bejeweled collars. Toenails painted. Ate better than I do. Believe me." His voice took on a relaxed humor, "I often wished I could come back as one of Eleanora's pampered dogs."

"Good to know. But Audrey is not quite like a poodle. She is one-hundred pounds and slobbers. I do all I can to wipe her lips, but sometimes, when she shakes, it flies." Alice tilted in the direction of the French doors. "Besides, I'm guessing the professional clean-up of the crime scene starts tomorrow, and Audrey is a hound drawn to body fluids. No matter how the police try to seal up or disguise odors in the parlor, she'll be aware of clouds of scent."

Both crooked their necks to look at Audrey beneath the table. She eyed them back as if she were in trouble.

Merritt smiled. "To find Cade, Eleanora won't mind if you want to begin your investigation tonight with Audrey. The professional crew has sanitized small areas, and yes, the police have cordoned off the parlor with heavy duty plastic sheeting. Sanitizing of that area will begin tomorrow. Any other cleaning—like slobber—will be handled by Elka and Carmelita, the Tasmanian devils of cleaning. Neither will mind Audrey. Cade's a favorite with family and staff." As if sharing a secret, Merritt leaned forward and said, "Eleanora never sees her two granddaughters to the first Mrs. Huff. To her, Cade is her *only* grandchild. A warning: Elka will scold you *into* searching for a clue to Cade's whereabouts whether Eleanora approves or not."

Alice pushed her reservations aside. With her lodging settled, she decided her next conversation should be with Elka.

A warm breeze drifted off the field of vines, carrying the soft music of two workers harmonizing.

"When I talked to Guthrie last night at dinner, I had the impression she and Eleanora are very different people."

"Not so very different." Merritt's eyes drifted to men leaving the field for shaded picnic benches. Alice checked her watch. Time flew: almost noon. "Guthrie wasn't happy to move to the vineyard, but Eleanora thought it would be easier for Cade. From the time he was a kid, he spent every summer here. I remember him from when she was a client of my dad."

"How long have you been Eleanora's lawyer?"

"Four years."

"So, what went wrong between father and son?" asked Alice.

Merritt tried to hide a scowl with a grin. "This house has been Eleanora's home since after O'Dare was born. He was raised here. Then his young daughters lived here until he and his first wife divorced. The relationship with that family has been severed. It's safe for me to say Eleanora didn't exactly welcome either wife. However, she didn't want her son developing a habit of divorce. Her intrusion into his divorce was a smack to his nose."

"How old are his daughters now?"

"Sage is twenty-eight. Sierra probably thirty-two, married and has two children. They all live south of Los Angeles."

Alice began to calculate. If it were over an hour to drive to Jess's house, then a drive to south of L.A. might take her two hours or more. That is if she wanted to casually snoop.

"Eleanora doesn't see her grandchildren?" asked Alice with disbelief.

Her protective side bristled. *What grandmother willingly dismisses a relationship with grandchildren?*

"All according to the divorce agreement." Merritt's smile hinted at something hidden. "O'Dare's divorce was difficult." Then, sitting straighter and leaning forward, he said, "Now it's my turn. Why are you interested in the children by his first wife?"

"Curious," said Alice. "Forgive me, but I'm guessing the Huff family has some wealth. A vineyard. Big house. A lawyer who pops in when a crisis hits." Alice looked at him for a reaction. Seeing no emotion, just a practiced grin, she decided to go for broke. "It seems to me that seven months after O'Dare's passing is an adequate amount of time for a will to be read. Maybe an ex-wife's angry and felt cheated. Maybe a daughter thinks an inheritance should be passed along to her young children. Or a boyfriend thinks it's time to strike it rich?"

The lawyer again smiled as if schooled in hiding judgment.

"I see your thinking. Follow the money." Merritt squared the napkins placed on the table, positioning them in front of the salt and pepper. "Seven months is actually lightning speed for a complicated will to be read," said Merritt his intelligent eyes guarded. "You and Eleanora will get along just fine." Merritt stood, ready to leave.

Alice didn't understand his comment about Eleanora and herself, but she followed up with a question pulled from the lawyer's unease. "O'Dare had a will, didn't he?"

"Professionally, I can't confirm or deny."

Alice took his comment to mean O'Dare's estate was probably in lengthy probate while the court, without a will to direct them, decided who got what.

"Does Guthrie have family we should contact?" asked Alice. "A mother perhaps?"

"I don't have that information on file. I'll leave that to Eleanora. Best you hear it from her."

His face looked amused, but critical as if he wanted distance from Alice. She was sure there was a story he kept close.

"Before you go," said Alice, "Guthrie told me there was something *untruthful* about Eleanora, yet you think she and I will get along. Can I trust what she says?"

Merritt wiped his mouth with the palm of his left hand. "She's a sharp business woman. That's all I can say. And here's our Elka with your lunch. Scallops? I'll leave you to it." With that said, Merritt grabbed a green bean from Alice's lunch tray and walked away.

A frowning Elka put down the tray with two large grilled scallops, orzo salad with tomatoes and basil, and long, wrinkly green beans. The glass of iced tea fogged in the warm air.

"I'll be out with something for dog," said Elka. "Let's see Mr. Big Lawyer steal a bite of that."

"Not necessary, Elka. Audrey eats twice a day."

"Will need her strength. Has work to do." Elka turned back to the house.

Audrey raised her head, but her nose seemed uninterested in scallops.

Wandering through the conversation with Merritt, Alice listed details she would have shared with Lena if her best friend weren't on a food adventure with Julian in the northern half of California, and if her friend could forgive Audrey, who hogged the king-sized bed in the back of the RV. Alice sighed with guilt.

Lena, Alice imagined, *Guthrie and her mother-in-law may not get along, but Eleanora does love Cade. There's a first wife with children and grandchildren. Then Guthrie and Cade, a second family.*

So, who's the dead guy in the vineyard? A thief? A lover? If a thief, why was a stranger allowed into the house late at night? I didn't see evidence of a break-in. No door was forced.

Or did he sneak in through the unlocked backdoor?

When did the struggle happen? Before the man was shot or after? One ran out a side door. Was that because of his confusion after being shot or part of an escape plan? The car was in the driveway and nowhere near that side of the house.

Guthrie was shot three times. A car pulled away. Guthrie's shooter had to be the driver.

Alice looked at her dog. "Audrey, we know thieves. Remember Phil? This just doesn't feel like a simple theft. In the wee hours of the morning, why was Guthrie still dressed in daytime clothing? My guess—she expected someone to arrive. After our dinner, the house was mostly dark, but the lights were on later when we entered. I don't think she surprised two strangers."

With a sigh, Alice added, "I wish Lena were here. I like Galati, not so much the lawyer. Audrey, I wish you could talk. I've never thought lawyers could hang around for hours. What do you think he's protecting? Is something poisonous going on?"

Chapter 9

Elka returned with a fresh bowl of water for Audrey, and Alice picked up a green bean with her fingers to show appreciation for Elka's efforts. The hound's mouth plunged into the bowl and came out dripping. Elka stood back several feet, and Alice held up her napkin as a shield against the dog's muscular shake.

"Sorry, she's energetic," said Alice.

"I know," said Elka, using her apron to dab at her face and arms. "Have Great Dane at home."

"Thank you for understanding. Why is Merritt still here?"

"He watch police."

"Why?"

"Don't know. You not eating?" Elka's tone was more accusation than question.

"I'm wondering about Cade," said Alice. "Can you take a minute and tell me about him?"

Elka pulled a chair back from the table and sat. Audrey's soft eyes followed Elka's every move, finally placing her face in the younger woman's lap. Elka's hands instantly went to the hound's wrinkles and ears, massaging the way only a dog owner knows while ignoring the water wicking from Audrey's face into her apron.

"She good dog," said Elka, "Very warm."

Alice nodded agreement, picked up her fork, scooped a portion of orzo, and said, "Guthrie told me a little about the argument that may have sent Cade away. Do you know anything about that?"

"Not here that night, but for days father and son make bad remarks to each other."

"Like what?"

"Cade drop out of college. Father call him lazy, a do-nothing. Call him disappointment since he born. Tell him he no good to take over yacht parties. Never will make money to take care of self. A burden. Cade say Father can't tell him what to do. Won't repeat the bad words Father uses or Cade's." Elka's eyes grew bigger, one eyebrow raised. "'Blank the business' Cade say. That's all I know about argument. But Father right. Is not good kind of business for Cade. He too gentle."

"O'Dare was good at his event business?"

"Nothing but birthday party on boat. I could do business. Buy cases of wine, trays of appetizers, blow up balloons. Then turn face and pretend everyone is still wearing clothes." Elka made a face and whispered, "He never make money. Always asking Mrs. Eleanora for a little something more to help him along."

"His business wasn't going well?" Alice quickly picked up that if she ate lunch, the younger woman was more eager to share information. She forked a whole scallop, finding she needed to store part of it in the pouch of her cheek while she rapidly chewed a portion, readying herself for the next question.

"Too high and mighty. Big shot. Want others to work," said Elka as if the failure of his business were obvious. "Two years ago, Mr. O'Dare and Mrs. Eleanora argue about money. I hear from kitchen. He asks for his inheritance. Mrs. Eleanora tells him no, not bailing him out for a fourth time. He say he need money for bills. I think, they moved here last year to punish Mrs. Eleanora. Get sympathy money. I think he not know how sick he really is. Sometimes a stupid man."

Elka's lips and nose wrinkled with judgment.

"His bills were medical bills?" asked Alice.

Elka tilted her head. "Why he have medical bills if don't see doctor about his head?"

"Mr. Merritt mentioned Eleanora and Guthrie were sometimes at odds," said Alice, encouraging more sharing.

"What is *at odds*?"

"Sometimes people don't get along. Not in a hateful way to each other but irritable," explained Alice.

"Yes. This true. Mrs. Guthrie and Mrs. Eleanora like olive oil and water. Everybody fight. Times this not a happy house. I feel sorry for Cade. Hard life, I think, even before the sickness of his father, not good.

"Did O'Dare ever talk about his daughters or his ex-wife? Did he ever consider giving his party business to his daughters?" Alice alternated between crunching green beans and scooping up orzo.

"Never hear him mention daughters. I work here eight years and never see other family." Elka dusted her hands together. "He finish with first family. Not have big heart. His way, only way. I think he see daughters as, what word I want?" Elka's hands swept an invisible nuisance aside. "Cade is son. Supposed to be a salesman. But shy."

Audrey's nose moved toward Alice's plate, but she flopped down with a groan. Alice forked a piece of scallop, salty and sweet, followed by a scoop of tomato pieces and basil.

"Describe the marriage."

"A show-up marriage," said Elka.

"I don't know what that means."

"He needs to appear in public for party, she show up. All other times like storm."

"Had to be hard on their son. Who were Cade's friends? Did he date?"

"Private eye boy ask me same question. Answer: I don't know.

Never see him with anyone, but he also away at school. I leave every day at two o'clock to pick up my children."

"Cade never invited anyone here?"

Elka frowned and leaned forward. "Don't know if invite, but Hector, worker in field, tell me he see Cade talk to someone dressed like a grape worker. All cover up. Hat hiding face, you understand me?"

"I do. I've seen the workers in the field. The sun must be brutal. The men need protection."

"Hector say man, about the size of Cade but stronger, talk to Cade long time behind the tractor barn. He say it look like argument both times he see them. Man grab Cade pretty good. Shook him."

"Two times?"

"Yes. Hector tell Mr. Nimble, the vineyard manager, stranger point finger, make a fist in Cade's face. Mr. Nimble have no idea about stranger. Not expect new worker, and man never join others in the field."

"Did the stranger drive away?"

"Don't know. Hector never say. He tell me because everybody know Mrs. Eleanora not like strangers on property."

"When was this?"

"During pick grape time. September."

"Did Cade ever talk to you? You know, come down to the kitchen in the morning when you were preparing breakfast. I think with all this turmoil in the family, Cade might look for one kind face."

Elka gave a sly smile. "Sometimes."

"What did he like to talk about?" Alice opened her eyes wide and smiled.

"Things boys like. He tell me about sports. I don't know sports, so I listen to him. Sometimes he talk about boring school." Elka eyed Alice's full glass as if disappointed. "Most of time, Cade talk food and grapes. He smell meat cooking and talk about grape flavors, olive, pepper, licorice, smoke. This, I don't know."

"He was interested in the vineyard?" Alice took a big gulp of iced tea.

"Yes. He only here when not in school, but he like grapes from the time he was boy. He ask me to teach him, but I'm in kitchen. Don't know about harvest or smashing grapes or wine taste like chocolate."

"The vineyard is beautiful. So peaceful. We saw wild turkeys a while ago. I could forget the rest of the world if I lived here. I'm surprised being here didn't repair Guthrie's marriage."

They both sat peering out at the vines as a hawk floated above on a stream of air.

As if a light bulb went on with a memory, Elka said, "Before argument, I tell Cade to talk to Mr. Nimble about grapes. Cade say he did as boy. Teach him about grape sugar. Raisins not good unless want sweet wine."

Elka looked at her watch. "Time for children," she said. "I arrived early, leave early. Dinner in the refrigerator. The detective tell me to lock all doors in case thief comes back." She fished around in her pocket and pulled out keys. "You need these. Lawyer say you to look around inside of house. Upstairs is five bedrooms. Mrs. Eleanora's is in front of house. Mrs. Guthrie's is in the back. Cade's and another on the south side. Two more across the hall. You look." Elka stood tall, like a warrior, her face fierce. Her eyes filled with tears. "Bring Cade home to Grandmother, whatever the case."

"I'll do my best," said Alice, touched by Elka's trust.

"Now, tomorrow's food. Who I cook for?" asked Elka. "Detective say he wants to talk to your daughter."

Alice tried to release the young cook from her responsibilities, but Elka took her job seriously, and Alice understood how everyday work helps people through a tragedy.

"I think my daughter and two grandchildren will be visiting tomorrow. Lunch will be lovely. Thank you."

"Is school day. Children will come?"

"I was supposed to spend part of today with them. I understand tomorrow is a shortened school day because of testing. My grandchildren are teenagers. If their mother has the chance to talk to a real, professional police detective, there is no way Juliana and Henry will miss the drama."

"I understand. Then I make big pasta lunch, salad, cannoli pie. Everyone sit down and eat, together like family. Mrs. Eleanora come home tomorrow night." Elka paused and bit her lip. "I talk to her. I think she afraid. Ask me if I be with her tomorrow night. I tell her no because of children."

"Audrey and I will look after her," volunteered Alice, and Elka nodded.

"Is dog passed out?"

Both looked at Audrey who was under the table, flattened like a puddle, her loose facial skin covering her eyes. But at Elka's mentioning of dog, Audrey's head rose. Her bloodshot eyes opened.

"Her schedule is off," said Alice. "She needs a nap."

Elka looked at her watch and hesitated. "One thing. Mrs. Eleanora tell me not to be nosy parker. I understand nosy but not parker. This talk our secret?"

"Absolutely a secret. A nosy parker isn't bad. It's someone who is curious," said Alice with a grin. "We've had a good chinwag, haven't we?"

"Don't know chinwag either." Her eyebrows drew together in a frown.

"It's an old way of saying as friends, we've had a good conversation."

"Chinwag. I like better than nosy parker."

With that, Elka-in-charge picked up the dishes from the table.

"Elka, do you like Detective Galati?"

"He a man." Her lips wrinkled as if she tasted something sour.

"What about Mr. Merritt?"

Her nose wrinkled and rose into the air before she retreated to the kitchen. Alice itched to snoop through the house and check out the bedrooms, but that could wait. She couldn't drag Audrey up the stairs just yet. The sanitation crew still worked inside, and her hound needed naptime and playtime. Besides, Merritt probably took inventory of everything they did—or was she being too critical of the man who wore loafers and no socks? Alice pictured smelly feet and slimy toes.

Wanting time to organize her thoughts, Alice stood to retreat to the cottage. In September Cade argued with someone in the vineyard, then in November he argued with his father and disappeared. Two weeks later his father died. In May Guthrie's murdered and one man shot. The same guy that threatened Cade with his fist?

"But why?" asked Alice aloud.

Interviewing Eleanora might take some mental preparation before her return. But first, Alice knew she needed to call Lena and tell her what had happened. Lena loved being involved in a murder investigation, but she and Julian were so far away. Were they still miffed about the overly long drive to California? Maybe telling Lena about the murder would help make amends.

Picking up Audrey's leash, Alice said to her hound, "You don't think Lena set up that website about us, do you?"

Chapter 10

Time: Monday, 1:26 p.m.

Alice felt the effects of a long day that began with a murder at two a.m. Her shoulders were tight, eyes burned, spine in need of a good stretch. Audrey, who loped back to the cottage, seemed to have her agenda set. Once inside the cottage, the hound pawed and gathered her blanket Alice had brought from home to protect bedding. As the folds of the blanket fell into the perfect rumple, the hound plopped into a tight knot. She eyed Alice with her disappointed look, *Well, you coming to bed or not?* In the time it took Alice to dial Lena, Audrey relaxed and flipped onto her back. Snoring followed. Alice spied one of her shoes tucked between her dog and the blanket.

"Alice," answered Lena, a brightness in her voice. "We just stopped for the day. This morning we dropped off the RV and rented a car. I'm liking the ocean off Carmel-by-the-Sea, but it's cooler than I expected. What a town for shops! I could spend weeks just in this town. Julian's anxious to leave. He's in a snit-fit about my shopping. But so many lovely things call to me. I had to buy. Wait until you see a snazzy nightie I found. Julian almost choked when he saw the price. How are your grandchildren? Fun?"

Alice took a breath at Lena's rush of information and smiled at the thought of Lena dragging Julian from shop to shop. Both of her friends were retired. She from baking; he from driving a truck. Julian liked to put on a crusty demeanor, yet Alice knew he had a gentle soul. Lena was often giddy with collecting bits to display in her already crowded home, but she was generous and forgiving to a fault.

"Not quite able to have fun times with the grandchildren yet. Lena—"

"Well, there's so much to do at the end of the school year. I remember parties. Cut the children some slack, that's my advice. Surprise them. Buy a bikini and join them at the beach. That will make their eyes pop."

"Bikini? When I'm in my sixties? Not happening," said Alice as she welcomed Lena's teasing chuckle. "The children are fine as far as I know, but Lena, I called because I awoke this morning at two-ish to a murder."

"Is this a *joke?*" Lena's voice sparked higher.

"I wish it were."

"Who died?"

Alice heard movement from behind Lena's end of the line and guessed Julian had taken an interest in the call.

"The woman who owns the house where I'm staying."

"Oh?"

"Today I spent the day with the police, giving them the information I have."

"Oh, Alice. Do they suspect *you?*"

"No. Maybe they're curious about who I am."

"Can't believe it."

Julian addressed Lena with a question, but Alice couldn't pick up all the words.

"Audrey and I have moved into a cottage at a vineyard. Our hostess was shot last night. The strange thing is, she asked Audrey and me to walk the vineyard because her son disappeared eight months ago, and she worried he may have been killed on the property and buried."

"Murder! A son and now a mother! I don't know what to say." Alice heard shock in Lena's voice. "OH! Yes, I do know what to say. Wait a minute." With her face away from the phone, Lena said, "Julian, Alice needs us. We have a murder case." Back on the phone, Lena said, "Alice, you're now on speaker so Julian can hear."

Alice thought she heard Julian say, "Hallelujah!"

"We checked into a motel," said Julian. "Can't leave tonight, but we'll be there late tomorrow. Where should we stay?"

"It's not really necessary for you to interrupt your vacation. I don't want you two to hate me after your sacrifice in driving us here."

"Nonsense," said Lena. "The streets in California have too much traffic. Everything costs an arm and a leg. And I can't possibly sunbathe on the beach with that biting wind off the ocean. Besides, when does a person get a chance to solve a murder case?"

"For you?" asked Alice, "I think that was last Christmas."

"Ha-ha. Very funny."

"What's the deal?" asked Julian. "We want to hit the ground running when we get there."

Enthusiasm's new for Julian, thought Alice. *He really must not like Lena's shopping.*

"The woman who owns the vineyard is in her eighties and has been away. Her name is Eleanora Huff and she'll be back tomorrow. She's a little creeped out about being in the house alone since a murder took place. She's requested someone to hang around with her. I may be overstepping here, but, Lena, you and Julian will be perfect to help set a safe tone."

"We'll take care of the old lady," said Julian.

"Don't you worry," added Lena. "In the meantime, tell us what we can do to help?"

Alice didn't really know what to expect from Eleanora. Was an elderly, California woman like Limekiln church ladies? Probably not.

"Will you look up the obit for O'Dare Huff? Guthrie, his second wife, was the woman who was murdered. They have a son named Cade. He's the boy who disappeared. And look up Eleanora Huff. I'm getting some conflicting information on her. A statement or two on O'Dare's travel business might be helpful. He supposedly planned parties on yachts, but again mixed signals about how or if the business made any money. Any newspaper stories might give us clues."

"You thinking somebody went after the kid if daddy didn't pay his bills?" asked Julian.

"Wouldn't be the first time that kind of muscle happened," said Alice. "For fun, maybe look up Roddy Merritt, the lawyer. He arrived early this morning to talk to the police. Lena, he doesn't wear socks."

Lena laughed. "I know how that makes your skin crawl. I'm not fond of gooey toes myself."

"Don't like lawyers," said Julian. "I don't mean that firecracker of yours, of course. She's okay. But you know what I mean."

Before Alice could respond, Lena said with glee, "Newspaper archives, here I come. Nothing hides from me."

"One more thing," continued Alice, scrunching her eyes and hoping Lena wasn't her website architect, "Do you know anything about my website?"

"You have a website?" asked Lena. "When did you do that?"

"I didn't. Someone else set up a site. I'm assuming you'd tell me if it were you."

"Alice, when have I ever kept a secret from you?" asked Lena.

"I can think of a time or two, but if possible, can you figure out how I can shut it down? It will be one more thing to put on my grateful-to-you-forever list."

"Are Julian and I mentioned on the website?"

"Not really. Only a picture or two."

"You're right. Information should be accurate," said Lena, her tone sounding a bit put-out at being neglected. "I'll look it up. If we can't shut it down, at least I'll make sure it gives a full picture of what we do."

"Lena, you understand, I'm not looking for search-and-rescue publicity. And I don't want people thinking I'm a professional detective when I'm not."

"Uh-huh."

"I'll appreciate any help you can give. Thanks for coming to my rescue."

Alice knew Lena's mind was off in a whirl of murder drama.

"We have a case," sang Lena. "The posse is back together. See you late tomorrow evening." Before she hung up, Alice heard Lena squeal to Julian, "Love Monkey, a California murder to solve."

It was useless to insist they weren't real detectives. Julian got a kick out of calling Alice Snoopypuss, and maybe that was the best description of what the three of them did.

"Maybe everyone has a Gladys Kravitz side," whispered Alice so as not to awaken Audrey, "Well, girl, danger or not, ready for the plunge?"

Chapter 11

Time: Monday, 6:10 p.m.

After a fitful nap with Audrey and a long walk through the countryside, Alice saw that the parking area in front of the garage was empty of cars and trucks. Elka was gone for the day, so were the police except for one promised police car at the bottom of the driveway.

"Come on," said Alice to her dog, "time to peek into the garage."

One key on the key chain Elka had given her opened the side door. Four cars sat parked: a black Jeep, a green Jaguar, a well-used, behemoth Lincoln Continental, and a black Mercedes-Benz.

"Wow," said Alice. "Guessing the Jeep is Cade's, Jaguar O'Dare's. Does that make the Lincoln Eleanora's and the Mercedes Guthrie's? Or the other way around?"

The hound showed no interest in the garage.

"Okay, dinner. We have been given keys to the house," said Alice, "and Elka gave you special dispensation should you leave a cord of slobber. Just the same—"

Alice reached over with a small towel and wiped Audrey's face and lips.

Then dog and owner went through the French doors to the glistening white, industrial-sized kitchen.

"Lena will love this," said Alice. "Last night I didn't properly notice the counter space and stainless-steel appliances. You don't watch HGTV, but this is what real cooks want."

One sheet of instructions on the counter and another posted on the refrigerator guided Alice to the prepared cold dinners for her and Audrey. Two trays: plates, napkins, and utensils on one, a stainless-steel bowl and plate on the other. Plastic wrap covered plates in the fridge.

"Elka has more chicken for you this time with rice and carrots, but I'm not ready to eat."

A quick peek into the pantry revealed can goods hand-labeled with expiration dates in magic marker. A stack of folded white aprons carried the odor of starch.

"Elka is very thorough."

As Alice continued to gush about the house manager's efficiency, the big farmhouse sink, and runway counters, Audrey broke her owner's admiration homily by stretching toward the swinging doors to the rest of the house. Alice felt a tickle of fear, hoping her dog's interest wasn't in detecting a new smell or the old one of blood.

"Time to check out Cade's bedroom."

Alice followed Audrey through the kitchen doors and into the hallway that led to the scene of the murder. The hound's head turned to look at the closed door of the parlor draped in opaque plastic sealing off the room. Yellow crime tape warned them not to enter. Audrey's nose worked, the plastic sheeting apparently not hindering the iron smell of blood.

"No, sweetie, not today. The police are preserving the crime scene. We're not allowed," Alice said.

They took their time to look at a series of other parlors, both elegant in cream and bawdy in maroon and black, all with French doors leading to the wrap-around porch.

"If this house were back home, I'd call it a Prairie style," Alice told her hound. "Big, wide wrap-around porch, a rabbit's warren of rooms. If last night's intruders didn't know the house, once the guy was shot, he could easily have become confused and run for the wrong door to escape. I won't tell the detective my guesses just yet, but to shoot someone in the neck, I think the person either has to be skilled or lucky. Wonder if Guthrie ever took lessons? But tomorrow, we'll walk down those rows of grapes and see what's on the other side of the vineyard. Was the young man running from the house or toward safety?"

A staircase near the front door led upstairs. Audrey took the lead in climbing the stairs covered in carpet with pink flowers on a black background. At the top of the stairs, Alice moved her dog toward the front of the house where Elka had indicated Eleanora had her bedroom.

"I know we shouldn't be looking, but this might be our only chance. But no jumping on her bed." Alice tightened her grip on the leash as she opened the bedroom door.

Eleanora's room was large and painted bubblegum pink. Her canopy bed sported elaborate ruffles. The dresser was covered with black-and-white autographed pictures of movie stars. But it was the bulwark of six mannequin heads against the wall that drew Alice's attention. Each one had an elaborate wig: curly blonde, long straight black, brown page-boy, platinum, in a style of the royalty in the French Revolution, and a red beehive of the sixties. One outdid the others: school-bus yellow mini-braids. Although all were cared for, Alice noted sections of the wigs had become matted.

"What a bedroom," whispered Alice, feeling very much like an outsider. "These wigs are old. And a bit odd, but then people have described her as a character."

Audrey's nose sniffed in the general direction of the wigs as Alice peered into a walk-in closet. "Lots of clothes. Enough for a lifetime. Or if you're Lena, enough for a month. But look at all these costumes hanging in the back. Hats, heels, scarves—many sized for children. Huh? Makes me wonder."

The carefully preserved clothing for little girls was decades old. A time-capsule for pretend games.

"Some people might be freaked out by this. However, Audrey, I think it's sad."

The expanse of every wall was broken by large windows and doors. Another door led to a bathroom. A third door without a doorknob popped open with a palm's touch. The room beyond served as an orderly office painted in gray. Heavy drapes darkened the window. Four file cabinets against the wall, locks pushed in signaled privacy. Shelves on one wall held black binders, each labeled with a year and standing aligned except for the last four. Alice found the untidiness curious. The last four did not butt up against the others as if they had seen recent activity. Yellow Post-it notes acted as page markers. Other markers littered the floor. Carefully, Alice removed one binder with three notes and flipped it open.

"Ledgers."

Columns of numbers written in small neat handwriting listed out both income and payments. Notes questioned numbers. In the last binder, twenty-some yellow markers peeked out. Feeling intrusive, Alice turned to leave.

"Huh. Eleanora is more than fluff. She is the business woman the lawyer mentioned. But look at this floor. I've never known police to be this messy. What's on your paw?" Alice removed a stray Post-it.

With one more sweeping glance and a tinge of concern, Alice and her dog left Eleanora's private space.

The bedroom facing the backyard was painted a cream-color and had white woodwork. Bedding was in white and blue. Alice peeked in, saw a woman's clothing lying about, and the tell-tale black dust of finger-print powder.

"Guthrie's." Alice's shoulders sagged. Death always brought work for family, tidying away a life, repurposing memories. Quietly, she closed the door. "We'll leave this room alone. The police may be back. We need to find Cade's room."

Another two bedrooms in green and beige seemed ready for guests. Cade's room was the one in brown and black. The single bed, chest of drawers, and chair didn't fill the room. Alice noted the lack of wall art.

"Well, this won't be hard to snoop. Cade lives in a cell like a monk." Alice momentarily dropped her dog's leash, and Audrey took the chance to leap up to the perfectly made bed. "All right. But don't snuggle down too long. I really don't want to explain to Elka why you were in bed."

On the maple chest were Cade's wallet, phone, tablet, and car keys. Alice slipped on latex gloves and opened the wallet to his school identification, driver's license, two credit cards, and one-hundred and twenty-six dollars. A knot hit her stomach as she ran through scenarios. If he had been abducted from home, his personal things might have been left behind. Yet, no one had mentioned a ransom. What was the motive?

If he left of his own accord to run away, thought Alice, *why is his wallet still here? Did he walk? Did a friend possibly pick him up? Why leave all identification and money behind?*

Opening drawers, Alice found clothing still neatly folded. The closet, orderly. The room held no bookcases, thus no books. No evidence of sports or music. Alice went down on her knees to check under the bed. During his teen years, her own son was a great one for hiding items under the bed.

"I've told you about Peter," she said to her dog. "He hid things, like graded essays under the bed. It was hard having a mother as a teacher in the same school. I knew his grades before he did."

Peter was an excellent student, but usually needed space. What boy doesn't want to surprise his mother with a paper marked with a big, fat *A*.

Audrey's paw reached out, tangling her toenails in Alice's gray, loopy hair.

"Ouch!" When Alice looked up, Audrey looked confused as her mouth touched her owner's forehead. "I'm okay. I found two big books on winemaking and one motorcycle magazine."

Dread hit Alice as she took in the whole picture of Cade's room. It was almost as though he were saying goodbye to his life. Something about the barrenness of the room reminded her of stories of suicide victims. A young man of twenty would hardly leave his tablet behind or his phone. Only one missing item kept Alice from drawing a dire conclusion.

"Where are his sunglasses?"

Alice felt cold as she and her dog went down to the kitchen and took the food Elka had prepared out to the porch. For Audrey, there was more pulverized chicken. For Alice: sliced chicken, salad, home-made bread, tiny bowls with condiments and . . . Alice swiped her finger through a tan smear on her plate. "Garlic hummus." Seated on the porch, Alice said, "We don't have all the pieces of information yet, so no reason to jump to conclusions."

Audrey licked her plate clean before Alice had forked the first bite of salad.

"Tomorrow Jess will be here and, if I know my grandchildren, so will Henry and Juliana. Henry's the one whose car we used when we first got here. You'll like Juliana. She plays softball like I did, but she is a much better athlete."

The babble about her grandchildren didn't calm Alice's thinking.

Apparently realizing no second helping was about to appear on her plate, Audrey stood and placed her head on Alice's thigh. Her eyes were soft with pleading.

"Okay, share-zies." Alice broke off a piece of her chicken slice for Audrey. "I have to eat dinner. Can't disappoint Elka. But I'm not hungry. Not liking what I saw in Cade's room or in Eleanora's."

A lone motorcycle buzzed down the road, shifting gears to reduce speed. Alice wondered if he were going home to his dinner. Or, remembering the motorcyclist who'd watched the driveway, Alice feared his trip was a reconnaissance mission to check out if anyone was home. She was grateful for the lone police car parked at the end of the driveway.

Chapter 12

Time: Tuesday, dawn

"Mrs. Tricklebank? Marci Breakiron. Did I wake you?"

"No, but I'm not up or dressed. Is it morning?"

Alice looked through the window to the half dark, her eyelids heavy. Even Audrey kept her head down, her face reflecting *make-that-call-go-away*.

"Dawn's just breaking behind the hills," said Marci, her voice sounded breathy. "I called because we have a situation."

"Please, not another murder," said Alice putting her palm to her forehead.

"No. A lost child. We've called for a German shepherd, but he won't arrive for another hour. I thought Audrey could help find the little girl."

"Give me five minutes." Alice threw off covers. Audrey bounded out of bed and stood at the door.

"I'm parked at the bottom of the driveway. I'll drive up to the cottage when you're ready."

Alice pushed her gray, curly hair back from her forehead and blinked, remembering when she shared the back of a police car with Audrey who saw the separation bars as a bigger cage.

"No. I'll drive Audrey. She likes to ride shotgun. I'll follow you."

When she hung up, Alice dressed in jeans and a turtleneck, harnessed a ready-to-go Audrey, and grabbed her backpack filled with gear.

"Audrey, where's your leash?" The dog stood still, cocking her head to the left. "Sweetie, we have to go. Did you hide your leash?"

All the while searching under the bed, through the bedding, in the bathroom, Alice said, "I'm truly sorry I forgot your favorite toy, but this new thing of hiding important stuff has to stop." She opened the closet door wider and there on the floor was the leash. Alice ran her hands over Audrey's wrinkles as she fumbled with securing the leash to the harness. "Here we go."

Snaking through wine country was peaceful at dawn as colorful balloons lifted into the sky. With the car window cracked open, she heard balloon fire providing a soft distant whoosh. The police car and rental passed a small white church with an old graveyard in front of it before the landscape returned to more vineyards. Seeing an old-fashioned farmyard windmill twist in the breeze, Alice reflected on how the precise organization of grapevine rows resembled young corn plants on the Fourth of July—only wider apart.

With Audrey tethered in the passenger seat, they followed Breakiron's car to a campground full of small cabins. Outside stood a cluster of people listening to Officers McNally and Garcia. In the gathering of people, a man and woman stood gripping each other. Breakiron joined Alice as the bloodhound jumped from the car.

"My daughter is five years old," said the mother to a cluster of neighbors and police. Her hair was light blonde, her face and throat mottled. She wore white shorts and a black tank top, revealing tattoos on her upper arms and one calf.

"I don't know where she went." The father's deep voice broke, becoming thin as he spoke. "This morning she was gone. We've searched everywhere in camp." He was a big man with broad shoulders, his hair rumpled. Jeans covered his legs but like his wife, his arms were tattooed creating a blueish cast to his skin.

"I put her to bed," said the mother. "We played cards with our neighbors." Two people casting their eyes downward, nodded. "I checked on her before we went to bed." The mother's eyes met those of her husband as if to affirm the truth of what she said. Alice wondered how many times she'd had to repeat this story to other neighbors and police.

The father bit his lower lip.

"Have you had kidnappings?" Fright was clear in the mother's voice. "Did someone take Kiley?"

McNally said, "There is no evidence of a cabin break-in."

"We have to do something!" the mother proclaimed. "Why are we standing here? Tell us what to do."

Breakiron appeared ready to comfort or explain, but Alice put her hand on the younger woman's arm as she turned toward the parents.

"Do you have a piece of your daughter's clothing? Pajamas work well."

The mother looked startled at Alice's question. The father said, "Yes, one of the officers said you'd need this."

Alice took the plastic bag with the child's T-shirt and turned her attention to Audrey.

"We're going to find a little girl," she said with bright enthusiasm to her dog. Audrey gave her an *Oh-boy!* face. "Take a big sniff." The hound's nose barely skimmed the bagged clothing when she pulled away. "Audrey, find."

Audrey first swept the ground around the cabin. Alice imagined her dog's long ears as two brooms collecting clouds of odor, waving the smells back toward her nose.

The mother said, "She hardly smelled the clothing at all. Make her try again."

But Audrey was off and trailing the scent. The sun was up, and the hound loped along a broken asphalt road. Breakiron convinced the small cluster of neighbors to fan out behind Audrey, looking for anything the child may have dropped. Alice knew the crowd wasn't given enough instructions for a true grid search. Breakiron was keeping them occupied, apparently trusting Audrey's nose.

"Up ahead, the road changes to dirt. Maybe look for footprints," ordered Breakiron. "The child is barefoot as far as we know. And listen for sounds."

Everyone moved in silence. The only sound—the padding of feet.

"Will conversation distract your dog?" Breakiron whispered. "Is there anything else I should mention to volunteers?"

"A hound with an odor to follow is pretty much zoned out of the world, virtually blind and deaf to distractions. She has a chance to show off. It's why handlers keep a bloodhound on a leash. She'd walk into a tree or out into traffic if she were on her own. Right now, the only thing she wants is to find that smell."

"What makes kids wander off?" asked Breakiron, more to herself than Alice.

"My daughter usually wanted something. Had to have it *now*," said Alice. "My son was different. He wanted an adventure. Wanted to prove something. Luckily for me, they usually wandered to a neighbor's house. I might not have known where they were for fifteen minutes, but they were always some place safe. A shout away."

"This little girl is five, and a tourist. How does she know where to go?"

"She might be headed in the wrong direction for what she wants, but I'm willing to bet she has a purpose. A pretty strong one if she left in the night." Alice recalled the elderly man with dementia who'd wandered off last summer to an old airport. He too had a purpose. "What's up ahead?" asked Alice.

Breakiron glanced over her shoulder, "Nimble knows this area better than I do. Nimble?"

Nimble? thought Alice and turned her head enough to see a thin man in jeans and a long-sleeved, blue shirt trot up to Breakiron. He was probably in his fifties, his face heavily lined, sparse graying hair cut short.

"Alice wants to know about the terrain," said Breakiron. "I rarely get down here."

"Just more blocks of grapes," answered Nimble. "A walnut farm a little further on. Then some small houses. Down this road, people are private, don't like company. They handle things themselves."

"As far as I know, we've never been called out here. They wouldn't hurt a child? Right?" asked Breakiron.

"Not at all." Nimble shook his head. "They won't like us walking their land, but for a missing kid, they'll understand." He dipped his face away from Breakiron.

"Why do you look concerned?" asked Alice.

"The river cuts in ahead. At this time of year, it's only a small stream, but can have a swift current."

"This is crazy," claimed the mother walking behind them. "That dog can't know where Kiley is. We've walked over a mile. My daughter's five. She wouldn't have walked this far in the dark."

"Mom's worried," mouthed Breakiron before she dropped back and spoke softly to the mother, offering comfort but also asking additional questions. The mother regained control in reviewing the previous evening. Kiley went to bed. The adults played cards. The little girl wasn't angry or upset before bedtime. In fact, she was eager to find a water park the next day. Their itinerary included splashing, sliding, and playing, before returning to the campground for an evening barbecue with neighbors. Kiley liked barbecue.

Audrey's head stayed down, her nose to the ground. Alice skipped along behind, careful to keep up.

The fast-moving stream about two car lengths wide but only six inches deep skirted the dirt road. The mother gasped as Audrey moved toward the water. Alice too felt the tension as she noticed the steep bank of earth, a nine-foot mudslide into the water. Alice shivered.

Even in the six inches of water, a child could drown. But after stopping at the edge of the drop-off, Audrey pivoted back toward the road. Her nose twitched as her head swept back and forth, making sure she had the trail.

"Besides the danger of drowning, wild boar and mountain lions come for fresh water," whispered Nimble to Alice. "Usually animals hide from humans. But a child? I don't know."

"So far, Audrey's body language tells me Kiley has a goal. I think she's determined," said Alice.

"You can tell that from how your dog moves? She looks like a dog sniffing."

"Exactly," said Alice. "The child didn't stop her walk. Didn't waver."

As a stand of trees came into view, Audrey's head lifted into the air, and her pace picked up. A gurgle came into her throat before she barked twice.

"What just happened?" asked Nimble.

"Audrey thinks she's found the little girl. I'll hold her back. Don't want to scare Kiley. Will you check the trees?"

Nimble waved Officer Garcia forward as McNally alerted the paramedics. Breakiron held onto the mother's elbow as the woman covered her mouth with her hands, fear in her eyes. McNally stood next to the father and grabbed his arm. Nimble and Garcia hustled to the stand of trees and disappeared behind them. To Alice, it seemed everyone in the group held his breath while Audrey barked and wiggled her success. She knew the child was there and wanted to do a final nose kiss of accomplishment.

"Please let her be okay," whispered Alice.

From where she stood, Alice saw Nimble's foot and lower leg on the ground, kneeling. The group watched as a small hand appeared from behind the tree and took hold of Nimble's fingers. Garcia came out from behind a tree and waved everyone forward. "She's okay."

The mother tore away from Breakiron. "Kiley?"

The group turned into motion as two paramedics rushed toward the trees. The mother cried and hugged her daughter, Alice braced for Audrey's paws to hit her shoulders for a customary hug, and the crowd of volunteers patted everyone on the back while laughing and wiping happy tears.

"Looks like she walked here until she got tired," said Nimble. "Her face's a bit swollen. Maybe from crying. But she had this flashlight. Smart kid."

Alice heard the father say "Where'd she find that? It's not ours."

"I wish Audrey wouldn't bark at a find." Alice took a deep breath and released tension. "Particularly with a child. Dogs can be scary, but it's also not good to announce a find if trailing a bad guy."

Kiley's mother insisted on carrying her daughter away from the trees and back to the dirt road. She buried her face into her daughter's shoulder. The paramedics trailed behind. Not letting go of her child, the mother plopped down on the grass, pulling Kiley onto her lap.

"Honey, why did you walk away?" asked her mother as a paramedic squatted beside them.

"I wanted to feed the bunnies," she said in a small disappointed voice.

"What bunnies?" asked the father.

"The ones coming to dinner."

Her mother looked up, shocked. "Oh, my God. I'm so sorry."

"You heard us last night?" asked the father.

Both turned to Breakiron. "We were planning a barbecue for to-night of fresh . . ."The mother mouthed "rabbit" and then whispered, "from a local farm."

Alice hunkered down and handed a dog treat to the child. "Oh, your mommy hasn't heard. The bunnies can't come to dinner tonight, but if you want to feed Audrey, that's okay."

Small fingers held out a dog treat, and Audrey's soft mouth accepted the offering. Kiley pulled back her hand, wiping slobber on her pajama top. Everyone laughed fear away. While the paramedics checked out Kiley, Audrey distracted the girl by downing six more treats. Both child and dog looked pleased.

After mother and child were in the ambulance, Nimble said, "There's a rabbit farm at one of those houses I talked about. People around here place orders for fresh rabbit. The family doesn't like strangers to know too much of their business. Scary for kids who grew up with Thumper."

Breakiron nodded. "For me too. I may carry a gun, but I'd rather shoot a bad guy than take out an animal."

Audrey turned to stare at the vineyard across the river. Her body was still, tongue tucked into her mouth. Alice recognized the robotic, serious face as her dog scanned the rows of grapes, puzzled. Was there a dangerous animal? But the symmetry of the grapevines on guide wires was all Alice noticed. Whatever her dog detected was nowhere in sight.

"What's attracted your attention?" asked Alice of her dog. Audrey moved with an awkward grace, but whipped back into a frozen stance, studying the vines. Alice felt a chill like the one she had when she heard the crackles the night of the murder.

The mother left the ambulance and approached Alice, Nimble, and the police officers.

"I want to thank you for finding my daughter. I was so scared. I didn't behave . . . I'm grateful for your help and for your dog."

"We're happy we found her," said Alice.

Grinning, the mother added, "She just told me a purple fairy with wings appeared and kept her warm. She told her to wait for her mum. That's when Kiley fell asleep." The mother wiped tears away with the heel of her hand. "I told her it was her guardian angel, but I think *all* of you are angels." As more tears fell, she walked away with her husband, back to her daughter and the ambulance.

"At least we're not purple," joked Garcia.

"Wasn't there a blue angel in some Disney cartoon?" asked McNally.

"Pinocchio," said Breakiron. "And it wasn't a blue angel, it was a blue fairy who came to comfort the wooden boy. You guys clearly don't have kids."

One officer swatted at the other. "Let's get people out of here."

The father caught Alice's sleeve before she could leave. "I want to thank you too. I don't live around here, but I have an uncle and aunt a half hour away. You need anything, call. Here's my card. I'm Jordan Shango."

Alice put the card in her pocket without looking at it. "My pleasure to find her. Glad everything turned out."

"Alice, can I get a lift back to Eleanora's vineyard?" asked Nimble. "One of the officers caught me and asked me to help because I know the area. Got a ride here with him."

Alice delighted in the opportunity. She had questions about vineyard safety for her dog. They walked back to the car with Audrey doing her proud, awkward shimmy and Nimble commenting on the search.

"I'll have to ask you to sit in the back. If you sit in front, Audrey will be in your lap. She's used to a bench seat of my pickup, and this car is small with bucket seats."

"Understood." Nimble climbed into the back and leaned his hands on the back of the front seat. Even with Audrey's tether in place, she managed to hang her head over the seat and leave slobber stripes on their guest.

"She likes nothing better than playing hide-and-seek. To her a search is play," said Alice.

"I've been in a couple of searches for lost hikers up in the hills," said Nimble working his thumbs into the wrinkles on Audrey's face. "This is a small community, and we all help where we can. But I've never seen a bloodhound in action. So, you're a detective?"

"No, not at all. Someone put up a website saying I am, but I'm a grandma in California to see my grandson graduate." Feeling compelled to say something about detective work, Alice added, "Audrey amazes me every time we go out on a search. Her nose is like radar. I guess that's why Guthrie asked for our help finding her son Cade."

"We were all sorry to hear about Guthrie."

"I ate dinner with her the night she was murdered. She asked me to search the fields with Audrey in case—"

"In case, her son was killed and buried on vineyard land?" finished Nimble. "She ran that past me, too."

"It seems unlikely, I know, but I promised her Audrey and I would try."

"Lots of reasons it can't be true. First off, the men in the field would notice if earth was disturbed. We're pretty particular about any kind of change in the vineyard." Alice caught his expression in the rearview mirror. His eyes narrowed into a frown. "Mold, mildew, insects, disease. The men are vigilant, on constant watch. One infestation can destroy a block of grapes to the point we have to rip out the vines and start over. Believe me, someone would have noticed if a body were buried."

"You told Guthrie this?"

"I did. But she's a mother. Worried. And O'Dare could be unpredictable, so I understand how she jumped to conclusions."

Nimble looked out a side window as if weighing something in his mind. Guthrie's request sounded unlikely to Alice, but she needed to know of any dangers to Audrey if they should walk between rows of grapevines.

"Is it safe for Audrey to walk through the fields?"

"Definitely. Most vineyards have dogs. Our men know they can bring dogs with them. You might see two yellow labs and a sprinting border collie tearing along rows or beside a cart. Of course, if you should see men in hazmat gear–probably not a good day to walk a dog."

"What do you think happened to Cade?"

Nimble's hand went through his hair. "He's a good kid. Far as I could tell the only one angry with him was his old man. Look, the kid's interested in grapes. The old man wanted him to take business classes, but he never finessed Cade, you know? Present the idea of the business side of owning a winery."

"Do you know anything about the last argument Cade had with his father?"

"No. Only of an early one when the kid went off to college. Not the details, though."

"I walked through Cade's room last night. I saw books on making wine."

"I loaned him the books," said Nimble with an air of guilt. "If you have a chance, I'd like them back. Never wanted to approach either Mrs. Huff with all that has happened."

"How'd Cade get interested in grapes?"

Nimble shook his head. "I'm not sure. Eleanora and O'Dare were only interested in contracting the sale of grapes. Cade, however, once told me there is poetry in growing them. Can you believe that?"

"I know farmers back home who'd agree with the poetry of the land."

"Well, I've never seen anything rhyme in the field."

"D.H. Lawrence was an English writer. He has a poem called 'Grapes.' The only line I remember is 'Down the tendrilled avenues of wine.'"

"For a moment, I thought you were gonna say *tendrilled avenues of murder.*"

"Well, that works too. Twisting, gnarling, avenues of motives." Alice smiled. "See, you do have a poetic side. She watched in the rearview mirror as one side of Nimble's mouth grinned back. "Saw a motorcycle magazine in Cade's room."

"Can't help you there."

"You ever see Cade with anyone? Did he have a girlfriend?"

"I manage a few vineyards for Penzberg Wines, so I'm not always here. They have a long-term contract with Eleanora and many other growers. The crop is trucked out to the winery. Never personally saw anyone talking to Cade." Nimble's eyebrows again drew together. "The men in the field, however, saw someone, twice. Asked me if we had a new man on the crew. I'll mention it to them and see if they can provide more description."

"Any chance I could see surveillance tapes of the vineyard?"

"Surveillance?"

"The wooden boxes on poles in the vineyards. All the vineyards seem to have them. I'm thinking the crop is precious, and you have an eye in the sky."

Nimble's laugh exploded. "I'm sorry. I didn't know what you were talking about at first, but you're right. We do have eyes in the sky. Many. Those boxes are owl nests. Vineyards keep barn owls to cut down on the rodent population. Grapes contain some sugar and attract all kinds of pests, and thankfully, young owls are hungry for rodent meat."

"Owls," mused Alice. "I like owls. More than one person has teased that I look like an owl."

"It's your eyes," said Nimble. "Big, round, and gray. An owl is a fine bird."

As Alice pulled into the vineyard driveway, she saw Jess's car parked next to Elka's and another belonging to Detective Galati. Several other worker vehicles were parked near the outbuildings. After they left the car, Alice and Nimble stood still allowing Audrey to sniff her interest in roses.

"Nimble, I have to ask. Do you have any idea what happened to Cade?"

"I don't know. Maybe ran off. Seemed unhappy."

"Was Cade the kind of kid who was discontent or despondent. I'm asking because I went through his room last night. Everything belonging to Cade is still there."

"I've never been in the house," said Nimble, his eyes downcast. "But if you're asking if Cade considered taking his own life, I can't believe he'd actually go through with it. He was kinda dreamy, you know? Dragged around here. O'Dare called him 'that fool boy.'" A hardness entered Nimble's eyes, his mouth tightened.

"You believe he's still alive?"

Nimble shrugged. "Your next question is going to be why he didn't come home for his father's funeral. The question after that is will he be home for his mother's funeral. You're not the first to ask about Cade's disappearance. My answer is I don't know. I mostly saw him walking to his Jeep."

Alice nodded. "How does Galati strike you?"

"I know him," answered Nimble. With a glint in his eye, he said, "He's a cool one. But he knows his stuff. If anyone can figure out Guthrie's murder, he can. Who are the two waving at us?"

Alice looked over her shoulder toward the house as two young people scurried out a door and down the porch steps.

"As I suspected," said Alice, "my daughter brought my two grandchildren."

"Lucky lady," Nimble said with a grin.

Chapter 13

"Gram!" Juliana put her arms around her grandmother in a big hug. "Audrey is huge! Want me to walk her for you?"

Juliana stood 5'9" and had a face more rounded than Henry's. Both had the same brown hair color, lightened by the sun. Henry stood well over six feet, wore jeans and a navy-blue T-shirt with a school logo, and looked like a young version of his grandfather Baer. Juliana's eyes mirrored the Okazaki side of the family. She wore beige shorts and a long-sleeved, olive shirt. Juliana's huskiness reflected Alice's family, specifically Aunt Lu. The surprise for Alice was Juliana's diamond stud in her nose. More evidence that she had Aunt Lu's flair running in her veins.

Alice gave both of her grandchildren big hugs and marveled at how Juliana had changed in a year.

Wearing a beige fishing hat, Galati sat at the table on the porch. This time he wore half glasses and held a tablet in front of him. His hand waved an invitation for Alice to sit next to Jess. Her two grandchildren stood near the other table. Behind Alice, Breakiron trotted up and took a seat at the table near Henry and Juliana.

"Back from a search," said Breakiron. "The other officers are finishing up."

Audrey's eyes drooped more than usual as she stared at Juliana. Being ignored even after a whine, the dog's nose slammed into Juliana's crotch. Juliana jumped back.

"Hey!" she yelled. "Not nice."

"Sorry," said Alice, "Some dogs smell feet. Audrey gets more personal." She pulled her hound away from her granddaughter and bent to whisper to Audrey while tousling her ears.

"Audrey could use some water."

As if she heard Alice's request, Elka walked out the French doors. "I see you walk up. Have water for dog. I hear search a success." Elka put down the huge stainless-steel bowl, and Audrey's face plunged into the water, even her nose.

Juliana's nose wrinkled as she watched water slop over the sides of the bowl and onto the porch. "Is she really that thirsty, or just messy?"

"I know you two want to visit," said Galati cutting off Alice's answer, "but you both agreed to give us some privacy." His voice and face were stern, and Alice's grandchildren retreated from the porch.

"Where are you going?" asked Alice.

"For a walk," said Henry, while pulling out his phone. Juliana rooted in her bag until she found hers.

As they left, Audrey's face again rose from the water. A jaunty shake sent streams flying. All questions stopped as Jess, Alice, and Galati dabbed at clothing, but only Jess gave Alice her stink eye.

Jess was always the serious one who carried responsibility for everyone around her. At 5'7" she was shorter than Juliana. Jess sat forward in her chair, forearms on the table, her ankles curled around the legs of the chair. She wore a salmon polo shirt, white shorts, and sandals. Her face, arms, and legs were heavily freckled. *How she hates freckles*, mused Alice. Alice reached out and took her daughter's hand.

"I'm allowing you to sit with your daughter," said Galati, "because she will tell you about my interview anyway, and some detail Jess says may recall a memory of something Guthrie told you. Since all of this is hearsay, might as well have it all at once." He turned to Jess. "Did Guthrie have any enemies that you know of? Anyone contentious?"

"Not that I ever heard," said Jess. "Not recently."

"Before?"

"Only her husband. But he's dead," said Jess. "Since the shooting, I've been trying to think of who might have wanted to hurt her. I can't think of anyone. We only met at yoga and stopped for tea afterwards. I don't really know of other friends."

"Let's work with that," said Galati. "What did you talk about? What drew you together?"

"Normal events like yoga. We were both beginners. We both wanted to lose weight. Both hungry after a session."

"Did she reveal any complaints?"

"Family." Jess stole a guilty look at Alice. "I told her about my mother being too *old* to investigate crimes." Jess rolled her eyes as if to say, *you know it's true.* "She told me about her husband, son, and mother-in-law."

Galati nodded and asked about the private investigator.

"O'Dare refused to allow her to hire an investigator and then Eleanora—that's her mother-in-law—delayed notification of the police once O'Dare was gone." Jess shook her head. "It was complicated. Both Guthrie and Eleanora expected Cade to return for his father's funeral."

"But he didn't show."

"No. That caused her to worry that something had happened to him."

"I would think a mother might file a report despite what anybody said." Galati's eyes were narrow.

Alice knew the tilt of Jess's head. She had something more to add.

"I would have," said Jess.

"You hinted that Guthrie and Eleanora might have issues with each other. What was her relationship with her mother-in-law?"

"I think they tolerated each other. Guthrie knew for years that Eleanora bailed out O'Dare when he was irresponsible. But in the last couple of years, when O'Dare needed cash, she didn't come through."

Galati took notes. In her mind, Alice underscored money. Eleanora had it. O'Dare not—despite arranging parties on yachts.

"This is all history. Anything current? Guthrie ever talk about being afraid, needing a gun?" asked Galati.

"No." Jess looked surprised at the question.

"She ever talk of going to bars?"

"She went to bars?" asked Jess turning to Alice, shock on her face. "I can't imagine that. She was a health nut. Even more than me, Mother."

Alice recognized another line of questions to ask Jess. How did Guthrie's wine drinking figure into that perception of health? But she'd leave that for another moment.

"Did she ever talk about her son going to a bar?" insisted the detective.

"No."

Alice found it too difficult to sit silently and observe. "Do you have an ID for the body of the man found in the rows of grapes?"

Galati looked annoyed with her question. "We do. Xavier Nettle, a bartender at the Hungry Fool, a bar about twenty miles south." Focusing on Jess, he asked, "She ever mention Xavier or the Hungry Fool?"

"No. I've never even heard of it."

"Mostly a beer bar. Frequented by bikers," said Galati.

Alice knew that with an identity, the police had already questioned the workers and patrons at the Hungry Fool for information about Xavier. If the previous night's incident were a simple robbery gone bad, there would be no reason to dig into Guthrie's story. And by now forensics would have the caliber of the gun used in the murder. But *bikers* caught Alice's ear—bikers on the road, biker magazine, bartender at biker bar.

"Detective," asked Alice, "what kind of gun was used to shoot Guthrie?"

"You also a gun expert, Mrs. Tricklebank?"

"Certainly not. Curious that's all."

"Well, this is my interview." Galati sounded like a scolding parent, but then he grinned. "The four bullets were .38 caliber, shot from the same gun. Guthrie registered a Smith and Wesson .357 revolver. Common gun, but I'd say unusual for the ladies. They commonly own .22s."

"Do you have her gun?" asked Alice clamping down her riled emotions ignited by *ladies*. At least he didn't say, *the little ladies like a .22 so it doesn't stretch out their handbag.*

"Elka thinks it's in the safe," said Galati, eyes narrowing. "We can wait for Eleanora to return this afternoon to open it. According to Elka, the safe combination was known to both Eleanora and Guthrie. We've finished searching the house, and as you can see, clean-up is in progress before Eleanora arrives. However, we will leave the plastic over the door to the scene of the crime."

Alice made a note in her head. Why was Galati willing to share that the bullet was a .38 but the gun Guthrie owned a .357? It didn't make sense. Why look for Guthrie's gun if the shells were different? When Julian arrived, Alice intended to ask him what he knew about guns. The detective was behaving as if Guthrie had her gun in hand, ready for trouble.

Sitting at the table, Alice stretched her spine. She felt a certain eagerness to move, to do *something*. She found it annoying that when Guthrie needed help, she hadn't alerted her. Shooting was not Alice's skill, but she could have called for help.

"Now, if I may continue with my questions, Alice," said Galati turning back to Jess, "She never mentioned fear."

"No, she didn't. Maybe isolation. She missed her former home and friends, not that she had many."

"Was she depressed?"

"That's hard for me to answer. I work in a mental health clinic, and we have specific descriptors for depression. Let's leave it at sad. Guthrie was sad." Jess's shoulders sagged. She took a minute, her eyes turning to the vineyard. "I think Guthrie was frustrated for a lot of years. I don't know why she stayed with O'Dare. When he became sick and his party business failed, he still binge shopped for big items nobody needed. Detective, money collectors were at their door."

"So, we could be looking for an angry guy wanting to be paid his money."

"Maybe. I don't know."

"I'm sorry to peel off in a different direction," said Alice, "but you said Guthrie was shot with the same caliber gun as the one that shot Xavier?"

"Seems so." His face was cagey almost egging her on.

"Did forensics find gunpowder residue on Guthrie's hands?"

The detective tilted his head, saying nothing. Alice took the silence as *Yes*.

"So, after Xavier was shot," said Alice, "maybe by Guthrie, the third party got into a skirmish with her, wrestled the gun away, and shot her three times. How did Guthrie get the .38 in the first place?"

The detective glowered. "May I continue?"

Alice nodded as her mind went to her imaginary whiteboard. Who had threatened Guthrie enough to cause her to kill. Who did O'Dare owe money? Had parties been canceled, the deposits not returned? Alice decided Guthrie's fear about other women didn't measure up because seven months had passed after O'Dare's death. The killer wasn't an angry husband.

"You said they had bill collectors at their door. Did Guthrie give any indication of his commitments coming here for payment?" asked Galati, apparently reading Alice's mind. "Maybe contact with a lady friend?"

Jess shook her head. "I don't know."

The Hungry Fool crossed into Alice's thinking. In the Midwest acquaintances weren't eager to share with the police if the information they had might be misleading? What if they accused an innocent person and caused trouble? On the other hand, people were very willing to tattle on someone they didn't like if the listener were non-threatening, like an older, retired woman who didn't dress well and traveled with a bloodhound. If she could steal away from the vineyard, maybe she'd brave a biker bar.

"Sorry again, but I have to ask," said Alice. "Do you know if Xavier was a good worker?"

"I thought you were going to ask if he was known to be a thief." Galati's chin dropped. He glared at Alice.

"Was he a thief?" asked Alice.

"Not that anyone said." Galati physically turned his back on Alice. "Jess, do you know of any difficulty that could threaten Guthrie or any person who might know detail about her?"

"We were in yoga class together, so other than some complaining and worry, I really don't know her that well." Jess looked at her mother with her born-and-bred Midwestern look. "What happens now?"

Alice gripped Jess's hand and smiled her support.

"We wait for Eleanora to come home and open the safe," said Galati as he rose to leave.

"Detective," said Alice, "I have two friends who will be arriving late this afternoon. Elka said Eleanora is afraid of being alone in the house. I've invited them to provide company."

Galati gave Alice a questioning glance before a grin broke on his face. "I'm not rid of you?"

"Nope. I promised to look for Cade."

"Those two friends, the older couple on the website?"

"That would be them, yes."

"Good."

"Detective," said Jess, her voice direct, "if I think of anything else, I'll let you know, but I want you to promise to watch my mother." Jess frowned at Alice. "She can be a little too trusting in her abilities. Always thinks she's supposed to solve problems." Jess's tone became sarcastic. "What is it Dad always said about baseball?"

"Watch the runner," answered Alice with an overly bright smile.

"When someone should be watching the catcher and what she's doing," scolded Jess.

Alice turned to Galati. "She means me."

"So I gathered. You both know the police here are pretty good, and we're in charge," said Galati.

"Goes without saying," affirmed Alice.

"You learn something, I'm your first call," said Galati.

"Absolutely."

"Make sure your friends know that too."

"Will do." Alice raised her hand in a salute.

Detective Galati walked to his car. Silent during the interview, Breakiron fiddled with her sunglasses, her hat, and checked her phone before she was ready to leave the porch. Alice knew the time-killing behavior and moved to her side.

"Xavier has a few disorderly-conducts on file," said Breakiron, barely moving her lips. "As a kid, he had a reputation for theft, but you didn't hear it from me."

Chapter 14

Time: Tuesday, 11:47 a.m.

After a family-size portion of spaghetti and salad, Henry polished off a mountain of cannoli pie. Juliana, Jess, and Alice ate less then picked at leftovers until all the pasta was gone. Audrey watched each forkful. The police were gone, so too was the professional clean-up crew.

Four sighs of accomplishment later, everyone sat back in their chairs while Elka scoured the kitchen, preparing to go home. Bees worked the lavender next to the porch and created a soft hum.

Alice asked, "Henry, are you willing to go upstairs and look at Cade's room? I'd like your male-take in case I'm being too sensitive about a boy's room."

"Sure."

"Not without me," said Juliana. "I'll hold Audrey in the hallway. She has to go along, right?"

"Right."

"I'm not sitting down here alone," said Jess.

Together the four plus Audrey climbed to the second floor. Before they entered Cade's room, Alice provided latex gloves for each of them and herself.

"Put these on first. I don't want the police hunting you down to identify prints you leave behind." Henry and Juliana obeyed. Jess did too but ended up outside the room as the holder of Audrey's leash. "Look around and tell me what you notice or what questions occur to you."

"Did he choose the colors?" asked Juliana. "Kinda dark. Who chooses dark brown for a bedroom?"

"We both know Dungeon and Dragon guys at school who like moody role-playing," countered Henry. "We've seen black bedrooms." He turned to his grandmother. "They decorate with chain-mail."

"Their rooms are all black?" asked Jess, winding Audrey's leash around her hand. "How do you know?" Jess's voice challenged their experiences.

"I know a couple of guys in band. Juliana heard me talk about them," said Henry way too fast. He opened a closet door.

Alice saw her two grandchildren give each other a look. Juliana rolled her eyes toward her mother.

"Mom, gamers aren't bad people just because they dress up," said Juliana. "You taught me that. They're a lot like Gram. Gathering facts, testing theories, drawing conclusions. Isn't that what you do, Gram?"

Henry cut in before either Alice or Jess could respond. "Where are his things?" His head moved from scanning walls to a desk and back to the closet.

"Like what? What are you expecting?" asked Alice.

"Clothes?" said Henry with a sarcastic tone. "These clothes are old. I mean, he can't be a poor kid."

Juliana pulled a shirt from a drawer. "No one would wear this any-more. I mean, it's okay for you, Gram, but he's twenty."

"Why?" asked Alice. "It looks clean and it's from a concert."

Juliana held up a shirt and raised an eyebrow. "The band fell apart four years ago. No one would wear an old concert shirt unless the band is still really, really respected. Like from your day. Maybe the Dead." She carefully folded the shirt and put it back.

Alice heard an echo of Lena's criticism, clean and useful isn't fashion.

"I thought you said they were rich," said Henry.

"I think I said comfortable, but yes I imagine rich captures his grand-mother at least."

Alice's grandchildren continued to look through the closet and drawers.

"Can I open his wallet?" asked Henry.

"Be careful not to disrupt the order."

After opening and closing the wallet, Henry moved away from all the items on the end of the dresser. He leaned against the wall and shoved his hands into his pockets.

"Gram? What happened to him?" Henry's expression reflected tragedy.

"Don't know. His mother thought someone may have . . . kidnapped him."

"Then it had to be from the house when he least expected to go out."

"Maybe. Why do you say that?" asked Alice.

"Because if it were me, there's no way I'd leave any of this stuff be-hind. I have a hard time remembering where I put my keys if they're not in my pocket. Ask Mom."

As they spoke, Juliana poked into the tablet left behind. She turned it on to readily available icons and one that demanded his password.

"It works?" asked Alice. "It hasn't been used for months."

"The power's at eighty-nine percent. Has someone else been check-ing out his tablet?"

"I'm guessing yes," said Alice. "What's on it?"

"Business text books. But that doesn't explain why there are no books in the room." Alice watched her granddaughter type information then hit exit. Tap more search words. Exit. "I checked Facebook and Twitter. He hasn't posted anything since last year. You want me to check Snapchat?"

"As long as you don't change anything."

Out of the corner of her eye, Alice watched Juliana fiddle with her bag and move back to the tablet, tapping, swiping, exiting.

"There's no way a guy would leave the house without keys, identification, and phone . . . look, his wallet even has money," said Henry. "No way."

"Was he kidnapped Gram?" asked Juliana.

"I don't believe so, because would the kidnapper leave Cade's possessions on the dresser? Henry's right. The wallet has money. The tablet could be sold. Keys to Cade's Jeep?"

"He has a Jeep? No way he'd leave that behind," said Henry.

"Maybe someone wanted to hurt his family," said Juliana, far more seriously than Alice liked.

"Okay, we've seen enough," said Jess. "Downstairs. Now!" As the two children marched downstairs, Jess grabbed her mother's arm. "This is what I hate about you snooping. You bring my children into a room of a boy who clearly committed suicide? Mother, really, I am so angry with you. We see this behavior at the mental health clinic. This boy was severely depressed, and I'm guessing desperate." With that, Jess shoved Audrey's leash into Alice's hand.

"You think suicide?" asked Alice. "You're sure?"

"He left everything behind that gives him an identity. What else can it be?"

Alice watched her daughter charge ahead away from her. Henry and Juliana looked over their shoulders.

"He killed himself? Why?" Juliana looked stricken.

"We're going home," announced Jess. "No more butting into this poor boy's life."

Both grandchildren hesitated before going down the stairs. "What about tomorrow?" asked Henry.

"You have school. If your grandmother can promise she won't involve you in her case, she may see us Thursday. But this murder or kidnapping is not our concern."

Alice wanted a moment to explain, but the opportunity had passed. Given a chance, Alice would have added, *This is California, where are his sunglasses?*

Juliana was the first to enter the car, followed by Jess. Henry pulled Alice aside, but said to his mother, "I got that thing to tell Gram." Jess nodded approval, and Alice saw Henry's strong shoulders carried distress. "I have to tell you—"

"I'm sorry if the room disturbed you," said Alice.

"No, it's not that. It's about graduation on Sunday." Henry hung his head as if he were a small boy. "I can only have four tickets. Mom, Dad, Juliana, and my other grandma, you know Dad's mom. Grandfather Okazaki is a professional photographer, so he has permission to take pictures for the online yearbook. He doesn't need a ticket."

The reality hit Alice like a punch to the jaw, and she felt a little dizzy. There was no seat for her at graduation.

"Oh." She could think of nothing to say. She'd come all this way, putting her friends in an uncomfortable situation, and now wasn't going to see her grandson graduate after all. Had she been too insistent about traveling to California? She never considered Audrey wouldn't be allowed to go to an outdoor graduation. Never considered limited tickets.

How stupid of me! I know better.

Alice fought tears, blinking and looking toward the tangling of grape vines to gain control.

"I understand, Henry. It would be nice to see you cross the stage, but I understand. I have Audrey but no dog-sitter." *And apparently no ticket*. "Even if you had a ticket for me, Audrey presents a problem. Sitting shoulder to shoulder on bleachers could be tight. It's okay. I'll look forward to your graduation party." She tried to smile as she squeezed his arm.

"No, no, you don't understand. I have . . . a special ticket for you." His head dropped again, and he didn't make eye contact. For a moment, he was a sad puppy. "The school has reserved seats down front for special needs. You know, like grandparents in wheel chairs. You have to be in place exactly at twelve-thirty. Graduation starts at one."

"Henry, nobody will think I belong in a wheelchair."

"I know." Henry's face brightened. "That's why I told the school you have epilepsy and need to bring a service dog to alert you if a grand mal seizure is coming on. There's a kid at school who has a dog for epilepsy. Gram, you have a ticket, but I had to lie. I want you there."

Alice swallowed hard, conflicted. "I'm not taking someone's place who really needs a spot?"

"No. I checked." Henry took on a naughty glee. "They have eight more empty places. You'll be seated on the end, close to the paramedics, because, just in case . . . but you have to be there at twelve-thirty. The school will allow regular family to fill in the empty seats after that."

Henry's eyes pleaded as Alice slowly closed her eyes, feeling morals decay for love. She held him in a big hug.

"Then I'll be there. Promptly at twelve-thirty." Alice felt her pulse keep pace with the drum beat of time.

"You can't be late."

Alice wanted to say something clever to cut the tension but thought better of a Cinderella comparison.

As she released Henry, Audrey apparently felt left out. Standing on her hind feet, the hound stretched to put her front paws on Henry's shoulders. Her grandson had Baer's grin as he hugged the dog.

"She is really big. I can't wait until my friends see her."

Chapter 15

Time: Tuesday, 4:27 p.m.

The afternoon sky took on a golden glow even though it wasn't anywhere near dusk. The vineyards appeared to be demanding quiet. Everyone had gone: Jess and her children, Elka to her children, Roddy Merritt, the cleaning crew, the police, including the lonely squad car at the end of the driveway, even the workers from the field—all gone. Alice locked up the house and stood on the porch to take in the peace and poetry of the vineyard. In every direction around the house, symmetrical rows of grape vines hugged guide wires. The land and man's effort brought forth bounty. Deep in the yard, an outdoor pizza oven anchored a picnic area. Overhead, patio lights swung in a light breeze. Without yet knowing Eleanora, Alice respected the woman who spent her life in the middle of a vineyard, wrapped in beauty and order.

Back in the cottage without her leash attached, Audrey swept every corner with her nose. The dog's gurgle reminded Alice that she promised her hound an hour of serious playtime at the dog park.

"Wait a minute, please. I haven't forgotten everything you like."

With the hound watching her every move, Alice secured her special surprise at the top of the backpack and quickly hunted for her hound's tennis ball. She found it in the bathtub.

"I'm still not forgiven for leaving your sock toy behind?"

Together they walked to the park built on the property of an abandoned soap factory. Audrey's nose twitched as they entered the gates. Alice, too, found the smell bitter but oddly familiar, as if she had walked into her grandmother's house on wash day.

"Audrey, this smells just like Fels Naptha. Rather curious for an old soap factory, particularly after all these years."

She unclipped the leash, and Audrey took off in an explosion of joy, leaping and charging, rolling in grass, climbing on benches, barking at tough beach balls, and proving she was besotted with smells.

"Did you think I forgot your bubble wand?"

Alice dipped the wand into the jar of soapy water and blew. Iridescent bubbles winged above Audrey's head. With determination, the hound snapped at the disappearing magic. Dunking the wand again, Alice twirled, holding the wand above her own head. Bubbles floated down. Bloodhound paws hit Alice's chest, leveraging a chance to catch a bubble. With one big sweep, Alice waved bubbles on another wild ride. Audrey took off at a gallop around the yard and cornered a big globe of soap before it exploded on her nose, causing her to sneeze.

For a half-hour, Alice stopped thinking about murder, and danced in bubbles. Her dog was every bit a clown. She caught herself laughing out loud.

When they returned to the vineyard, Alice went through her dog's routine, cleaning face and wrinkles, brushing fur, inspecting paws.

"No irritants for you. Besides, we need to go into the main house. Eleanora will be arriving soon."

As one last precaution, Alice grabbed a bedsheet she'd brought from home to cover any furniture Audrey might choose for lounging. One parlor inside the house had a slouchy couch draped with a worn golden slip cover. Audrey tap-danced with expectation as Alice covered it with her dog's sheet.

"The lawyer said Eleanora once owned two poodles. Is your nose telling you this is where they slept?"

Before corners were tucked into place, the hound jumped up and settled. Alice smiled as she gazed out the front window. Galati texted a squad car was following Eleanora's limo back to the vineyard.

Out of the corner of her eye, Alice saw a shadow cross a side window, heading toward the back of the house. She hadn't heard a car, and it struck her as odd a woman home from a trip would walk to the backdoor.

When she opened one of the doors to the porch, a woman dressed in a long purple wool coat with a knitted stocking cap on her head stood outside. For the warm weather, Alice thought the woman's attire was curious. She was small, just over five feet tall and looked as if under her wooly coat she weighed less than Audrey. Her hair hung in thin gray dreadlocks down to her waist. Worker boots, too big for her feet were laced about her ankles. Alice was taken aback. Audrey, nose working, stayed behind her owner and stared.

"Can I help you?" asked Alice seeing an expression she couldn't decipher. Was the woman afraid or angry? She held a package close to her chest, a brown paper bag crimped and tied with string. She backed away from Alice.

"Are you here to visit the family?"

The woman shook her head before she turned, and with her sleeve and then her palm, rubbed a chalk spot from the trim on the corner of the house.

"Do you need something? Are you hurt?"

Again, a head shake.

Reasoning that coming to the backdoor was somehow connected to Elka, Alice asked, "May I tell Elka you were here?"

"She'll know." The woman turned to leave but looked back at Alice with studying eyes. "Do you color inside the lines?"

Alice was taken off guard. "Mostly. Pretty much. Haven't colored since the grandchildren were young, but I guess."

"Pah!" said the woman in purple. Still hugging her package, she stomped toward the rows in the vineyard.

"Thank you for standing guard over the child this morning," called Alice. "Why did you leave before we arrived?"

The woman stopped, turned. "I heard all of you coming down the road. You all marched like an army. The child was safe."

"I'm sure the mother wanted to thank you," said Alice. "Kiley told her mom a purple fairy kept her warm."

The woman kept shaking her head. "I'm not foolish or stupid."

"Of course, you're not. You recognized a child alone at night was in danger. It was good of you to give her the flashlight."

"Not everyone would see it that way," said the woman. "I have to be careful. Imaginations take people to terrible places." Her voice became a breathy whisper as her eyes darted between the house and the vineyard, perhaps plotting her escape. "Why did the child disappear? Find a dirty homeless woman by the river? Must be a bad person. Maybe crazy. Need to lock people like that up. Put them away. Maybe hurt them." She hugged the package closer as if Alice might take it.

"I'm glad you kept her safe. So, *I* want to thank you."

The woman nodded.

"Are you Sunny?" Another nod. "I have a message for you. I was in Mitten, and Mrs. Rotolo asked to tell you she has packages of hand wipes for you." The woman lowered her chin and gave a small smile. "I think you have many friends, Sunny. It's a pleasure to meet you."

Sunny turned toward the vineyard but before she disappeared down a path between grapevines, she stopped and deadheaded a rose bush. She created a tidy pile of debris.

Alice closed the kitchen door and said to Audrey, "So, what do you think? A very interesting person to have in the vineyard. Elka must create packages of food for her. I did see a cooler on the porch, but never thought anything about it. Women look after Sunny. Breakiron is willing to relay messages. The librarian furnishes hand wipes. On our next walk into town, we're buying her a new flashlight and extra batteries."

Audrey returned to the parlor and climbed onto the slouchy couch.

"You know, Sunny's right. People do judge what they don't understand. If she knows something, maybe she's reluctant to tell."

Alice wondered what Sunny knew about the night of the murder or why Cade vanished. "We'll see the purple fairy again," said Alice. "This protector of children."

Chapter 16

Time: Tuesday, 6:42 p.m.

Alice sat and waited for Eleanora to come home. Her fingers made circles on Audrey's belly. The hound was sound asleep. Alice allowed a piece of her conversation with Guthrie to replay in her mind.

"At twenty I was in a relationship when I met O'Dare," said Guthrie with an embarrassed grin. Her chin fell slightly, preventing eye contact.

To Alice it seemed this was a confession, a long time coming.

"O'Dare was in his forties, divorced, but with . . . someone. Funny how things turn out. That weekend we drove to Vegas and married."

"Love at first sight is possible," said Alice.

"I was so sure." A dismissive laugh came into Guthrie's voice. "His intense brown eyes were like his mother's but needy, you know? I believed he was throwing the world away for me. And believe me, telling my parents and family wasn't easy. After all, they had received letters from me saying I expected a proposal from my current boy-friend. Even sent them a picture of us together. My mother talked to our minister about scheduling a wedding. When I married O'Dare, it was a shock to everyone, even me. My family, particularly my sister, stopped talking to me."

"Your marriage lasted twenty years," said Alice, encouragement and appreciation in her voice.

"The license lasted," said Guthrie with derision. "Love dropped off after Cade was born."

Both women sat on the porch and watched the falling sun paint the sky. Wispy clouds took on pink and yellow coloring, adding a sheen to the grape leaves.

"I don't believe O'Dare ever matured any more than an eighteen-year-old. He saw every woman as a post-prom date." Guthrie used her napkin to cover her mouth and chin. "Whenever he disappeared from our marriage, Eleanora's money forced him back."

Alice had nothing to say.

Sitting on the couch with her dog, Alice smiled and remembered those powerful first moments with Baer. He was taller than she was— a definite gift. She asked if he minded having a girlfriend six-feet tall. He smiled and said he would never grow to be a bent-over old man for stealing kisses. The universe seemed to smile on eighteen-year-old Alice Signal with her wild, loopy hair, overly big eyes, and wide shoulders. She understood Guthrie's fall for O'Dare.

A livery service pulled up the drive and stopped outside the main house. Alice watched as the driver opened the back door of the car and helped a woman in her eighties, who extended her hand like a princess. Breakiron's car followed.

"So that's Eleanora Huff," said Alice.

Eleanora was a small woman, not slight, but not heavy. *Sturdy, solid, stocky* stuck in Alice's mind. She wore a matching pink dress and coat, much too delicate for her body structure. For all the wigs Alice found upstairs in Eleanora's bedroom, the woman herself traveled with her own white hair exposed, flattened in places, rumpled in others, as if she had just risen from bed. Red lipstick bled into the creases around her mouth. Her face was soft and rutted with wrinkles. She clutched a large handbag with fingers covered in rings. Alice guessed the colorful stones were real.

The driver, close to Alice's age, had a sloppy grin on his face as Eleanora leaned in close to him, giving an air kiss. Alice heard her say, "Be a dear." The driver collected her four bags and put them near the door.

"Now how am I going to carry these in?" She mounted her sunglasses on her forehead, and her fake black eyelashes fluttered.

"I'm not supposed to enter a house," said the driver.

"Who's gonna tell?"

"She might," said the driver pointing to Alice who peered out the window.

"Then she can carry them," said Eleanora, both her mouth and eyebrows rose in displeasure.

The older woman lumbered into the house and sat in the first stuffed chair she found. The driver leaned in to put down two suitcases, going back to retrieve more.

"You. You the detective?" She rummaged in her purse, removed cigarettes, and lit one. "You here to find my grandson?"

"I'm Alice Tricklebank. I—"

"Roddy filled me in." She waved her hand like a queen and rolled her eyes. After rummaging in her purse once more, she pulled a folded stack of bills and handed them to the driver who brought in two more bags and tipped his hat in appreciation of the tip.

"Guthrie thought—"

"Oh, I know what Guthrie thought," said Eleanora. "That Cade was murdered by my son. It's all nonsense because Cade's not dead."

"You know that?" asked Alice.

"Of course. He's off somewhere. Now that his mother is dead, his conscience will bring him home to me. I made sure Roddy placed several stories of the murders in the news with a specific request for Cade to come home." Eleanora puffed on the cigarette, holding it between her index finger and thumb and looking every bit like a tough movie gangster. Maybe Edgar G. Robinson in drag. "When Cade sees the news story, he'll come home. You'll see."

Officer Breakiron entered the house.

"Mrs. Huff."

"Yeah, I know. Your boss wants Guthrie's gun from the safe."

"Yes, ma'am."

"You don't want me hiding or tampering with it."

"No, ma'am."

"Give me a minute, will ya?" Turning to Alice, Eleanora said, "This the dog?"

Not usually one to hang back from new smells, Audrey stood her ground and seemed to eye the cloud of smoke rising around Eleanora.

"Audrey's a bloodhound," said Alice. "Guthrie thought we should search—"

Again, Eleanora cut her off. "Search, don't search. All the same to me. Dogs like walking in the vineyard, but she won't find anything."

"I thought your lawyer said we should look."

"For appearances," said Eleanora. "Don't need nasty rumors about the vineyard to spread. Nothing like a bloodhound to make people feel safe. I rather like that soft expression people have in their eyes when they think I'm a poor grieving soul."

"Do you want Audrey and me to find other accommodations?"

"No, why would you think that?" She threw her head back, taking a long drag and then released smoke so that it curled about her face. "Besides I like your dog. She's got pizazz."

"Thank you," said Alice, unsure if she liked this woman or not. Audrey's tail wagged, but she kept her distance.

"After we take care of business, I'll be going upstairs for a nap," said Eleanora stubbing out the cigarette. "Will you be sleeping in the main house tonight?"

"No," answered Alice. "I have two friends who will be arriving, and with your permission, they will sleep here tonight. They have helped me in the past."

Eleanora waved her hand and dismissed further explanation. "A man and woman? The ones pictured on your detective website?"

"Yes," said Alice without her usual disclaimers.

"Do what you think is best. Always good to have a *man* in the house. I may be down later for dinner. Or not."

"Shall I carry up your bags?" asked Alice.

"Of course. You're receiving free room and board, aren't you?" Eleanora waved Breakiron to follow. "Come on, honey, your law enforcement job has got to be hard enough without me keeping Detective Mucky-muck waiting."

With that said, Eleanora climbed the stairs, carrying every one of her years on her shoulders.

After stowing luggage in Eleanora's room, Alice met Officer Breakiron at the front door.

Seeing the evidence bag in the officer's hand, Alice asked, "Was the gun there?"

"Not there. Only Eleanora's .22. Doesn't figure in the investigation. But I found .38 ammo." Breakiron shook the evidence bag.

"Galati said Guthrie gun is a .357," said Alice energized by the disparity in numbers. "The shells that shot her and the young man were .38s.

Breakiron bit her cheek. "We need to find all the evidence."

"I met Sunny. She was the purple fairy who kept the child safe."

"I figured she was, but please don't give her publicity. People are kind as long as she's in the background."

"She said the same."

"You going to be able to handle Mrs. Huff?" Breakiron gave a cynical grin.

"Maybe. I've known women like her. Right now, she's living on hope."

"Could be a hard fall if she's wrong," said Breakiron.

"How's Galati doing with the case?"

Breakiron's expression told Alice the question was inappropri-ate. "Fine. He'll be happier seeing these." She jiggled the evidence bag again and opened the door. When she turned toward Alice, she was biting her lip. "Wadcutters," said Breakiron. She fast-stepped to her car before Alice could ask the next question.

Chapter 17

Time: Tuesday, 7:17 p.m.

Breakiron drove away from the vineyard and Nimble Cipriani pulled in. Alice and Audrey waited at the front door, but Nimble drove to the back of the house and entered through the back without knocking.

"I saw you through the window," he said. "Didn't think you'd mind. I need seven wine glasses."

"Eleanora's home and upstairs. Are other people coming?"

"I'm not here to see Eleanora," said Nimble. "Is this a good time to have a wine tasting?"

He tipped a large canvas bag and showed Alice six bottles, each with two or three inches of red wine. The bottles had white labels with hand-written numbers on each one. Audrey's neck stretched toward the counter, eyes curious.

"I don't drink much," said Alice as she opened cabinets to look for glasses.

"You won't be drinking much now. Tablespoons. One of the vineyards had a wine seminar. These bottles are the leftovers. Let's go outside. About time someone near this family understands Cade's passion for wine making and his skill. You game?"

"Sure."

"Good."

Audrey watched Alice lace her fingers around glasses, but she followed the man shuttling bottles. Her nose twitched in their direction. Without detecting interesting odors, Audrey settled on the porch, head up, watching.

Once they were seated, Nimble said, "Galati came to grill me today about Cade. He saw Guthrie's obit and Eleanora's invitation for Cade to come home. You know Galati suspects the kid killed his mother."

"Why?" She didn't reveal Cade as a murderer also occurred to her.

"He's focusing on Cade's unhappy life, running away, maybe wants something from the house, knows about the gun, gets in an argument." Nimble sat straight. "Galati's crazy wrong about Cade. He's not that kind of kid."

When Alice first met Nimble, he had a calm kindness. She pictured the lost child reaching out to him. Now Nimble's eyes held fear and desperation, his body angry and on alert.

Nimble lined up six bottles and six glasses and poured an inch of wine into each glass. Alice noted the colors from see-through pink to inky purple. He handed her the seventh empty glass.

"Is Cade coming back home?" asked Alice.

"How would I know?" he said, a little too irritated. "Galati thinks he is. He plans to invite Cade into the station for a talk. You and I know it will turn into an interrogation."

"You think Galati will stop looking for the real killer if Cade does come back."

"I wouldn't like to see that if he does." Nimble's hands made fists before opening with a stretch.

Audrey lined up at the table with them, eyeing the glasses, nose working.

Nimble held up the first glass. "Imagine you are a wine maker and all these different wines came into your winery. Do you bottle them just as they are, or do you blend to create something new?" Holding a straw, Nimble dipped it into the first wine, using it as a pipette, and drew a portion into the straw then dropped it into Alice's empty glass. "Try this one and tell me what you taste."

Alice took a sip. "It's sort of sweet, like a citrusy strawberry."

"Good. You got it. Do you think clients might like it? Would you buy a bottle?"

"Not really."

Nimble emptied her glass by flinging the remaining drops at a wisteria plant. He drew more wine into the straw.

"Try this one."

Alice sipped the darker colored wine. "Cherries."

His behavior continued as wine droplets went airborne.

"Now this one."

"Plums?"

"And now?"

"Cherries, but not bing. More like black cherries?"

Two more followed. Chocolate and one that was dark, almost offensive.

"Don't like this one. I'd never buy this."

"That's a grape that produces a dark taste of tobacco. Cigar smokers love it in their wine."

Alice frowned, and Audrey jiggled at being left out of the conversation. A high-pitched hum followed. First patting her pocket to get Audrey's attention, Alice withdrew a treat and slipped it to her hound.

"A wine maker has all these grapes, and it might be impossible to market each as a single vintage. It's not cost efficient because not enough people drink strawberry or straight tobacco. Time for us to blend. What two would you combine?"

"Chocolate and cherries. Chocolate and strawberries?"

Nimble extracted small measures of wine for blending, dropping a quarter pipette of each into Alice's glass. "Now try a sip."

"I like it," said Alice surprised at the taste.

"Now, let's add a half straw of plum and a straw inch of tobacco."

Alice prepared her criticism before taking a swallow, but after the wine blend hit her tongue, her big round eyes became wider. "Wow, that's good. I'd buy this."

"Even with the tobacco?"

"It makes the wine taste linger in the mouth, but not in a bad way. I think the strawberry taste hits first and softened the darkness. Am I right?"

Nimble smiled but didn't answer. He stroked Audrey's head before sitting back. "That's why Cade wants to have a career in the wine industry. Grapes come into the winery, and we know how we want them to taste, but nature can play tricks. Every year the grapes taste slightly different. You've tasted only a few, but there are hundreds of descriptors: spice, leather, rosemary, current, bell pepper, rose, bread. Literally hundreds. The wine maker uses his creativity to juggle the different tastes to blend something magical. And here's the kicker—Cade can define them by using his nose not his taste buds. He's a wine bloodhound."

After recorking bottles and slipping them back into the canvas bag, Nimble asked, "Do you understand? Can you guess how valuable he can be to the industry?"

"Thank you for the lesson in wine poetry," grinned Alice.

"Still don't understand poetry in wine," said Nimble, standing and hefting the canvas bag to his shoulder.

"You're saying winemaking is an art, and each performance or production is a momentary experience, not to be duplicated."

"I guess I am. I can't match the talent Cade has, few people can. O'Dare wanted Cade to make money? You know what the industry will pay for a nose like Cade's? Nobody in this family had a clue what the kid can do."

Audrey pawed at the vineyard manager.

"If Cade comes back, I'm hoping someone like you will be on hand to moderate Eleanora's reaction. And keep Galati off his back. He's a good kid."

"You expect temper from Eleanora?" Nimble nodded and Alice continued. "Other than being a run-away family member, what has peaked Galati's interest?"

Nimble's eyes closed briefly as if shutting out truth. "Officers talked to teachers at the business school. They didn't hear about the same kid I knew. One said Cade was impulsive and had a quick temper. Said Cade got into a skirmish with a guy. Maybe a student, maybe not."

"Did you counter that when you talked to Galati?"

"I tried. The kid doesn't deserve that reputation. But there's that business with Cade and a disguised intruder here at the vineyard. Maybe the same guy at the school. I never saw him, but my men reported the confrontation to Galati."

"But you told him about Cade's character?"

"I did, but he had already interviewed a couple workers and students at the college. My information can't knock down what other people saw."

Nimble's face was tight as if he expected Alice to criticize his assessment.

"Thank you. I promise to do what I can."

The manager of Eleanora's vineyard nodded and left. As Alice washed wine glasses, she said to Audrey, "Why was Nimble so insistent about giving this wine lesson tonight? What's coming?"

Chapter 18

As Alice walked Audrey back to the cottage, still feeling a little light-headed from one pipette too many, a car pulled into the drive. Her best friends Lena and Julian got out, and Alice gave a big sigh of relief.

"Whew! That was a drive," said Lena giving Alice a hug. "I think everyone in the United States is visiting California. The traffic!" After sweeping big round sunglasses she no longer needed from her face, Lena rolled her eyes. A halter sundress of yellow-green hugged Lena's curves. Her arms were sunburned. A charm bracelet jangled on her wrist as she held it up. "Like it? Julian bought it for me in Carmel."

"I like it. Now, let's go into the cottage first," said Alice. "Eleanora is resting upstairs in the main house, and I want to fill you in on what's been happening."

"Oh, good. We need a little excitement, don't we, Cuddle Bug?"

Julian kept his growling low in his throat. Not a shorts-wearing kind of guy, Julian dressed in long beige pants but because he wore them low on his hips, the cuffs curled under his heels.

"Have you changed his nickname?" whispered Alice, eyeing a frowning Julian.

Lena grinned. "If he's going to call me Magpie, I'm calling him Cuddle Bug or Love Monkey."

Alice apologized for ruining their vacation. "I also apologize for the trip to California. You two were very generous." The friends went into the cottage where they sat in the small sitting area. Audrey snorted and went belly down near the bed and watched.

"No reason to apologize," said Julian. "We've had rough spots before this. At least this time nobody has broken bones."

"Only baggy eyes," said Lena with a grin and blinked her eyes. "A nice murder investigation will make all of us chipper. No harm, no foul."

Alice gave a Cliff Notes condensed version of the two murders and the missing boy.

"Ya want us to investigate Guthrie's murder or the missing kid?" asked Julian.

"The police are handling the murders. We're supposed to be investigating what happened to Cade. But, I can't help think the two are related."

"If thieves were casing the joint and knew one woman was gone and the other home alone," said Lena, "could be they decided on a robbery. So maybe they aren't related. Just a string of misfortunes."

Alice dug out a large dog bone from a box and offered it to her dog who immediately rose to accept the treat.

"What's got you rattled?" asked Julian of Alice.

"The gun. The police know Guthrie owned a .357 revolver. Both she and Xavier were shot with .38 caliber bullets. Julian, can a .357 fire a .38? I thought the numbers were supposed to match."

"It can. A .38 is a shorter shell, that's all."

Alice took a deep breath and watched her dog clean crumbs of bone from the floor.

"Then, I'm guessing Guthrie had an inkling that two people were coming to her house and may have felt threatened enough to pull her revolver from the safe. Whatever happened among them, Guthrie shot the young man, then struggled with the second man. He got the gun from her and shot her three times. Today a police officer followed Eleanora's transportation home from the airport and checked the safe for Guthrie's gun. It's gone."

"The bad guy took it," said Julian. He went to the sink for a glass of water. "Three shots. Excessive. Musta been angry."

"There is no sign of a break-in," said Alice.

"Backdoors left unlocked? Like back home?" asked Julian.

"Yes."

"An intruder would have to know that. Right?" asked Lena.

"A stranger came onto the property before Guthrie's son went missing eight months ago," said Alice, "but if his intention were to scope the house or break-in, why did he wait all this time? There had to be evenings when neither Mrs. Huff was home."

"Police say whether the robbers were armed?" asked Julian. "Is there another gun in this story? One they pointed at Guthrie?"

"So far, there is only the .357 belonging to Guthrie. A .22 belongs to Eleanora and is still in the safe. The police officer took the .38 ammunition." Alice paused at not being able to make the puzzle pieces fit. "If they know anything about another gun, they haven't shared it with me."

"It's not easy to take a gun away from someone who's ready to shoot," said Julian. "Of course, maybe the first shot was an accident, and it scared her. Maybe she never realized the damage a bullet can do. You said the young man died?"

"He did," said Alice.

"I bet Special Forces could strong-arm a woman with a gun," said Lena. She folded her arms across her chest. "Did the police name any military men who might be involved?"

Julian frowned.

Alice smiled. She was used to Lena's wild, entertaining leaps. "Nothing military has been mentioned. The police found a motorcycle tire iron," said Alice. "I'm guessing probably not Special Forces."

"If we're gonna help, who do we need to know?" asked Julian.

"Elka is here in the morning until two in the afternoon. She likes to be called the house manager. Mostly, she looks after the meals. No cooking for you, Lena."

"Of course not. I'm on vacation."

"Roddy Merritt is Eleanora's lawyer. Nimble Ciprani is the vine-yard manager." Alice held back on identifying Sunny. "The vineyard has workers here seemingly every day. Detective Galati works for the county police force. Officers Breakiron, McNally, and Garcia are with the town of Mitten."

"What do you think about the missing grandson?" asked Julian.

"Hard to imagine he's dead. A few people think he ran off. He's twenty. Not many people were interested in looking for him until his mother was murdered."

"Sounds to me like someone wanted to rob the house," said Lena. "The woman heard a noise and went for her gun. Bang. She shot a stranger."

"No," said Julian. "Doesn't fit what Alice told us. Why didn't she shoot both intruders right off?"

"Do we know she didn't?"

"One intruder was shot once, Guthrie three times," said Alice. "The lights were on in the house, and she had on the same clothing as she had at dinner. She wasn't surprised in her pajamas."

"Could the second guy who drove off be Cade?" asked Lena. "Maybe he came back to the house for cash and got caught."

"No," said Julian as if speaking to a child. "The kid may have taken the gun away from his mother, but why shoot her three times un-less there was really bad blood between them. Any reason he hates his mother? And I mean hate." He leaned to rest his forearms on his knees. All the while his brow wrinkled. "Alice, do you think it was Cade?"

"Can't say. Don't know enough," said Alice. "I'm guessing no, because Eleanora's expecting Cade to come home for his mother's funeral. However, his room is odd."

"Meaning what?" asked Lena.

"If you walk through my house, you know my life is dog-centered: toys, towels, treats. Your house is filled with collections: the joy of owning, preserving, sharing. Cade's room is empty of personal items. Not to mention, all his identification is still in his room."

"I don't know what to say," said Lena looking to Julian.

"Tell Alice what you found about the old lady," said Julian.

"I've only started. The historical museum here in town has a regular posting of Eleanora, the young actress. She was quite in demand in 1950s television. However, I'm guessing it's not how she made her money. Her Hollywood status doesn't come up when I type her name into archives. If I Google her, I see newspaper stories of current events she attended. Three pages into the list of items, are references to someone called Eleanora Whipkey. If the two women are the same person, then her money came from Enoch Whipkey, who, decades ago, invested in streetcars in a place called Redlands. There are lots of stories on Enoch. His children passed around the inheritance and squandered much of it. All the men who inherited the fortune died before fifty, but it seems Eleanora, a great-granddaughter, has a head for business and has built up the fortune since she was twenty-four. Of course, this is all assuming both are the same Eleanora. I'll keep looking."

"What's the old lady like?" asked Julian.

"Hard to say," answered Alice. "The house has some rooms with Hollywood glitz and her bedroom has signed pictures of movie stars, but Eleanora strikes me as having a big slice of Marge Schott in her. Remember the owner of the Cincinnati Reds?"

"I hear ya," said Julian. "I liked her team. Never cared for her mouth or disrespect. Got her into hot water.

"Oh, Alice," said Lena. "I'm so glad you called for help." Lena clapped her hands at Audrey. The dog ambled to Lena with a face full of expectation. "Audrey, a movie star, an heiress, a missing boy, maybe Special Forces? This is so our case?" Lena's hands held the dog's head tousling it back and forth.

"Yeah, yeah," said Julian, his face sour. "Clear enough you two gals can't do this one alone."

Chapter 19

Alice helped her two friends unload their car and carry bags to the main house. Neither had stopped for dinner, and Julian's stomach growled, causing Audrey to tilt her head and wrinkle her forehead. Alice's brain puzzled over Lena's information. Had O'Dare's life and death followed the pattern of his ancestors? Instead of mentioning it to her friends, she opened the front door.

"Eleanora's probably asleep."

"We'll be quiet," said Lena as they slipped into the house. "This place is huge."

A breeze from the open door caused the plastic sheeting that covered the parlor door to ripple.

"That where it happened?" asked Julian.

Lena's eyes were merry with anticipation. "Can't wait to see the crime scene."

"It's closed off and sanitized, I think. I'm guessing the police may want to keep it in tact in case they need a second look. Elka prepared open-faced sandwiches and salad for your dinner," said Alice. "It's better if it comes up to room temperature." She hurried to the kitchen and quickly returned. "Wait until you see the counter space in that kitchen. Please go into the parlor on the right."

Audrey stopped in front of the sealed parlor door. Her nose twitched at some odor Alice missed.

Both Julian and Lena tilted their heads back to look at the ceiling with paintings of chubby, naked babies. The walls of the room were covered in red brocade wallpaper, the furniture in maroon leather.

"Does anyone else think this looks like an old-time movie whore house?" asked Julian.

Lena swatted his arm. "It's Victorian." Then swatting him two more times, she said, "Don't let the owner hear you say that."

"A woman who spits nails and could live in a place like this, wouldn't care," said Julian.

"Well, here you are. Were you talking about me?" Eleanora made a grand entrance, sweeping down the stairs.

No one spoke. Lena's mouth fell open. The Eleanora before them wasn't the grief-stricken grandmother. Her stocky body was draped in a long pink gown with a neckline showing ample cleavage. On her head was the long-haired black wig, the bangs skirting her painted-on eyebrows. Her cheeks had smudges of dark rouge.

"Don't let me interrupt. You two must be my guardians. I didn't know if you'd bring your own gun, so I removed this one from my safe. A gun in a man's hand makes me feel safer."

She batted her eyes at Julian and handed over the gun before her palm caressed his chest. Eleanora then rolled her eyes and nodded in Julian's direction. Alice put a calming hand on Lena's forearm. Julian moved to a bookshelf and placed the gun alongside some books. The hound ignored Eleanora, choosing instead to stand still and stare at the parlor.

"Mrs. Huff, I read about your career," said Lena. "So sad television shows from the early days were lost," said Lena.

"It has been a continual disappointment to me." Her mouth made a little bow as she took Lena's hand and patted it. "Will you be a dear," she said in Julian's direction, "and pour me a bourbon. Two ice cubes. You look like you have a generous hand at pouring."

Alice saw Lena almost pull her hand away from Eleanora as if her Julian-radar again pinged. The women took seats in the red room. Julian moved a chair close to the door.

Once Alice and Lena denied joining her in a drink and Eleanora lit a cigarette, the older woman with an all-business voice said, "Now, tell me what the police know about Guthrie's death."

"There were two intruders that night. One was a young man named Xavier Nettle. Do you know him?" asked Alice.

"Me? No." Eleanora flipped her hair. "Who is he?"

"A bartender at the Hungry Fool." Alice waited for Eleanora to react, but she continued to puff on her cigarette. Alice imagined her playing poker. "Can you think of any connection between Guthrie and the bar?"

"Not one," responded the older woman while making eye contact with Julian as he handed her a drink. "Who was the other intruder?"

"So far the police haven't shared that information."

"You know, Guthrie's gun went missing after she moved here." Eleanora's voice became coy. She kept her eyes averted. "I don't think that lady officer today believed me when I told her."

Alice found her sympathy for the older woman draining away. The look in Eleanora's eyes challenged the three listeners to call her a liar.

Turning to Lena, Alice said, "Maybe I'm wrong. I thought Guthrie might have gotten her gun because she felt danger. Shot Xavier and then after a struggle, the other intruder shot her."

"My .22 can't kill anyone unless the gunman is a crack shot. Are you a crack shot?" Eleanora eyed Julian before draining the bourbon from the glass.

Julian didn't answer but asked, "Was Guthrie's gun reported as missing?"

"How would I know? It was her gun," said Eleanora. Her shoulders swished like an irritated cat's tail as she pulled her filmy scarf closer to her throat.

"Pardon me," said Lena sitting straighter, "but if I were to hear one of my daughters-in-law being shot, I'd be distraught. You don't seem upset."

"Of course, I was upset when I heard," said Eleanora, stubbing out her cigarette only to light another. "But you certainly see what this means." She paused as if waiting for the reveal. "Come on, you've got to see it. There is no way my grandson will neglect his mother's funeral. After all these months, I'll see Cade."

Alice felt a shiver along her spine.

"Didn't you promise sandwiches?" asked Lena looking to Alice, her cheeks reddening.

"Yes, I did. You two must be hungry."

All four rose.

"Then be a dear and pour another drink?" Eleanora's eyes twinkled as she took Julian's arm with one hand and clinked the remaining ice cubes in her glass. "This time fill the glass with ice. Pour bourbon to the tippy-top."

Julian looked to Lena before he left the room in silence. By the slouch of his shoulders, Alice knew he wasn't happy.

"Are you married?" asked Eleanora of Lena.

Lena stammered, "No."

"Good for you. I never wanted to wash a man's undies, either."

Lena looked embarrassed and followed into the kitchen as Julian came out with a tumbler filled with ice cubes.

"They're a cute couple," said Eleanora. She balanced a cigarette between her lips, grabbed the glass from Julian and the bottle of bourbon, then headed for the stairs. "You have dinner. I have all I need right here. See you in the morning but not too early."

The three friends picked up trays of food and moved outside to the porch. Audrey finished her plate of chopped duck before the humans took their first bites. Conversation starters about Carmel-by-the-Sea and Henry's graduation fizzled. The three nibbled at dinner mostly in silence. Flatbread with sliced duck and goat cheese drizzled with balsamic softened their mood. A citrus fruit salad complemented the duck and disappeared too fast. Dessert was a creamy tapioca concoction with toasted almonds, plump raisins, and bittersweet chocolate chips. Julian even smiled.

"How's Audrey doing with the food here?" asked Lena.

"We're probably both destined to put on a few pounds. As you can see Elka is a wonderful cook, but her whole body sags with disapproval if people don't lick their plates. Did you notice Audrey's plate of pulverized duck? Elka expects her to eat three times a day."

"Well, Alice, at home she goes through quite a few treats."

The bloodhound stretched out on the porch, belly down and closed her eyes.

Julian's gaze went off into the dark distance of the vineyard. "It's beautiful here. What's that smell?"

"Wisteria. Tomorrow, check out the other plants on the porch. I've counted five dishwasher-size pots holding wisteria. They climb up the columns and across the beams. The flowers are beautiful in the daytime as they drape above. Wait until you see the vineyard in the full sunlight. The gold and purple colors. The perfume from roses and other flowers—I find myself at a standstill, inhaling. It makes me feel like Audrey."

Hearing her name, Audrey rose from the porch and pushed her face into Alice's middle.

"How's she doing?" asked Lena.

"She's hiding things. I'm thinking it's revenge for me leaving her special toy behind."

"Any room in your cottage for us?" asked Julian.

"No. Sorry. But there are two lovely guest bedrooms upstairs. You have your pick."

"I'm not carrying our luggage up there alone," said Julian as he looked at Lena. "We do this together." Then to Alice, "Does the guest bedroom have a lock on the door. We're protecting her from an intruder, but who's protecting me from her?"

Lena's eyes glistened as she swatted him again. "You're such a hunk. I'm sure Eleanora can't help it."

Audrey moved with resolve to the edge of the porch and stared into the vineyard.

"We'll talk in the morning," said Alice. "There is something else I need to explain."

Chapter 20

The sun was high over the hills and warming the day. Audrey walked up the driveway after a much-appreciated moment of relief. Her overly long tongue lolled out the side of her mouth. Alice spied Lena leaving the main house and hurrying toward her. Seconds later, Julian closed the backdoor and followed.

"Morning," said Alice with a wave.

"Morning," tossed off Lena as she glanced over her shoulder. "Is it too early to talk? There's no sound from Eleanora's room and Elka hasn't arrived."

"Not too early. We've had our morning walk to the soap factory dog park. Come in. You can make coffee while I give my girl water." Bowing toward her dog, Alice said, "Then it's time to clean dust from your feet."

"I swear you treat that dog like a kid."

Alice grinned as she filled a stainless-steel bowl with water. "She's my buddy." Eyeing her dog, she said, "Aren't you? Aren't you the most gorgeous thing ever?"

The hound's face went into her ha-ha-ha expression before slopping down water from her bowl.

Lena busied herself pouring water into a coffee pot as Julian came in and sat at the small kitchen table.

"No way I'm staying in that house alone," he said.

Lena massaged his shoulders as she looked at Alice, her expression intense. "I have questions. What's your take on Eleanora?"

"Well, I—"

Lena cut her off. "I know artists have a different way of seeing the world, and Eleanora is an actress."

"She—"

"Has lost her grandson, I realize that," said Lena, "but she's denying what happened. I get that, too. I do. But I'm worried about how she's treating Julian."

"Me, too," said Julian with a slap on the table. "Last night the old bat came to our bedroom door. Asked me if we heard the noise at the backdoor. Wanted me to go downstairs *with her* to confront the threat. When I said to wait a minute until Lena was ready, she said never mind." His eyes grew big as if the story were all anyone needed to know regarding the woman in her eighties.

"Then she told him to make the morning coffee because Elka doesn't arrive early enough," added Lena. "And ordered him to choose fresh flowers from the garden for her breakfast tray."

"I'm guessing she was tipsy last night. She can't be up this early. Did you make coffee?" asked Alice.

"No way. I'm not waking her up. Not picking posies either. As far as tipsy? I'm thinking more like blotto when she came to our door."

"She's apparently a handful," said Alice trying to keep from smiling at the shock of her two friends.

"Bless Julian's soul, he's taking her guff. Seething, but taking it," said Lena.

"I'm sorry this is difficult," said Alice. "None of us have to cater to her. Maybe we need to scout out a new place to board."

"Not on your life," declared Lena. "After you left and before we went to bed, she came weaving downstairs to tell us about the private detective. *He* found nothing. I'm certainly not letting this go. Who do you think is the murderer of that poor woman?"

"I got my own ideas," said Julian. He tilted his head in the direction of the house.

"You can't be serious," said Lena.

"Think about it," countered Julian. "How many times did she say the mother's death will bring her grandson home?"

"She's eighty. Who was her partner?"

"Lena, she's got money up to her ears. She doesn't have to do the killing herself. She's got people. What about the cook? Or one of the grape guys?"

Their voices seemingly disturbed Audrey who came forward with a woof. When silence took her companions into thought, the dog jumped back onto the bed, rumpled the covers, and fell into the middle with a groan.

"I'm not seeing Eleanora as anything more than a lonely woman," said Lena. "Seems to me the murder happened during a simple theft. Alice, what do you think?"

"Two intruders may have wanted to steal cash or jewelry. Maybe they knew Eleanora wasn't home. But—"

"An inside job!" proclaimed Lena. "They expected the house to be empty. Julian may be onto something. Do we like the cook?"

"Guthrie instructed Elka to make dinner for two," said Alice. "If she were involved, Elka would have known about me. Also, Guthrie had her gun out of the safe and ready. I think she knew danger was coming."

"If it was in the safe to begin with," added Julian. "The old lady says the gun was missing."

The duet of Lena and Alice said, "That's a lie."

"How do you know?"

"It just is," said Lena.

"No eye contact," added Alice. "Besides, most of the time she fiddled with her cigarette or twirled her whiskey glass. Did you notice the way she pleated the hem on her sleeve?"

"Women," declared Julian.

"Men," countered Lena.

"Look," said Alice. "If Eleanora were involved, she also would have known I was at the cottage. Too much of a chance for a witness. The second intruder didn't skedaddle when Xavier was shot. He waited until after he shot Guthrie."

"We're pretty far from the nearest neighbor," said Julian. "Nobody to hear the blast and call the cops."

Alice waggled her head back and forth. *Nobody to hear* knocked around in her head. *Not even Sunny?*

"Second," said Alice, "did the two intruders come from some business connection to O'Dare? He apparently didn't pay his bills. Maybe a client or investor got tired of waiting for his payment and sent two thugs to collect from Guthrie."

"That kind of guy wouldn't expect a woman to be armed," said Lena. "They'd get aggressive wanting cash. She has a hint they're coming. Gets the gun because she's scared. Blam! Damn thing goes off. The other enforcer takes the gun. Pow! She's shot. Plausible?"

"Thugs would have their own guns," said Julian.

"That's what I'm saying. Come in with guns blazing."

"Not blazing." Julian's voice squeaked. "The place would have been shot up. No. They'd come in cool and threatening. After all, they want money."

"Oh."

"O'Dare's first family has possibilities," posed Alice. "He has two daughters, one with children. The lawyer said they received a good settlement when O'Dare and the mother divorced, but after twenty-some years, was it enough?"

"Didn't you mention a lawyer guy?" asked Julian.

"He and his father have represented Eleanora for years. Can't see him hiring someone to do his dirty work."

"Gotta know plenty of bad guys. He's a lawyer," said Julian.

"I didn't get the impression he's a trial attorney."

"What's the difference?" asked Lena.

"Knows bad guys in suits," said Julian.

"We know one of the intruders was Xavier Nettle, and we know he worked as a bartender at the Hungry Fool," said Alice.

"No information on him?"

"Not yet," said Alice. "Lena, if you have a moment, will you look up newspaper stories about Xavier?"

"Absolutely."

"What do you want us to do today?" asked Julian.

"Hang around the house. Get to know Elka. Talk to Eleanora. Drive into Mitten when Eleanora gets under your skin."

"They have nice shops?" asked Lena.

"German Christmas stores."

"Cupcake," said Lena in a naughty way, "shopping."

Julian closed his eyes and furrowed his brow. "And you. What are your plans?"

"Keep looking for a trigger event. What one event caused Cade to leave when he did? What caused two intruders to visit Guthrie on that particular night? Let's face it, last summer Audrey and I would never have been called to Dingle Grove if Clifford Twine hadn't been frightened by his son repairing the house. A trigger-event."

"Cat and rat," said Julian. "This is the cat who ate the rat that lived in the house that Jack built."

"Exactly. They had years of family discord and bad business management. What triggered Cade to disappear, and what's the relationship to his mother's murder?"

"We'll keep our eyes and ears open," said Julian.

"Thank you. Sometime today I need to make amends with Jess."

"Why?" asked Lena.

"Her experience at a mental health clinic tells her Cade committed suicide. She's angry because I asked the children to observe his room. Absolutely barren of personality, but he hid two books and a magazine beneath his bed. If he were off to a new life, he didn't take anything from his old one. Even left money behind."

"Maybe kidnapping?" questioned Lena. "I hate to think of anyone so lost that they'd—you know."

"Me, too."

"Time to get back to the house," said Lena. "And for me to protect Julian from Lady Hands."

Chapter 21

A text came in from Lieutenant Robert Unzicker. *Call me.*

Alice always smiled thinking of Bobby, a former student who'd gone into law enforcement. Fate and bad guys threw them together on many cases.

"Unzicker."

"Bobby, this is Alice."

"How's California? Things are dull with you out of town. Galati solve the murder yet or did you beat him to it?"

"California's fine. Vineyards are heavenly. Galati's still working on the case. 'Course he's not willing to share with me, but he has me on snoop duty here at the vineyard." Quickly she explained the night of the murders. "Can you give me information about guns. Can't ask Galati because I don't want him to know I found out."

"That sounds about right coming from you. What's your question?"

"A .357 revolver can shoot a .38 bullet. Right?"

"Yes." His voice was matter of fact. "But it dirties up the barrel. Requires the gun owner to do more cleaning, but some guys use .38s."

"Why?"

"Guys I know choose the smaller shell for target practice. Thirty-eights are cheaper and there's less recoil from firing because the velocity is diminished. Was a .38 found in the body?"

"Yes, but the other victim owned the .357 revolver."

"You thinking she met the intruders with her gun?"

"Yes." Alice explained the timeline.

"I agree. She expected a threat and was ready," said Bobby.

"One more question. What's a *wadcutter*? I heard one of the officers mention it."

"That adds to the picture." His voice sounded conclusive.

"What do you mean?"

"A wadcutter is an old term for a flat-fronted bullet designed for target practice. You know bull's-eyes printed on paper?"

"I do."

"A wadcutter slices into paper more smoothly. It creates a more circular hole in the target. It's a good way for checking accuracy during practice."

"I'm not picking up the significance," said Alice.

"Okay. Your first victim was shot by the owner of the gun. Her ammo is primarily used for target practice. The lady practiced with that gun. A .357 loaded with .38 wadcutters *can* be used for defense but is only deadly if aimed at the soft tissue of the body. Where was the first victim shot?"

"In the throat area. I don't know that officially, just from observation."

"Then the significance is your woman practiced with her gun, and when forced to use it for defense, she knew what she was doing. She had the skill to hit the neck rather than torso and did so because she knew her bullet could only cause real damage if it struck soft tissue. It was no accident, Alice. She meant to take him down."

Alice felt cold and shivery.

"How was she killed?" asked Bobby. "Where did the shots land?"

"All over." Controlling her emotions, Alice took a breath. "On her left side. I think below her ribs. One in the chest. One near her clavicle on the left side."

"Maybe they struggled. Bad guy takes gun. Did you notice powder burns?"

"I don't know what to look for."

"Forensics will tell the detective. Here's my thought: If the gun were loaded with normal ammunition, one shot from a .357 at close range would have killed her. But your bad guy didn't understand the kind of ammo or the slower velocity. Probably kept shooting her because he wanted her dead. Maybe out of anger. Maybe fright."

"So probably not a thug?"

"Your bad guy still has the gun?"

"That's my guess."

"In my experience, amateurs are unpredictable. You be careful."

Chapter 22

Alice, Lena and Julian had just polished off poached eggs, biscuits with warmed fresh strawberries, and coffee when they heard yelling coming from inside the house. All, including the hound, bolted for the French doors to aid Eleanora.

"You couldn't call me? I had to read about my sister's death from obits online?"

The woman was wild-eyed, waving her arms up and down with every few words, her voice pitched high with indignation. Eleanora sat on a big overstuffed chair, her chin and one eyebrow raised, defiant.

"What the hell happened that night?" yelled the woman in her late forties. "You're not answering me. I'm not good enough to talk to?"

Julian walked forward and took the woman's arm. "Hollering doesn't work on her. Why don't you tell us who you are?"

The woman jerked away from Julian's grip and took two steps back. She looked confused. Staring at Julian, she wiped her mouth with the back of her hand. "Rayne. Rayne Musgrave. I'm Guthrie's sister."

Audrey flattened near the stairs and watched.

Alice thought Rayne once was a beautiful woman. Her cheekbones were high, her neck willowy, her eyes big and almond-shaped.

But Rayne dressed hard. Even though her body was thin, her black clothing puckered as it stretched to cover her skin. The tights exposed sharp hip bones and a heavily tattooed tummy. Around her neck was a choker with a cascade of yellow beaded strands falling like a bib over a tube top. Her ears, eyebrows, nose, cheek, and lip were pierced.

"Look," said Julian, "Eleanora wasn't in California when the murder happened."

"Still, she's responsible. I *know* she's responsible."

"Then give that information to the police," sneered Eleanora.

Rayne took two more steps back, and Julian pulled a chair from a grouping to offer her a seat. Rayne sat down. Her face contorted as if she fought an explosion of tears.

"I didn't call you," said Eleanora, "because I don't have your phone number. I didn't even know you were still in California." Eleanora's voice filled with boredom. "Did you give up crafting earrings for whatever that yellow thing is?"

"You're vile. You know I'm in Guthrie's phone contact list." Her words were razor sharp with judgment.

Lena went to Rayne, her palm slid down the other woman's back as if comforting a distraught child. Rayne pulled forward with a scowl, and Lena retreated to Julian's side.

"Rayne, I wasn't here when it happened," said Eleanora. "I came home yesterday. As far as I know, the police have Guthrie's phone. So how could I have called you?"

"Really?" Her doubt was obvious. "Poor you. Has Elka left you? Oh, no, there she is in the doorway." Elka retreated into the kitchen. "No lawyer to do your bidding?"

"There simply wasn't time."

"How about this? What are the funeral arrangements? When is her body being released?"

"The police haven't said." The older woman lit a cigarette. "My only contact with them was opening the safe to search for Guthrie's gun. I have no idea when her body will be released."

"No contact, huh? Then how did you learn she was shot?"

"My lawyer called." Eleanora picked a piece of tobacco off her lip and looked at it, brushed ash off her clothing.

Rayne's eyes went on alert as she glared at the others in the room. "See who I'm dealing with?" She perched on the edge of the chair as if ready to launch herself at Eleanora's throat, but said softly, "Am I allowed to see her body?"

"That's up to the police. Will you be planning the funeral service?"

Rayne face reddened with fury, and she stood clenching her fists. "You miserable old skank. You know I don't have that kind of money."

Eleanora made a face, sighed, and conceded, "That's right. You make jewelry." Her hand flicked, dismissively. "Okay, I'll pay for the funeral."

"It's probably too early to ask about the reading of Guthrie's will," said Rayne, her eyes becoming slits.

"I don't know if she had a will," said Eleanora. "Did she?"

"How would I know? She lives with you."

Lena looked at Alice as if pleading for her to do something. This conversation was mired in history with each woman assaulting the other. To Alice, Eleanora was winning at ripping scabs off wounds. But what to do?

"You're her sister. Didn't you two ever talk?" asked Eleanora.

"Are you saying I need to search Guthrie's room? I can do that. I can march up those stairs and clean out her stuff."

"Certainly not. This is my house. Besides, Guthrie's estate, if you can call it that, will go to Cade."

"Cade? Cade's dead." Rayne's eyes were big. Her dark mascara smeared with her facial contortions. "My nephew is dead. Have the police questioned you about that?"

"He's away," said Eleanora. "Not dead. He'll come home for the funeral."

"Then you're crazier than Guthrie said. The private eye you hired found nothing."

"He's alive. As his grandmother, I feel it."

"When have you ever acted like a proper grandmother? Or mother? All you've been to anyone is a cash cow."

Eleanora winced and stubbed out her cigarette. Her face took on a desire to hurt Rayne. "Over the years, I'm sure you were a fine auntie."

"Cade's not coming back." Rayne was back to yelling. "I'm Guthrie's sister. That makes me her heir and his heir."

"What do you think Guthrie owns?" asked Eleanora, her voice controlled, cool.

With a sassy face, Rayne said, "O'Dare's money had to go to Guthrie because she was his wife. With Cade dead, that money comes to me whether you like it or not. That's the law. I'm a blood relative."

Eleanora shook her head and lit another cigarette, taking her time to enjoy a long drag and releasing a steady stream of smoke. Alice could almost see the older woman plotting.

Rayne straightened. "Be reasonable. Guthrie's death puts a burden on me. Grief, you know? I want her jewelry to help pay for grief counselling." She rose and pivoted to the stairs. Julian and Alice moved to block her.

"The court will decide who receives the jewelry," said Eleanora. "My guess is they'll choose Cade. But settling her estate may take a couple of years."

"Years! She's *my* sister."

"And Cade's her son."

Out of the corner of her eye, Alice saw Nimble walk past a window. Rayne saw him too.

"Who's that? Outside?" asked Rayne. She went to the window, placing both hands on the glass.

"That's Nimble Cipriani," answered Alice. "He manages the vineyard."

Rayne paused before she spoke. "Who are you?"

"This is the woman who found Guthrie and called the police," said Eleanora.

"You're a witness?"

"No, I found her after she passed," said Alice as gently as she could.

Rayne studied Alice. "Keep that dog away from me."

"Why were you concerned with Nimble?" ordered Eleanora. "Do you know him?"

"No. He just looks kinda like a guy I met years ago. Before Guthrie and I met you." Her voice sounded confused again. "Okay, what if we work a deal. You give me Guthrie's Mercedes. If everything's tied up in the courts as you say, the car won't be drivable in a couple years. I may as well have it."

"And *you* may as well know," Eleanora puffed, sending clouds of smoke around her, "the car's in my name. Everything of value is in my name. Car, house, even O'Dare's attempt at running a travel business. It's all mine."

Rayne sat down hard on a wooden chair next to the wall. To Alice she appeared skeletal as if all that remained were bones of anger. "I get nothing?"

"Sorry," said Eleanora, but the gloating in her voice was formidable.

Rayne jumped to her feet. "You're a hateful old cow. Bitch. Years ago, you were conniving and wicked. You kept O'Dare from marrying me. Someday you'll pay. I hope Cade *is* dead. Because you'll be left with nothing, same as me. Choke on your money."

Rayne pivoted and stomped toward the front door.

"I would have stopped Guthrie's marriage if I had known," said Eleanora, "but your sister trapped O'Dare, and they snuck off like rats."

Over her shoulder with defeated eyes, Rayne said to Alice, "I wish I could slice every bit of skin off her body." When she left, the door groaned as it swung shut.

"What a pity," said Eleanora, "I was about to offer her Guthrie's shoes."

Alice stood back, shocked at Eleanora's insensitivity. Julian's eyes narrowed, his chin rose. Lena's hand went to her mouth as she gasped.

When Eleanora's head dropped, Alice thought the older woman stifled a laugh, but when her shoulders shook, the weeping began.

Chapter 23

Time: Wednesday, 10:45 a.m.

"She cried," said Lena in a soft voice. "That proves she's upset by all that's happened."

"Don't buy it," said Julian. "She's an actress. They're taught to cry on demand."

"Rayne didn't have to be so . . . so loud." Lena crossed her arms.

"If my sister died and that old bat didn't tell me, I wouldn't be forgiving either." Julian sat back from the table and patted his leg. Audrey rose from the porch floor and nuzzled into him. Alice and Lena nodded to each other at this new bonding event between man and dog, but Alice knew what a comfort her hound could be.

"Julian, that's not fair," offered Lena. "She didn't have Rayne's phone number."

"She's got a computer. Got a lawyer. Bet he's got a secretary to look up numbers. Pretty hard to learn of a sister's death by reading it in the newspaper."

"Julian, I'm not fond of Eleanora either," said Lena, "but her grandson is missing, her son passed away, and she wasn't even in the state when Guthrie's murder happened."

"I'm not saying she fired the gun, but think about it. She said it herself." Switching his attention to Alice, he asked, "Didn't you say there was bad blood between granny there and the daughter-in-law?"

"Jess said the two women had a rocky relationship, but during summer breaks, they agreed Cade should spend time at the vineyard."

A young man's face hid behind thick, wrap around, blue-lensed glasses. He hugged a tablet and stood ten yards away from the house. His shoulders rounded as if he were afraid.

As he came forward, he asked in a soft voice, "Mrs. Tricklebank?"

"Yes, can I help you?"

"I'm not supposed to be near the house." His eyes scanned the windows. Using his head to point to another location, he said, "I'm Witt."

Alice had no idea who Witt was, but she grabbed Audrey's leash and left the porch. Witt began to walk away from the house at a rapid pace toward the outbuildings. Alice followed, turning once to look back at the main house. Elka stood at the window, waving her hand and shooing her to follow.

Behind the garage was a log bench. Witt sat down first. Alice joined him. Audrey gave a good sniff.

"What's up?" asked Alice.

"Didn't Elka tell you about me?"

"No. A lot has happened. She probably didn't have a chance. Who are you?"

"Witt. I'm the private investigator. I look younger than I am."

To Alice, Witt looked like he could be twelve. Skinny, dressed in jeans with pant legs folded about his ankles and held by wide elastic bands, sturdy sandals, and a T-shirt with a picture of a kangaroo. He still wore braces on his teeth.

"I didn't hear you arrive," said Alice. "Where is your car?"

"I'm not supposed to be here. Mrs. Huff won't like it. I rode my bicycle so she wouldn't hear a car."

"You're the investigator who looked for Cade."

"I am. Elka said you wanted to talk to me."

"I do. What did you find?"

"Not much. Didn't find anything on social media."

Alice was disappointed. "Why then does Elka want us to talk? And why are you chewing your lips?"

Alice tightened her jaw. So far it had been a difficult morning. If Witt didn't know anything, why was he here?

"I don't want Mrs. Huff to see us talking." He glanced over his shoulder as if he expected her to appear. "You see, I think she never wanted me to find anything. I mean I could have done a search, old school, you know, on foot, interview lots of people. But she didn't want that."

"Wait. I've talked to people who said you interviewed them."

"I did. But Mrs. Huff only paid me for an online search. Only an online search. I don't think she wanted me to talk face to face with people."

Alice questioned why Eleanora would limit the search, but Witt shook his head to every question. Elka recommended him as a private detective, the lawyer insisted on writing up the contract, and Eleanora granted one interview. The limits of the search were clear. He was to investigate online.

"Mrs. Huff said I wasn't to tip him off that she was searching for him."

"In the search, you didn't find him."

"Wherever he is, Cade isn't sending messages or posting pictures." Witt's wide front teeth raked his lower lip. "Someone who hates him, however, is. You probably don't know about revenge sites." Alice shook her head. "A guy ripped Cade a new one just before he disappeared. The revenger posted all kinds of promised violence from beating him with a pipe to someone shooting him in the head. The guy writes under the name of Noose."

"Does Mrs. Huff know?"

"The lawyer said not to mention it because Mrs. Huff would be distressed. He said he'd tell her in his own way."

"Did he?"

"According to Elka, he may have sugar-coated it."

"When did the postings stop?"

"Not for a while. That's the crazy part. After Cade went missing, the anger continued for maybe another two months. I wrote down the website if you want to see it, but it's weighty. Made my skin crawl."

"Did you tell the police?"

"No." Witt took a breath as if reinforcing his defenses. "When I find specifics, it's for a client to share information. After all, a revenge site is mostly guys letting off steam. The posting of anger is supposed to be the actual revenge."

Alice recapped what she had learned. Eleanora may not know the whole story, but the lawyer did. He knew about the threats from Noose and so did Elka. Curious about why Elka was informed, Alice asked.

"She knows my mom and she recommended me." He sounded like a kid.

Alice couldn't help but smile at the young man, who regardless of age or experience, allowed his twelve-year-old self to share information with his mom's friend.

"And now me," said Alice more to herself.

"Elka also told me to tell you Noose started up again about two weeks ago. He posted that if Cade was alive, he wouldn't be for long. Told of nasty ways he could die. I mean sick deaths. It's bad. He even threatened again to kill Guthrie and Eleanora if Cade came back."

"Threatened to kill Guthrie?" asked Alice. She felt her heart quicken, and Audrey moved to stand in front of her knees. "Wonder why he felt threatened by Cade? Do you know of anything that happened two weeks ago?"

Witt shook his head. "Other than talking to Elka, I've been keeping away from the family."

Alice pictured her calendar. It was about two weeks ago that she received Guthrie's invitation to stay at the vineyard. Jess had held out the possibility of her new friend being generous, but Guthrie took the time to mail an invitation, mentioning her mother-in-law had planned a vacation in Pennsylvania, the vineyard was lonely, and having company would be a treat. She welcomed Audrey by mentioning the comfort a bloodhound could bring by walking the vineyard.

"Witt, will you monitor what Noose posts? If you see any more threats, let me know?"

"I will." He removed his blue-lensed sunglasses and squinted in the light. Alice heard his sigh of relief. "Mrs. Tricklebank, Elka said you know how to fix things. Thanks."

Chapter 24

Alice and Audrey pushed past Lena and Julian, through the kitchen and up the stairs to Eleanora's bedroom.

"I was thinking of taking a nap," said Eleanora as Alice entered.

"I'll be quick. I have two questions. Did you make any changes two weeks ago?"

"What do you mean? I don't think anything changed." The older woman turned her back to Alice.

"It doesn't have to be big. Any new instructions? Any strangers visit?"

"Nothing worth mentioning."

"Did Roddy Merritt tell you about the threats to Cade that were posted online?"

"Of course." Eleanora killed time by shifting a coffee cup to a new location. "Boys are like roosters. They posture without any intention of acting on it."

"I'm from the Midwest. The roosters I've experienced have a pecking order and are quite ready to blind a rival by pecking or scratching out eyes."

Eleanora sat on the edge of the bed. "What do you want to know?" She sounded weary.

"Change. I'm looking for change because two weeks ago, the threats to Cade's life resumed."

The older woman paled.

"What ordinary thing shifted? What tilted in a new direction?" Alice felt heat rise around her neck at Eleanora's lack of concern. "You've heard of Noose? What made him angry."

Audrey sat down with an air of authority and a snort. Eleanora picked up her nightgown to fold. "Yes, I've heard of Noose." Her hands quivered.

"And?"

"My instructions to Roddy were ordinary."

"What did you tell him?"

She faced Alice, irritation tightening her face. "It's been seven months since O'Dare passed. I told Roddy I'm not honoring any payments for my son's debts or obligations as of June first. It's a common practice."

Alice didn't know if it were a common practice or not, but her nose tickled at debts not being paid.

"What did Roddy say?"

"He suggested I wait for one year from O'Dare's death, but he was agreeable."

"Do you know of companies or individuals seeking payment or backpay?"

"No. My accountant and Roddy take care of that."

"They have that authority?" Alice knew she was pushing her luck with these questions.

"Roddy's father did when he was my lawyer." Eleanora's lips wrinkled as they tightened. "Now Roddy does."

"You've never been suspicious of what's paid out?" It was a personal question. Alice knew she had revealed her earlier snoopy intrusion into the office, but she didn't care. She was tired and irritable from the lack of sleep and worried about the vineyard murders interfering with

Henry's graduation. Her hand went to her hip, creating her teacher stance that warned many a past student against misbehavior.

Eleanora stood, drawing herself up, her face stern. "I know every penny that leaves the trust."

"Do you really?" asked Alice.

"What's this about?" demanded Eleanora.

"I talked to Witt. He said threats to Cade appeared online about two weeks ago. You tell me you ordered a stop payment of O'Dare's debts, also two weeks ago. Too much for this to be a coincidence. I'm wondering if there is a connection between Noose and money."

"Noose? What a name." Eleanora sat down on the bed. "You see what this means, of course. Noose thinks Cade is alive. It's what I've been saying all along. But why would he or anyone threaten Cade now?"

Alice chose not to reveal where her thoughts were traveling. "I wonder how many people knew about the threats to Cade. Did you tell anyone?"

"Of course. Guthrie had this insane notion O'Dare killed the boy. I had to tell her of another possibility. I even told her that evil character threatened her." Eleanora threw her nightgown down on the bed. "But it's the gossip that's horrid. I had to stop it from spreading."

"Still, when I had dinner with her, Guthrie persisted in telling me she suspected your son," said Alice.

"She didn't believe me when I said Cade was alive, and she didn't believe someone wanted her dead." Eleanora hung her head and her shoulders sagged.

"Might she have shared the threats with anyone?"

"Maybe. Elka and Nimble knew. I mentioned it to Sunny. Nimble probably shared it with the men because he wanted them to watch for strangers. When I had my nails done in town, I might have mentioned it." Scrapping her guilty face, Eleanora said, "We live in terrible times when anyone thinks he can bully another online."

Both women went silent. Audrey rose from the floor and pawed Eleanora's knee.

"Dogs are dear," said the older woman. "She detects more than smells, doesn't she? She spots pain. Alice, did this Noose character kill my daughter-in-law? Is he Xavier Nettle's partner?"

"Maybe. Witt told me Noose threated Cade with a severe beating. Remember Xavier arrived at the house with a tire iron meant for motorcycles. He dropped it after he was shot and ran out toward the vineyard."

"I don't get it," said Eleanora. "What does any of this have to do with whether I pay O'Dare's bills?"

Alice believed the older woman really didn't imagine a connection. "Could your son have possibly hired Xavier as a bartender for one of his yacht parties? Maybe Noose joined his friend behind the bar or as security? Maybe O'Dare didn't pay them."

Eleanora's eyes flashed. "Very likely. Tell you what. I want to see for myself what kind of people we're dealing with." Eleanora stood, and in response the dog came to attention, tail wagging. "I want to visit the bar where Xavier worked," demanded Eleanora.

"Probably not a good idea. From what I understand, the Hungry Fool is a biker bar. This is something the police should handle."

"The woman officer told me they already visited the bar." Eleanora's hard strength flashed in her eyes. She was a woman used to getting her own way. "If you won't take me, Lena will. I'll make sure she does."

Standing in the doorway, Lena caught Alice's eye, her expression too bright to be good. Alice's heart sank.

Chapter 25

Time: Wednesday, 1: 37 p.m.

"Everybody says you're a detective. You got a website," said Eleanora.

Alice was tired of explaining the website wasn't hers, nor did she have private detective credentials. "I'm not a professional. I don't take money if Audrey and I poke into a situation," said Alice.

"But we're good," countered Lena. "We're subtler than the police, and people like us better than any professional P I. We check out rumors other people might think are nutty. And Alice has a squadron of helpers."

The four sat on the porch after lunch. Warm mesmerizing breezes slipped through the vineyard. Their faces focused on acres of grapevines. The blocks of manicured grapes halted Alice's interest in motives or plotting. To Alice, weather in California was perfect, perhaps too dry, but perfect. Every day was peaceful yet extraordinary with colors and fragrances. As a hot-air balloon floated above, all four waved and shouted to the people peering down at them.

"Isn't it late in the day for a balloon ride?" asked Julian.

"That's why they're low in the sky," said Eleanora.

"This is simply beautiful," said Lena as the balloon continued south.

"I told you I want to visit the Hungry Fool," said Eleanora. "If

Xavier worked there, someone knows something. Alice, Lena's up for the challenge. If you don't want to go for a beer, then Lena and I will have to go alone." Eleanora's face was serious but reflected she had already won this battle. She reached over to pat the back of Lena's hand and gave a simpering smile.

"Not without me you're not," said Julian. "Tell them, Magpie."

"It's a biker bar," said Lena. "I Googled it. We can't waltz in and interrogate bikers." Alice blinked at Lena being reasonable for a change until her best friend's face twisted into a naughty expression. "*I* have an idea."

"What do you suggest?" asked Eleanora. Her demeanor hinted that she already knew and approved of Lena's scheme.

Before Lena could speak, Alice jumped in.

"Bikers come from all professions: teachers, lawyers, construction workers. I don't think many are thugs, but patrons of the bar may be loyal to Xavier Nettle." Alice tried her warning face on Eleanora. "If anyone goes, I think Audrey and I should go in alone, be low key. Look at her expression. Who can resist a bloodhound?"

"You're not going without me," said Eleanora.

"Or me." Lena brightened in a way that made Alice uneasy.

"I'm certainly not letting any of you go alone," countered Julian.

"You can't go," said Eleanora. "We want no heroes pretending we need protection."

"Love Monkey, you have stay here." Lena angled her chair closer to Julian, rubbing her shoulder on his. "Someone has to watch the house. You know in case the police come back."

"Am I the only sane one?" asked Julian. "None of you are going. You said low key? What's low key about three biddies invading a biker bar with a dog? Who's gonna talk to the three of you unless you're in black leather and chains?"

Alice again saw Lena's zany expression that flirted with trouble. Yet she couldn't allow Lena and Eleanora to go into the bar alone.

Alice's heart kicked and added a reminder of time. But graduation was still days away. A small investigation at a biker bar was possible.

"He's right, Alice," said Lena. "Stealth-mode won't cut it. I know. We'll *invade* in style. Alice can ask questions, but Eleanora and I will be the diversion. You up for it, kiddo?"

"You betcha," said Eleanora.

"But—" Alice was ignored by the other two women.

"I do look good in black, shiny leather, but for this I think Julian's right. We can't blend into the scene, so we put on a show. And I know just how to draw attention to us," said Lena, her eyes flashed with whimsy as she pointed at Julian.

Julian threw up his hands. "We're all toast. Should I call the cops now and have them arrest us before anyone gets hurt? This is a mistake!"

I won't be late, Henry, thought Alice. *I promise.*

Chapter 26

With Lena and Eleanora occupied upstairs, Julian shoved Alice out the front door and onto the sunny porch. Audrey took no coaxing to obey. She looked up at Julian as if ready for a mission, a treat, or a jolly good roughhouse. Julian's eyebrows drew together, and his calloused hands made flapping gestures of frustration.

"I don't like you girls going to a biker bar by yourselves," he said without making eye contact. Alice quietly stood, quite accustomed to Julian's protectiveness of Lena. "I told Magpie I want to come along, but she bit my head off. Said you all had this covered. But you don't know bikers."

He turned to face Alice full on, his eyes fierce and challenging.

"You're concerned, naturally, so am I, but Julian, we'll keep a low profile. I want to stop in quickly, express condolences for the loss of their bartender, talk to a customer or two, and leave. All I'm looking for is a name of one of Xavier's friends. Then we're out of there."

Julian's face expressed doubt.

"I'm happy to go alone with Audrey," said Alice, "but if Lena gets wind of me leaving, she'll follow. Eleanora is also determined."

"True. But hear me on this: low key may be your plan—dangerous enough—but it's not Magpie's. She's working up something with Grandma Looney Tunes."

"What?"

"Don't know. They won't let me into the bedroom where they're plotting."

"I promise to do my best to talk her down. I'll keep her safe."

"You better," said Julian with his fat-chance expression. "I'm afraid Eleanora is encouraging her to jump the rails. You know what I mean?"

"Lena can be impulsive, I know." Alice put her hand on Julian's forearm.

"In case you need help, I can follow without Magpie knowing. I'll wait in the weeds. You can text me a sign."

"Not necessary. Julian, I don't want confrontation. It's better if . . . the three of us quietly go in."

"Okay, not me. Plan B: I called our friend back home to get suggestions for biker bars. I asked him how to keep everyone safe."

"Friend? Who?"

"Lorenzo Skree. The guy from Chicago. Remember he said if you need an army of bikers to call him? Well, now's the time."

"I can't believe he meant that literally. Besides this is California, and he lives in Illinois."

"All the same, Lorenzo said he met up with some California folk in Sturgis. He said he could make a call. Knows a guy who knows a guy."

"I don't want this to be a big deal," said Alice puffing with her own frustration, fear rising. Audrey stood alert that something was wrong. "Julian, remember I said no fuss? No confrontation."

Alice envisioned two motorcycle gangs meeting in the parking lot for a rumble, *West Side Story* style.

"You may not want a big deal, but three old bats entering a biker bar with a bloodhound? Seriously? How you gonna know if the customers belong to a biker club or a gang? What could possibly go wrong when our gal upstairs begins to sing?"

"She's planning to sing?" A lump formed in Alice's throat, and she looked at her hound. "Audrey howls when Lena sings."

"No kidding," confirmed Julian. He eyed Alice with his Popeye face, one eye closed, mouth twisted and tight. "Anyway, Lorenzo texted me a name. Doubleshorn. The guy promises to be there. I just got to tell him when."

Alice pictured a beefy-armed man dressed in black leather, ready to defend the honor of three grandmothers. She closed her eyes at the thought. Her mind raced through ideas of how to escape. Maybe she could delay Lena for a day but go early by herself. She knew she'd need a cover story for Lena and another story at the bar. Why was a six-foot tall woman with a collage of age lines on her face entering a biker bar with a bloodhound? On her own, she was sure to attract too much attention, and Lena did promise to be the diversion that would allow Alice to question a customer or two.

How can I talk her out of singing?

Alice's body sagged. The whole thing was a bad idea. And a good idea.

"Thank you for your concern, Julian. And thank you for a name." Alice tucked the piece of paper into her pocket. "How do I find him?"

"I'm guessing he'll find you. You three girls will stick out like a sore thumb."

"I know."

"Lorenzo gave me some biker rules. Don't let Magpie touch any of the bikes on her way into the bar."

Alice stopped her thought from becoming a question. *Why would she touch a bike?*

"If a man touches another guy's bike, it's a challenge," said Julian. "If a woman does it, the owner considers it an invitation for sex."

"Really? That's ridiculous. I've never heard that."

"Just repeating what Lorenzo said." Julian shrugged his

shoulders. "And if the bike's dusty, don't let her write any messages. Not a cool idea."

Alice couldn't find words to reassure Julian that all would be well. She felt a throbbing pulse in her throat. A singing Lena unleashed was frightening. A howling bloodhound, unnerving. A bar filled with bikers—*Yikes!* What was she thinking?

Both Julian and Lena had been seriously hurt in the past during murder investigations. Alice knew this scheme had the beginnings of a bad joke. *Three old ladies walk into a bar with a bloodhound. The bartender says—*

Chapter 27

Phone calls in the dead of night always sent Alice's heart racing. She reached for her phone and croaked, "Hello."

"Did I wake you?" asked Julian, his voice raspy but soft.

"Yes, but what is it?"

"You didn't hear anything, did you?"

"No, what happened?"

She blinked several times and sat up, forcing herself into wakefulness. Audrey lifted her head and shoulders from the bed, her eyes questioning sleep or fun.

"I'm calling from downstairs. Don't want Lena to know yet." Julian took a deep breath. "Remember I told you how last night the old lady wanted me to escort her downstairs to check on a noise? I thought she just wanted to make Lena jealous. You know, how some women want to think they still got something."

"Julian what happened tonight?" Alice put her hand to her forehead and closed her eyes.

"I got up to go to the can and heard the doorbell ring, over and over again, like someone was desperate to get in. I thought you might be in trouble, so I went down to answer the door. No one was there."

"Did you hear anything once the door was open?"

"Nothing. Reminded me of when I was a kid, and we played Ding Dong Ditch. You ever do that?"

"Can't say I did."

"Funny, now I can't imagine why we found it hysterical. Ring a doorbell and run away. Kids."

"Think someone is trying to figure out who's home before making his move?" asked Alice hoping to get back to the purpose of his call.

"Guess they know Eleanora's home. Found a note under the welcome mat."

Alice slowly waggled her head with frustration. Julian could have led with that bit of information.

"What does it say?"

"*Eleanora, come out.* What do you think?"

"I think we tell the police. They may be able to match the handwriting to a suspect."

"Not in handwriting. Cutout newspaper letters and letters from a shiny paper, like a magazine. Stuck on with tape."

"Sounds even better. I've never managed to tape anything without leaving finger prints on the sticky side. The police will be able to match it to a suspect or to whomever they arrest."

"Alice, after this note, I don't want any of you to go to the bar tomorrow. You gotta stop Lena."

"Put the note in a plastic bag. Then show Lena. Tell her your reservations. But Julian, we both know once she has her mind made up, it's almost impossible to deflect her attention."

"Should I wake up Eleanora and show her?"

"No. Show her in the morning. No reason she shouldn't get some sleep tonight."

When she hung up, Alice struggled with a sleep position. Thoughts tumbled and spun out in vectors to the guilty. Who wanted Eleanora out of the house? What was the point?

Alice pictured a man ringing the doorbell and running to crouch among the dark vines. Another fear tactic? Why?

Audrey snuggled into Alice, aligning her head with Alice's feet, her tail draped over Alice's shoulder. As Alice finally calmed her thinking and was about to drift off, Audrey had a happy dream and her tail thumped with pleasure. This second awakening catapulted Alice into two hours of questioning secrets: Eleanora's family, the Tricklebank website, O'Dare's daughters and grandchildren, Sunny's foraging for food, Lena's song selections, and Audrey's disruptive hiding of things. Finally, she settled into guilt and texted Jess. Thursday was a promised day with her grandchildren, one she needed to cancel. But if she were lucky, maybe she could give information to the police and make Henry's graduation on Sunday.

The universe has this conspiracy going to keep me from sleep. No wonder I can't figure anything out.

Chapter 28

Time: Thursday, 12:28 p.m.

For their adventure to a bar, Alice dressed in her normal look of blue jeans, an apple-green T-shirt, and walking boots. Audrey had her leash attached to a simple harness. The dog knew they were off somewhere and her body wiggled with anticipation.

"Soon," said Alice as she waited downstairs for the other two women to appear. "Soon, girl."

"I called the cops," said Julian. "They're sending a car to pick up the note."

"You say anything to them about Eleanora's plans today?"

"No. Kept my mouth shut. Lena'd kill me if I messed up her debut."

"I'll do my best to keep her safe."

"We both know once she has a crazy notion, she runs headlong into trouble. I know you'll do what you can."

Alice heard the upstairs floor creak as the two women walked to the top of the stairs. Their arms linked at the elbows. They descended with noses-held-high, full of attitude, but neither were what Alice expected.

The two women dressed like stereeotype tourists. Lena's baggy white shorts exposed her chubby knees. A tight hot pink T-shirt hugged her marshmallow-curvy body. The beige safari vest with cargo pockets hung loose, unable to meet in the middle to button. Anklets and orthopedic shoes finished the look. She had pinned her blond hair into a messy bun with a sequined head band holding stray hair back from her face. Around her neck hung an old-fashioned camera. The look wasn't the Lena Alice knew. Her Lena preferred glamorous.

Eleanora's thin white hair was moussed into spikes. She wore cropped pants and an overly long flowing T-shirt. Knee-high stockings didn't stay up, and as she walked down the stairs with a cane, the tops of stockings slid down to her mid-calves. Without makeup, she had no eyebrows. Age spots dotted her cheeks. Glasses hung on a black rope around her neck.

Alice took a deep breath, wondering if their cartoon-like attire could possibly charm customers at the Hungry Fool.

At the bottom of the stairs, Lena said, "I wish I had my gun. My insides are all shaky."

"No problem," said Eleanora. "Between the girls." Her index finger hit something hard on her chest and she winked.

Lena's nervous laughter shook her body. "Good to know you're packing."

"Please keep your gun hidden," said Alice.

"My .22. In my bra," Eleanora said with pride and pointed again at her cleavage. "Just in case."

"Bikers are accountants, computer programmers, doctors . . ." said Alice losing her train of thought. Her fear rose, not because the bar might be populated by a smoldering biker gang, but because her two companions might cause a riot if anyone realized they were not the people they portrayed. "We're going there for information. Don't really want to attract attention."

"We got this," said Lena placing a finger to her nose. "Our plan will give you space to snoop. And that's why we do need attention. Everybody's attention."

On their way out, Julian said to Alice, "Warned you."

Alice drove, Audrey sat shot-gun, Lena and Eleanora entertained each other in the back seat, discussing old television shows and actors Eleanora had met.

When they arrived, the three grannies and Audrey wove through rows of forty or more motorcycles to reach the door. Eleanora led off, followed by Alice and Audrey. Lena swiped her fingers across several Harleys.

"I remember Julian telling you not to touch any bikes." Alice's voice arced higher than she wanted. She knew Lena rarely listened to advice and often found trouble.

"No one's here to see."

"Julian said owners believe touching is an invitation to hook up."

"Really, Alice, dressed like this you think anyone sees me as a hook-up?"

"I'm just saying we don't know who's inside. You nervous?" asked Alice.

"No. Just admiring these motorcycles. Look. This one has a face on the dash-board. That what you call it?"

Alice grabbed Lena's arm and pulled her toward the door.

"Lena, you don't have to do anything. Sit with me, and we'll ask questions together."

"Don't be silly. You need someone to keep their attention. I can do it."

Lena pushed past and entered first. The women blinked to adjust to the dark bar. Faces turned. A young man came forward, wiping his hands on a towel.

"Can I help you ladies? Are you lost?"

"Is this a real cowboy bar?" asked Lena, her voice overly loud with enthusiasm. "Because we escaped from a dreadful bus tour and are looking for some action."

Alice heard laughter from several men at the bar.

"Do you serve . . . what's it called . . . a boxcar?" asked Eleanora.

"Gin, Cointreau, lime juice? I think we can manage," said the man with the towel.

"And egg white?" Eleanora had an impish air and raised one eyebrow.

"No! Dearie, you don't want that," said Lena. "Don't cowboys drink white lightning?"

The man at the door bit his lip and closed his eyes. "Tell you what. Why don't you have a seat at a table, and I'll look for cowboy hooch. Would you like a slice of pineapple in it?"

"That'd be lovely," said Lena as she turned to wink at Alice.

The con was on. Alice had told them to be non-threatening, and their plan might be nutty, but it was working. Everyone at the bar was laughing. Even Alice had to grin. *What does their get-up say about how the younger generations see us more experienced women?*

The three plus Audrey moved to a table in a dark corner. The dog pushed into Alice before slumping to the floor. Alice hoped dog fur didn't pick up anything sticky.

Lena leaned in Eleanora's direction. "Did you see the piano?" Eleanora nodded. "Do you play?"

"Not a note, but I can make sound effects." With that she began making sounds of airplanes landing, sirens, and her version of rap. "Boof de-boof. Boof de-boof."

"Good enough," said Lena. "I thought I'd begin with 'Itches in Me Britches.'"

"Tavern songs?" sputtered Alice. "Maybe not right off. Do you have a tamer song than 'Itches'?"

"'The Keyhole in the Door?'"

"Don't recommend it."

"Well, I'm saving 'Roll Your Leg Over' to be second to last."

Alice found her jaw tightening. "You haven't considered 'My Darlin' Clementine'?"

"Clean or bawdy?"

"There are naughty words to 'Clementine'?" Alice found heat rising on her neck.

Lena turned to Eleanora. "She's been teaching school too long. Didn't get out much." Eleanora looked at Alice with a grin. Lena continued, "Okay, I'll start with 'The Scotsman.' It was written by Mike Cross, so it's not as old as the other Renaissance Faire songs. Just as soon as I have my first couple of swallows of courage."

The young bartender arrived with three drinks on a tray.

Alice whispered, "I've been around enough to know the girls in 'The Scotsman' tie a blue ribbon on his . . . his happy place."

"Alice, you can be so cute," said Lena.

The bartender put down a boxcar for Eleanora, a mai tai for Lena, and an iced tea for Alice.

"I'll get you something else if you like, but Keesha said you prefer tea."

"Keesha?"

"Keesha Doubleshorn." He looked toward the bar where a tall African American woman waved back. She was dressed in black leather pants and a black sleeveless top. Her hair short.

"Oh yes, she promised to meet us to give advice on our adventure," said Alice.

"Whatever you say. Enjoy, ladies."

Eleanora sipped her drink, but Lena swallowed half of hers in a single swig. She nodded, and both she and Eleanora carried their drinks to the piano.

"Gentlemen, this place reminds me of a hall I used to sing at one summer when I had fewer pounds and less experience." Lena's hand went to her hip, her index finger to her chin. She rolled her eyes. "I was once a singer in demand. Still can . . . do many things from my youth, if you know what I mean. Roguish young men like yourselves used to like . . . my *pluck*."

Alice looked at the bar crowd. A couple of customers may have been in their twenties, a few more in their thirties, several in their forties, most, however, were gray-haired with ponytails. Every merry eye was on Lena. By their expressions and salutes with beer, they all appreciated what Lena meant.

"Want to hear a tavern song or two?"

The audience approved and banged hands on the bar and tables.

"Well, then, I'll need your help. When I give the nod, rap your knuckles three times on wood." Again, she rolled her eyes and then nodded. Knock, knock, knock followed.

She's going to begin with "The Chandler's Wife," thought Alice feeling the heat of worry and embarrassment rise to her face. *Please let her be a hit. And not too offensive.*

"Once more," said Lena with a nod. Knock. Knock. Knock. Eleanora provided rap. "Boof, boof, boof."

Alice stood up as Keesha walked to her table. The two women looked each other in the eye and shook hands.

"Are they for real?" asked Keesha.

"They are."

"Wait 'til I tell my grandmother." With a head tilt, Keesha sat and pointed in Lena's direction. "When I heard three women were investigating a murder—" She dropped the rest of the sentence. "I'm a physical therapist for patients after knee and hip surgery." She looked at Lena, who was well into the spirit of "The Chandler's Wife."

"Well, this tailor being a bold lad, up the stairs he sped," sang Lena. "And very surprised was he to find the chandler's wife in bed."

"I'm Alice Tricklebank," repeated Alice a little louder than she wanted, "Thank you for meeting with me."

Lena sang, "And with her was a fine young man of most incredible size. And they were having a . . ." Knock. Knock. Knock. "right before his eyes."

"A friend of mine introduced me to a guy from Chicago when we rode to Sturgis," said Keesha, throwing furtive glances in Lena's direction. "I guess he's your friend?"

"Lorenzo Skree. Yes."

"My friend told me you're curious about Xavier's murder. Your guy thought you might need protection. But look around, nobody dangerous here."

"Lorenzo's cautious. I met him during a murder investigation. Please sit."

Across the room, Lena finished her song with gestures indicating an earthy woman's need and said, "Let's thank the barkeep for these excellent drinks." The crowd howled and clapped.

"Did she just say *barkeep*?" asked Keesha. Her voice pitched higher with disbelief.

"She did."

Audrey greeted her by placing her head on Keesha's thigh.

"I heard about your dog. The finding of the little girl was on Facebook, and the story made the rounds at the bar. I asked the owner of the Hungry Fool to joins us. He may have more information than I do."

"Thank you."

Keesha raised her hand, and a man in his forties, wearing jeans and a Hungry Fool T-shirt walked forward. His head was shaved, and he had holes in his ears big enough for horseshoes to slide through. His neck was blue with tattoos. He held out his hand.

Lena entertained with off-color jokes.

"Steve Cohen," he said, focusing on them but checking out Lena. "Keesha said you want to know about Xavier. You a cop?"

Alice explained her relationship to the crime and the entertainment going on in his bar, letting him know the older woman was Eleanora Huff, the mother-in-law of Guthrie.

"We weren't sure three older women would be welcome in a biker bar," said Alice.

Steve's hand went to his scalp. "Well, this crowd is okay with fluff, but I don't recommend a Friday or Saturday night. Those bikers can be unpredictable."

Keesha nodded agreement. "They're the bikers you see on the news doing tricks on the highway and threatening drivers. What do you want to know?"

"I realize the police have been here with questions," said Alice. "Eleanora wonders how Xavier knew her daughter-in-law or if the choice of her house was a random theft."

"I don't know," said Steve.

"How about another song?" asked Lena. A cheer went up from the crowd as Lena began "The Keyhole in the Door" with a jiggle and a wiggle. Steve looked over his shoulder, his mouth shifting from a grin to tight and serious expression. Soon the three at the table were drowned out by the clapping from the audience. And Audrey's throat gurgled when Lena voice took on a siren tone.

Lena sang, "So taking off his trousers, he set off to explore, the keyhole at MY door." Lena's eyes grew big as her hand went to her chest with both shock and delight.

"She's very good," said Steve. "Is she available for gigs?"

"She's retired," said Alice.

"Where were we?" asked Keesha. The three pushed closer to each other.

"The evidence the police have seems to point to a robbery gone bad," said Alice, "but there is other evidence that doesn't make sense. Does Xavier have a history of theft?"

After clarifying anything he shared was rumor, Steve said, "He's a good worker. I hired him a couple years ago even though he had been in trouble. Petty theft. Snatching a purse. That sort of thing. But he was a kid at the time. Maybe twelve or thirteen."

"He was a good bartender. Quiet. Maybe moody," said Keesha. "Saw him tangle with a few customers, but they were giving him grief."

Alice noticed one guy at the bar wasn't paying attention to Lena's show. Instead, he stared in her direction, his face quizzical. Alice felt discomfort showing a picture of Guthrie. "She ever come into the bar?"

Audrey drew Alice's attention. With all that was going on, the hound stared at Lena, making grumbling noises as if she wanted to join the singing with a howl. Alice's hands became busy with the dog's face to distract her.

"The police had the same picture. Never seen her," said Steve.

"Xavier have any particular friends here?" asked Alice. She glanced at the bar again. The same guy stared back, but this time nodded. "Anyone close to Xavier?"

"We heard Xav was shot first, so you're fishing for the other guy, the shooter?" asked Steve. "I told the police Xav pretty much kept to himself. Rode with the Saturday night customers so the guy had his dark side, but he kept that out of here."

"OHHH!" sang Lena as she fell into the spirit of another song. "Me britches are tight, and I cannot undo them. There's a knife on the window, Love, Love take it to them."

Audrey barked before she threw her head back and her mouth circled into a baritone "Oooooo." Alice gave her dog a roughhouse scratch and flopped her ears to keep her quiet, but the bar picked up the hound's wolf-like howl and joined in. Their chorus of harmonized "Ah-ooo, ah-ooo" followed, and Audrey threw her head back again and embellished their wild refrain with her baritone howl.

"Who is the kid who trailed Xavier once he got off work?" asked Keesha once the noise settled. "They seemed tight."

"The skinny kid?" Keesha nodded and Steve turned to Alice. "He's maybe sixteen or seventeen. Hangs around across the street from the bar, kinda like a wary coyote. Never talked to any of us. He's only been here at best once a week around three o'clock. Xav never allowed him to come in. Kid's too young anyway."

"Does the kid have a Harley?" asked Alice.

"An old one, but yeah."

Alice remembered the lean biker from the walk she and Breakiron took. The biker had turned his head toward the vineyard driveway. Was he curious or Xavier's younger pal?

"Do the police know about the kid?" asked Alice.

"I never mentioned him," said Steve, but quickly added, "to me, their questions were all about Xavier. Wanted to see any paperwork I had on him."

Keesha made a face. "The old cop asked some of the bikers if they had seen Xav's friend in the last eight months. So I'm guessing someone gave him information."

"Like I said, the kid was here, at most, once a week, never on weekends."

"When did he first appear?"

"A few months ago," answered Keesha. "The detective asked us if the kid had his learner's permit," said Keesha, "but no one knew."

"Why would he ask that?"

"Maybe testing if they knew more than they were saying. Maybe looking for new places to search. Checking if the kid was really under eighteen and not an older skinny guy."

"Are you familiar with 'Roll Your Leg Over?'" called out Lena, her face shiny with sweat. The crowd banged on the bar, affirming they were all acquainted with a roll in the hay. Lena sang of flowers and bees, riding waves, and pistons. Verses went on creaking, squeezing, pounding, and throbbing. "If you were a hare and us ladies white rabbits, you'd teach us all very bad habits." Lena did a little suggestive jig and fanned her face while flirting with an older gent at the bar.

Alice tried to concentrate but had this urge to hide her face under the table. *Thank God, Julian's not here.*

"What was Xavier's mood lately?" asked Alice changing the subject. Her knee jumped giving her a warning.

Steve sat silent for a moment, checking out the songstress.

"Xav turned in his notice. The plan was to work until the end of the month. He spoke about a big opportunity."

"Where was he going?" asked Keesha. "Who'd take him on?"

"I don't know. But he seemed to think his luck had turned. Said he was coming into some money. He looked forward to a lot of beach time and a boat. Happiest I've ever seen him. Not that anyone would call him a happy guy."

Lena had been through her song list and finished up her show with an encore of "The Chandler's Wife." The audience went from robust knock-knock-knock to clapping, and Lena took her bows.

"I could fill this place any time of the day if she wants to try another session. For pay, of course."

"Probably not. She and I will be going home to the Midwest soon."

"Too bad. Could use her for Monday lunch. That's when our retirees on wheels come in."

Alice choked back a question, picturing many of the bikers she had seen on roads with white ponytails hanging below their helmets. "You mean bikers with motorcycles not . . ." She gestured with both hands to indicate wheel chairs.

"No. No." Steve gave a big grin. "But ready to ride. They'd love her."

"I must say your customers are very welcoming," said Alice trying to recover some calm.

Keesha smiled. "You get that with this group. Not exactly chain wielding. These old guys are mostly retired teachers. The younger ones are medical — two doctors, three nurses, CNAs, therapists like me, and there's a dentist, oh, yes, I forgot about the judge."

"I don't think I'll pass along to my friends that we were never in danger. By the way, who is the unsmiling man at the bar?"

"Shango. He usually doesn't come in until Saturday. Surprised to see him during the day."

Lena's concert broke up. Her face flushed as she accepted hugs and handshakes from the audience. Eleanora's eyes found Alice. With a nod Alice confirmed this was a helpful interview.

On the drive home, Lena reminded the other two women of all the compliments she'd received.

"And the manager said if I ever want to come back and sing, I'm more than welcome. He gave me his card. I can't, can I? Wait until I tell Julian. I could be a celebrity. A star. One man said I should record my songs. Put them on iTunes. Said he would buy a whole album of songs."

Filled with Lena's enthusiasm, the trip home seemed long. Alice found her mind wandering to the younger biker who met up with Xavier. Was he the one who struggled for Guthrie's gun and then shot her three times? Was he angry or afraid?

Lena said, "It will be good to get home and have a drink of water. My throat is so dry."

Alice agreed as she pulled into the driveway of the vineyard, but almost drove off the path when Eleanora screamed.

"Stop the car! Stop. Stop."

Alice jammed on the brake, and they all flew forward, only held in a safe position by a seatbelt and Audrey's tether.

Alice turned to look at Eleanora's pale face. She was crying but her eyes were large and not blinking. Her finger pointed to a group of men standing outside of the main house. Both Alice and Lena glanced at each other for help to identify what was significant.

Several field workers formed a half circle. Julian had his hands in his pockets, his shoulders rolled forward, chin down. Her index finger in the air, Elka apparently scolded the cluster of men. Alice puzzled at the scene, something in Elka's gesture reminded her of Sunny's attitude toward conventions. One rule-oriented, the other critical of those who colored inside the lines. Nimble stood with his hand on a young man's shoulder.

"Cade!" said Eleanora, her hands trembling. "It's Cade! I knew he would come back. Knew it."

Cade was tall, wore a rust colored, collared shirt and faded blue jeans. His face was mottled with emotion. Was it anger or embarrassment? He wore sunglasses.

Eleanora struggled out of the car and stumbled toward her grandson who moved toward her. Eleanora fell into his arms, placing her head on his chest.

By the expressions on the faces of the others, Alice knew something was very wrong.

Chapter 29

Time: Thursday, 5:10 p.m.

"It doesn't matter why you left. You're home now," said Eleanora after Alice, Lena, Julian, and Cade moved to the porch surrounding the house. "So, what do you mean you're taking off after your mother's funeral?"

"Nana, I can't live here. I found a place in town for a few nights." His fingertips found his pockets as he avoided eye contact and paced the deck, but he couldn't hide his calloused hands. Whatever his work experience, his deep tan revealed Cade spent time outside.

"Nonsense. Why not sleep in your own bed?"

"I can't." Cade's neck, still blotchy, deepened with color.

"Cade, this is ridiculous. After all you've put me through, you come home for five minutes and intend to leave? I don't think so, *mister*." Eleanora puffed up, asserting her grandmother authority.

"Maybe you should talk more privately," suggested Nimble. "In the house?"

"No," said Eleanora, her eyes narrowing. "How did any of you know to be here for Cade's homecoming? Cade, how did you get home?"

"I hitched." His eyes glanced toward the garage. Alice detected the lie.

"From where?"

"Called Nimble when I arrived in Mitten. I asked for a ride."

Alice studied Audrey and wished Eleanora would call out Cade for his second lie. Together she and Audrey made the walk into Mitten, twice a day. For a young man used to heavy labor, the walk from Mitten was a snap.

Eleanora took on the demeanor of a seventh-grade teacher disciplining boys in trouble. She looked at Nimble and placed blame. "You gave him a ride?"

"I did," said Nimble standing straight, eyes crimping. "He called me. I called Elka. Figured she'd have things to prepare for the homecoming."

Before Eleanora's head swiveled in Elka's direction, the younger woman said, "I call Mr. Merritt. *You* say any funny business, call him. So, that's what I do." She checked her watch. "Now I go. Already very late for children. Look at time."

Eleanora's eyes followed the vineyard workers as they disbursed toward their cars and trucks. "Did Roddy say when he would arrive?"

"He say he be here pronto," said Elka over her shoulder. "At beck and call, he say. I leave now." Elka walked down the stairs and turned to face the group.

"How about I make some coffee?" said Lena as she rose from her chair and beckoned Julian to follow her.

"I leave now," said Elka. "Dinner in fridge." Her head was down. Alice wondered what she had to feel guilty about.

"Yes," said Eleanora. "You go. Say hello to your children for me." Her attention switched back to Roddy's absence. "He and I have paperwork to discuss." She fidgeted and scowled. "Cade! You called Nimble but not *me*."

"Nana, I needed a ride, and I didn't want to walk into the house and give you a stroke."

"Very *considerate* of you," said Eleanora, a fierceness coming into her face. "You take off without a word. Didn't even send a note when your father died. We had a private detective searching for you. I was heartbroken. Your mother was out of her mind. She thought you were dead. Almost had me believing it. Where were you?"

Cade paced the porch before he turned to face Eleanora. "I know. I'm sorry," he said with a stronger voice. "I couldn't breathe here. I had to go."

Alice thought the rehashing of events needed to be private. She moved to the far end of the porch and crouched next to one of the washer-size planters filled with thick vines with purple wisteria flowers. She fiddled with Audrey's leash and thought a walk with her dog would be a perfect escape.

Nimble, who kept a low profile with his hands grasped in front of him, rose and said, "Time for me to go." He looked back long enough to say, "Good to see you, Cade." He put a little kick in his step as he rushed from the porch.

"The rest of you can have coffee. I need a drink." Eleanora looked to the open kitchen door and yelled, "Bourbon, two fingers, two rocks."

Eleanora's eyes danced as her bravery caved in. Her hand swept a trickle near her eye. "Can I have that bourbon, please?"

She's afraid, thought Alice as she dropped her hands unconsciously into Audrey's fur. At least the hound wasn't disturbed by the tension among the adults. Audrey stood with her back to the house and her nose in the air. In her stillness, she appeared to be zoned out, staring at the beauty of the vineyard. Alice crouched down, putting her back low to the big planter and untwisted a kink in the harness. Curiosity made her want to peek in the direction of her dog's nose. Was Sunny watching?

"Will you please leave that dog be?" said Eleanora with disgust. "For heaven's sake, stop crouching over her like she's about to attack. She doesn't bite."

Alice's attention was drawn back to Eleanora.

Audrey slumped down on her belly, but kept her shoulders high, jowl to Alice's cheek. Wetness collected around the hound's mouth. Absently, Alice wiped it away with her hand.

Eleanora sat at a table by herself, coloring with frustration or anger.

Cade stood, continued to pace, and stopped again to stand still.

As he turned to face his grandmother, a shot caught him in the back of his right shoulder.

For a second or two, Alice didn't move, but then another shot shattered the glass in the French door. Another took out a kitchen window. Alice lay on her side with Audrey behind the planter and reached for her phone as the gunman continued to fire. Her call went to 911. Audrey's head dropped to Alice's hip as she peered around the planter toward the gunman.

At least Eleanora had the sense to hit the deck. Or had she too been shot? Alice wasn't sure. Three more shots splintered a wooden chair, a flower box mounted to the porch railing, and skidded a gouge in the wooden table where Eleanora had sat before it lodged in the trim around the kitchen door.

The following quiet was almost more frightening than the shooting. Alice had counted six shots. Was the gunman reloading?

Alice and Audrey peeled off the porch and headed for the rows of gnarly grape vines. Out of the corner of her eye, she saw Julian race from the kitchen with towels and kneel over Cade.

"Looks messier than it is. You'll be okay, kid."

She heard Lena say, "Eleanora, are you all right? Careful, there's lots of broken glass."

Alice had no scent from the shooting to give her dog, but she trusted that if a man was sprinting, Audrey wanted to do that too. The dog's head was up as she raced forward.

"You're chasing the man, right?" Her heart kicked into full pounding, and she ran as fast as a fit woman in her sixties could. She chugged down air. "You better not be chasing a rabbit."

Too late she heard a car speed away. When they broke through the end of the block of vines to a hardened dirt road, the car was too far away and drove into the sun. No chance to identify make or license plate. All Alice knew, the car was black. She took a breath, mad at her sluggish thighs that once pumped around bases to bring a run home. Reluctantly, owner and dog walked back to the main house.

In her head she heard Baer's spirit criticize, *What the hell are you doing? Alice, you don't have a gun.* Her foot kicked at weeds and dirt. "Baer, he fired six shots. Unlikely he had anything left to shoot me."

By the time she returned to the house, the police and paramedics were on the scene. Breakiron and McNally stood on the porch with guns drawn. The paramedics left their truck with some caution but went directly to Cade. Julian, once a medic in Vietnam, stepped back but gave detailed observations and instructions. He had seen gunshot wounds in his day.

Julian leaned toward Lena. "What are the chances a guy comes home to get shot?"

Lena helped Eleanora to a chair on the side of the house, away from the glass. Seeing Julian capable of lending a hand, one paramedic left Cade and checked the older woman.

"I'm okay. Before the shooting, I was mildly annoyed with my grandson. Now I'm downright angry. Who wants to shoot Cade? You're the detective," she yelled at Alice.

"No, she isn't," said Galati, hustling toward the porch. "I am."

No one had noticed Detective Galati's car pull into the drive.

"Now, we all will go into the house away from this glass," continued the detective. "Second, the paramedics will take the young man to the emergency room. Watch him," he ordered the officers. "Got some questions once he's bandaged."

The two officers nodded, followed Cade as he was placed in the ambulance, and waited.

To the others, Galati said, "Takes time for the hospital to assess damage. In the meantime, *we* will talk. Then," he pointed to Julian, "can you drive Mrs. Huff to the hospital to be with her grandson? You two," he waved at Alice and Lena, "I have no idea what to do with you two, but I'll think of something. Got it?"

All three nodded and mumbled they were there to help.

"Why is he so angry?" whispered Lena.

Alice shrugged one shoulder.

"Thank you, detective," said Eleanora, "but I really do need a drink. Four fingers, two rocks."

Galati grabbed Julian's sleeve. "I'll allow two fingers. She's gonna need her wits."

They all went into the red parlor, and Julian poured amber liquid into a glass. This time Galati was more to the point.

"Where were you when the first shot hit?"

They all recounted their positions: Lena and Julian in the kitchen. Eleanora on a chair. Cade standing. Alice and Audrey, protected by a big planter of wisteria.

Each added memories of the gunfire. The first shot hit Cade. The second and all the following shots went into windows in a slow spray, almost like target practice.

"You got any ideas about the gunman?" asked Galati as he looked square at Alice.

"A bad shot whoever it was." Alice's voice was soft.

"What do you mean bad?" Eleanora sat straighter. "He hit Cade."

Alice and Galati shared a look as she offered, "It seems to me Cade moved at the wrong time."

"Have any of you received threats?" asked Galati.

"I imagine you mean me," said Eleanora. "No, no threats. I've been away and despite everything that has happened, I'm glad Cade's home."

"Did he mention where he was all these months? Did he tangle with anyone in Mitten?"

"I really haven't had time to talk to him, Detective. We came home, and Cade was in the driveway with several workers, Nimble, and Julian. He got shot before I could coerce any information from him."

"Where were you ladies?" Galati's flashed a look as if he expected their next answer to be *shopping*. Guilt-faces all around announced there was a story. "Well?"

"We went to the Hungry Fool," said Alice. "We thought——"

Before Alice could tell him their motivation, Galati said, "You thought three charming older women could outmaneuver the police and get information from bikers about Guthrie's shooter."

"We had a plan," said Lena ignoring Julian's cautionary hand on her arm.

Galati opened his hand and made circles in the air, encouraging more confession details.

"Well," continued Lena, "I was the diversion. I sang songs and got the attention of the customers. Alice talked to a couple people."

Two of Galati's fingers rubbed the skin between his eyes from his nose up to his forehead.

"And you learned that Xavier had a young sidekick and jumped to the conclusion that the two of them were the thieves the night Guthrie was shot. Sorry to disappoint you, but we already checked it out. Like your grandson, Alice, the younger kid's getting ready to graduate high school, depending on him completing a mountain of school work. The night of the murder the kid was out past curfew, buying projects off other students to scam the educational system. Our officers chased him down. Also spoke to the essay providers. Having us nose around yesterday didn't make his mother happy. She worried we'd inform the school, or worse yet the kid's dad. She's a piece of work, more piercings than I've seen in a while."

"It was worth a try," coaxed Lena.

"I appreciate the effort to help. But please leave the investigation to the police. You're aware that two off-duty officers were at the Hungry Fool while you serenaded the audience? Before the back of the house was shot up, I was on my way here to have a talk about that."

"We're sorry," said Lena.

Galati nodded. "Now, my job is to figure out if your visit made the shooter nervous enough to try to kill Cade or if the tactic served a different purpose. I'm going to start by asking your grandson, Mrs. Huff, a whole lot of questions."

Eleanora glared at the detective and lit a cigarette.

"What's the kid's name?" asked Alice. "Xavier's sidekick?"

"My investigation. My business. Don't need you double-checking our work." Standing in front of Alice, Galati asked, "You learn anything new from the tavern?"

"Your information covers it, Detective." Alice chose not to mention Xavier's dreams of big money coming his way. The detective probably knew that.

Breakiron came into the room. "The ambulance left with Cade. We'll be off. Detective, Alice followed the gunman into the vineyard."

"And?" Galati looked peeved about Alice not mentioning this.

"I'm not as young as I used to be. When I reached the dirt road, the shooter was in the black car, but too far away. Looking into the sun blocked detail."

"The path is used by joggers and dog walkers," said Breakiron. "We'll try asking around."

Ready to leave, Galati instructed Officer McNally to call for a boarding up service once they all reached the hospital. "In the meantime, the forensics team has work to do."

Eleanora downed her drink, stubbed out her cigarette, and stood. "Lena, will you call Roddy. His number is in the book near the phone in the blue sitting cove. Tell him I'm cross that he didn't come running when he heard Cade was home." Lena nodded, and Eleanora grabbed Julian's arm. "Lend a girl support, will ya, handsome?" Julian flashed an I'm-stuck look to Lena before leaving with Eleanora for the hospital. Lena and Alice were left alone.

"I suppose I should be getting used to shootings, but my heart is still aflutter," said Lena.

"Mine, too."

"It will be good for me to clean up the glass in the kitchen. You keep Audrey well away. We want no cut paws. Besides, Elka slaved all day making nice meals only to have shattered glass hit the plates. I don't want her to know the extent of the damage when she comes in tomorrow."

"Change clothes first. I think we'll have lots of time before we clean. Forensics just arrived."

Galati poked his head through the door. "Stick close to home. I'll call for another officer to watch tonight."

"Really, Detective, I don't think it's necessary we have an officer for the whole night," said Alice. "The real targets are in the hospital. Eleanora and Cade need protection. Don't waste manpower on us."

"Alice, if he wants to," interjected Lena, her voice weakening as she spoke.

"We'll lock the doors after forensics and the boarding up service do their thing," said Alice gesturing in Lena's direction. "Lena, we won't be alone."

"Ever occur to you ladies," said Galati, "that Cade may be involved? A falling out among thieves?"

The two women didn't answer.

"Alice, we researched Cade's background," said Galati. "Grandma kept him on a tight leash. Do you know Eleanora promised to turn her money over to him at twenty-one and then changed her mind? When you're twenty and have entitled thinking, the loss of her kind of money could rattle your cage."

"We didn't know," said Alice as she wondered who was Galati's source.

The detective opened his mouth as if to say more but dropped his next comment and left as a man and woman carrying forensic gear entered through the back of the house. Officer Garcia took up his post outside.

"I'll be upstairs changing my clothes," said Lena. "Want to wear different shoes to clean up glass."

"Forensics will be here a while. Do you want me to join you?"

"I need to be alone." Lena pulled a Hungry Fool business card from her safari pocket. "We had a good time, didn't we?"

"A very good time. You were a star." Alice hugged her best friend. "Thank you. I need to walk Audrey in a little bit."

Questions buzzed through Alice's head. Who had notified the shooter that Cade was home? Why did the gunman delay a second or two between shots? Why choose to create so much noise with shattering glass? On the white board she kept in her mind, Alice carefully edited facts she thought were true, convinced that the shooting had been staged. But, was the detective correct in his suspicions about Cade? Had he taken a bullet to prove his innocence in killing his mother?

"Audrey, why did the bad guy shoot Cade when Eleanora is a much more likely target?" Audrey's tongue hung out of her mouth and her eyes almost closed. "I know, ha-ha-ha. You probably know of a clue, and I can't read your mind. I'm the silly one."

She gathered the hound's leash and went down the porch stairs to Officer Garcia's car. "I'm off to call my granddaughter and then walk my dog. Is that okay?"

"Yes, ma'am." Garcia gave a small smile and tapped his fingers on the steering wheel.

When Alice entered the cottage, she said to her dog, "First, we call Juliana. See how she's doing with the files she downloaded from Cade's tablet. She doesn't think I saw her. Then we take our chances and try to find Sunny. Maybe she's frightened or at least curious about what is going on with all this noise. Anyway, I need to warn her about glass around the cooler," said Alice. Her spine straightened and her overly big eyes grew bigger. "I can be absolutely dim. We don't have to play hit or miss searching for Sunny. You have a nose. We can trail her scent." Alice pictured Sunny rubbing away the chalk mark on the house trim, the mark that told her available food was in the cooler. "Yep, we're back in business. And boy, do I have questions about what she knows."

Chapter 30

Time: Thursday, 7:06 p.m.

"Gram?" Juliana's voice was soft with surprise.

"Sorry, are you busy? Do you have a moment?" Alice heard loud music in the background.

"Sure. I'm at my friend's house. Is everything okay?"

"A lot has happened. I'll fill you in tomorrow."

"Got school tomorrow, Gram. This time I really have to be there. Maybe when I get home?"

"Good. And I want to hear about everything you do in school, but first, were you able to break into Cade's files on his tablet."

"Gram, I—" Juliana's voice was breathy as if weighing whether she should lie.

"You're not in trouble. But I know you downloaded some file or two. Just tell me everything you know."

"I . . . I downloaded a password protected linked file, but it's been a devil to open." Alice smiled at her granddaughter's phrasing, so like Jess. "Nothing I try works. The rest of the junk on his tablet doesn't tell anything. It's stuff any guy might have."

"Tell me about the junk."

"The odd files are his birth certificate and his parents' marriage license. I mean who keeps a picture of his birth certificate? Can you travel out of the country with a birth certificate? And then he didn't take it with him."

Juliana posed theories of difficulties that came with no ID.

"Tell me the names of his parents listed on the birth certificate," asked Alice.

"Mother: Guthrie Dani Musgrave. Father: O'Dare Michael Huff. Is that helpful?"

"I don't know yet. In what state was Cade born?"

"Here. California."

"When were his parents married?"

Juliana read Nevada and the date. "Oh, I see where you're going." Her voice took on the thrill of discovery. "He was born seven months after his parents got married. But, Gram, people do, you know."

"I'm not judging."

"What does this mean? Why is it important?"

"It's important because he saved the documents. Read the two documents to me."

Juliana read each line of information. "What do you think?"

"I think," said Alice, "we don't have a full explanation yet. If you open the protected document, call me."

"I'll keep trying. I wish I were the one graduating." Juliana went into a long lament of when a girl has made up her mind about how she wants to spend the rest of her life—namely as an investigative report-er—being in high school is senseless. "No offense, Gram, but I can't understand how you spent your life in a classroom. It's so boring. Your life now . . . wow! Finding dead people is much more important."

"You are important," said Alice. "The students in my classroom were also important. I know old people always say this, but time is about to fly. You'll be in college before you know it. And Juliana, Audrey doesn't find bodies every day. Mostly we play hide and seek with neighbor kids."

"Remember I get to spend a summer with you. If Henry can, I can.

Living with you will build up my journalism skills. I'm keeping a diary of every minute with you."

"Well, Henry has paved the way. Your mother can't say no, and I will cherish a summer with you. You're writing things down in a diary?"

"I am. Someone needs to remember what you and Audrey do."

Alice's nose tingled. She put pressure on her upper lip to keep from sneezing.

Bloodhound searches for posterity, Juliana? Huh. Gotcha.

Before they hung up, Juliana said, "I'll keep trying to break into the Sunny file, but what if I can't?"

"It has a name?" Alice felt her heart quicken.

"Yeah. S U N N Y," spelled Juliana. "Why is the title important?"

"Not sure. But the title tells me who to ask."

Chapter 31

Time: Thursday, 7:27 p.m.

Alice leashed Audrey, grabbed her flashlight, and walked back to the side of the house. She moved a chair and waved her hand next to the spot where Sunny blotted out the chalk mark after retrieving food from the cooler.

"Take a good sniff."

Audrey stood on her hind legs and braced against the siding, her nose swiping across the exact spot Alice wanted.

"You know what to do. Audrey, find." The hound's nose went to the floor of the porch and moved toward the back of the house where a forensic team of two still worked.

"No, no, no. This way." Alice pulled her dog off the porch and toward the rows of grapevines. Audrey looked over her shoulder toward the porch. "I know, but we're taking a shortcut away from glass." Alice stomped her foot on grass. "Find Sunny."

After sweeping the ground next to the vineyard, rejecting some smells in favor of others, Audrey caught a scent, and with her nose to ground followed it into the vineyard. The early evening was lovely with birds singing. In the distance, Alice heard cows mooing on one of the low hills. A soft, warm breeze blew through grape leaves.

"If this weren't a murder case, we'd walk to the river, and you'd go for a swim. The land is beautiful, and you do like water."

Audrey didn't pay attention to her owner. Her ears were sweeping a scent, her nose taking it in. Well east of the house, the vineyards opened to the narrow river protected by tall trees. First Audrey turned right, stopped, and backtracked left, following the river north. The hound's head rose, and Alice scanned the horizon, spotting an olive-drab, nylon-looking, mound of a pup tent tucked among the trees.

"Look, girl," Alice whispered to her dog, "collapsible and easily transported."

A black open trash bag revealing supplies and clothing rested next to Sunny whose back curled as she sat on the ground. Her bony fingers peeled back the paper surrounding a half-eaten sandwich. She nibbled with care until she saw Alice. Her mouth dropped, food still on her lips.

"I found this. It wasn't stealing."

"I know. We only came because we're worried about you."

"How'd you find me?"

"Audrey found you. We need your help."

"I help nobody." Sunny went back to eating her turkey sandwich. The hound's normal sad expression reflected disappointment at the woman not sharing her dinner. Alice slipped her hound two treats, pronouncing her a good girl for finding Sunny.

"Nonsense," said Alice. "You've been helpful already. I know that. But first, I want to replace your flashlight." Alice gave Sunny the flashlight. "It was kind of you to give yours to the little girl."

"She was afraid."

"Very kind. Secondly, did you hear the gunshots today?"

"I heard them. Didn't see them." Her shoulder crimped away from Alice as if signaling rejection. But Alice remembered all the tricks students used to avoid being called on in class. She wasn't so easily dismissed.

"You need to know that Cade has returned." Sunny's face

brightened. "But, he's been shot. Not seriously, but enough for him to spend a night in the hospital."

Sunny hung her head and kept silent.

"I know you want privacy. But one time you colored inside the lines, followed the rules, and helped a lost child. Another time you helped Cade. He created a computer file and sealed it with a password." Sunny turned her head away. "Sunny, we need to know what Cade wanted from you. I think it's important. It may be the reason he was shot."

"I want to be left alone in my garden."

"Your garden?"

"Closer to God in the garden than anywhere else on earth." Her voice challenged as her head turned toward the vineyard.

"The poem by Dorothy Frances Gurney," said Alice remembering the poet.

Sunny raised her index finger marking points in the air. "Sun for pardon, birds for mirth, where a soul of the world finds ease."

"It's a comforting poem. I live in a small town surrounded by corn fields and dairies, chicken farms and bee-keepers. I understand your love of the land."

Taking a deep breath, Sunny put down her dinner and said, "Okay, I'll tell you. I used to work for a lab. Still do, at times, if they need help, and if I've taken my meds."

"What kind of lab?"

"Animal DNA."

"I don't understand. My science knowledge is spotty. A whole lab just for animal DNA?"

Sunny peered up at Alice with a knowledgeable, superior glint in her eyes.

"Farmers and breeders want to know if a young animal is healthy, worthy of breeding, for example. Cattlemen don't want genetic problems in their livestock. Horsemen want to assure the parentage of their Thoroughbred. Breeders of pigs and dogs the same. What's an animal's pedigree? Breeders charge big money for a perfect product such as sperm for artificial insemination, providing they have certification of lineage or health."

"You worked for this lab where specimens came in and were tested for DNA information?"

"I did. Mostly, for health predictions but pedigree too."

"Did Cade come to you to test his DNA for health?"

Sunny nodded, shifting her position as if measuring how far she could run. "He gave me hair from his father and his own spit." She paused, her face twisted as her fist hit her thigh. "I'm good at what I do. I'm not a crazy old tramp. The lab trusts me. When I next worked for them, I tested Cade's specimens also. You can't tell them."

"I won't tell. When was this?"

"Maybe a month before his father died."

"Does Cade have a health marker for an aneurysm?"

Sunny's face registered surprise. "No, not at all. You don't understand DNA or aneurysms." Sunny began to fidget. "Aneurysms can be inherited. But Cade is healthy."

Sunny folded the paper around her sandwich and put it into the black plastic bag.

"I have to be somewhere," she said.

"Please don't leave," asked Alice. "I think you learned something else." Sunny stopped packing up. "Right after he learned of his health, he and his father fought. A nasty fight with terrible things being said to each other. Cade left."

"I remember. I'm not stupid." She faced Alice and laced her fingers together. "I shouldn't have told him. Cade asked about his health. Would he get sick like his father?"

"It's pretty scary stuff for a young man to think he will become angry and violent as he gets older. So, your news took away his fears. You told him O'Dare wasn't his father," guessed Alice, and Sunny nodded.

"I did. Hospitals and labs testing DNA of a fetus have waivers for parents to sign. They ask if a parent wants to know everything a test can reveal. The animal lab doesn't have waivers. I made a mistake. I thought it might make him happy to know he's not inside the lines of his father. He can be who he wants."

"Build his own garden," said Alice softly.

Alice could see the whirlwind of Cade's mind. With O'Dare not his father, Eleanora wasn't his grandmother, yet crazy Noose threatened his life and the lives of those he loved . . . even if they weren't his biological family.

No wonder his room is empty of any personality. For most of his life with a disrespectful, domineering father, he must have felt he didn't belong, thought Alice.

"Do you know if he told his father what he learned?"

"No idea." Sunny shook her head, and her gray dreadlocks whipped around her shoulders. "Why would someone want to shoot Cade?"

"Or his mother," said Alice. "I'm trying to figure out all of it. Thank you for telling me about the test. It explains so many things."

"I'll be around," said Sunny, "if you need me for anything else." She patted and lifted her dread locks off her shoulder. Alice liked her spot of vanity. As she walked away, Alice heard Sunny flick the flashlight on and off.

Once they were out of ear shot, Alice said to Audrey, "Why is it every bit of information, triggers more questions? Does Eleanora know Cade isn't her biological grandson? I'm guessing not. Do I tell her or keep my mouth shut?"

But if I don't tell her, will Cade? Maybe he'll up and leave without an explanation. And that would be too cruel.

"Oh, Audrey, when does helping become interference?" asked Alice, "I can tell you all grandmothers walk a tightrope."

Chapter 32

Time: Friday, 12:18 a.m.

"You better come," said Julian while standing at Alice's cottage door.

"What time is it?" Alice rubbed her eyes and looked back at the bed. Audrey nuzzled into her own blanket from home.

"A little after midnight. I brought Eleanora back from the hospital about an hour ago. Lena's sitting up with her. The old lady's stinking drunk and asking for you."

"I thought she'd want to be at the hospital with Cade?"

"Kid's not talking to her. 'Course they got him looped on painkiller. She's giving him space but insisted Cade wasn't to be alone. Police got a cop outside his door. Eleanora wanted a friendly face around should the kid want to talk. She called that guy Nimble. He's got no family and is willing to sit at Cade's bedside. Not that the kid's in bad shape. He's not, but Eleanora wants someone to nag an explanation out of him."

"Well, that's good. Cade's guarded on two fronts." Alice pinched her lip and wrinkled her nose. "Julian, he didn't say anything to you when you were there?"

"You joking? He's got that noble, guilty face on. He's keeping his trap shut."

Audrey joined Alice with a whine for attention, and Alice ran her hands over her dog's face.

"Has the lawyer gotten in touch with Eleanora?"

"She called a few times, but no answer. Any idea where he could be? Not answering his phone. She said it goes straight to voice mail."

"Huh? He never came to the house even after Elka called to tell him about Cade."

"One more thing, police yanked the car at the end of the driveway from watch duty. Can't waste manpower on a stand-alone surveillance here and cover Cade at the hospital."

"Let me get dressed."

"I'll wait out here," said Julian who shuffled away from the door toward a chair.

Audrey's head was up, but once Alice walked toward the bed, the hound jumped back and dipped into the rumpled covers.

"Don't get too comfy," said Alice stripping off her indigo pajamas. "We're going to the house."

After dressing in jeans and an overly big black pull-over, she strapped Audrey into her harness. Alice, who habitually carried the dog's backpack of wipes, treats, and emergency medical supplies, found a bath towel covering the backpack.

"Aud, are you trying to hide this? I'm sorry you're upset by change. I promise next time to remember your favorite toy." Alice gave her dog a treat before they joined Julian outside and walked to the main house.

"What's going on with Eleanora?" asked Alice.

"I'm not good with women when they get all weepy, and Lena playing mother-hen isn't helping. She saw the old lady's tears, and her overactive mother-heart shifted into full speed."

"Julian, Lena's always been sensitive."

"Don't I know it."

Alice wasn't sure what she could do to help Eleanora. The woman had a right to grieve the loss of her son and daughter-in-law and now the shooting of her grandson.

In a small parlor decorated in brown leather and plaid furniture, Eleanora sat with a bottle of Elijah Craig on the table next to her. She held a glass with two small ice cubes and four fingers of bourbon.

When she left for the hospital to check on Cade, she'd dressed in a peach-colored suit and her brown wig. Back at home, she plucked the wig from her head, revealing her helter-skelter white hair. Her face was red, eyes glassy but at least not crying. Alice thought, *This isn't just grief, it's despair.*

Audrey made the first move by leaving Alice's side and placing her head in Eleanora's lap. The older woman smiled at the dog, her hand patting Audrey's head.

"Good doggie," said Eleanora as her thumb stroked Audrey's face. To Alice she said, "You come to join me in a drink?"

Lena grabbed Alice's elbow and whispered, "She's been talking about her grandson." Alice nodded, and both women moved to chairs across from Eleanora.

"No drink for me," said Alice, "but thank you. How's Cade?"

"Repairable," said Eleanora. "He decided not to talk to me. Cade's acting guilty. He knows running off hurt me . . . and his mother. But he doesn't realize his mother and I also did something stupid. She held up her glass to the light of a lamp and saluted. "Got my best friend, here. A couple or three more glasses and I can sleep." She took a deep drink, closed her eyes, and pressed her lips together, trapping the amber liquid in her mouth until she swallowed hard.

"The detective thinks Cade killed his mother," said Eleanora, "and the dear boy won't tell them a thing to prove them wrong."

"He'll feel better in the morning," offered Julian. "First time you're shot, it's hard to get over the violation of it. Ya realize somebody wants to hurt you. Hard to take."

"Nimble said Cade will bounce back." Eleanora opened her glazed eyes. Her lip trembled. "I'm not so sure. He's taken nasty verbal shots over the years."

All sat in silence for a moment.

"I enjoyed your sound effects backing me up at the Hungry Fool," said Lena. "When you were young, did you arrive in Hollywood to make musicals?"

Eleanora made a face. "No. Did any of you see me in *Gunsmoke* or in *The Twilight Zone?*"

"Sorry," said Alice. "I understand you have a reward posted for anyone who can find the lost episodes."

"Lost episodes," said Eleanora with contempt. "In Hollywood everyone needs a gimmick, especially as you age."

"I don't understand," said Lena. "What do you mean?"

"My ten-grand's not in danger. I never was in television. There are no lost episodes. I started out in the movie business as a gal delivering food. Got pregnant, then married. He took a hike just before my uncle died. Can you beat that? My uncle left me the Whipkey money. I decided I didn't want my husband back. Had no reason to share with a louse. Know what I mean?"

"Unfortunately, I do," said Lena.

"When you want to hide who you are and you got money, you can create a new identity. I hired a photographer to take head shots. When O'Dare was little, we hid out in Mitten for years before I revealed my Hollywood actress stories. Now people focus on lost episodes. Anyway, no harm in them dreaming of winning ten grand."

Lena sat up straighter, indignation in her eyebrows. "But on internet, I saw a picture of you on the *Gunsmoke* set, outside of Tucson."

"Really? I'd like to see that. Sure it's me?"

"Pretty sure. Matt Dillon and Chester are in front. Miss Kitty stands off to the side. You're behind them in the background, holding a tray. You were a very pretty woman."

"Were?" Eleanora had a sour grin. "No one has ever found that picture. Not even me. Probably a Miss Kitty fan saved it."

With Lena appearing to fire up for more Hollywood questions, Alice asked, "You ever act in small theater?"

The older woman laughed, and tears fell down her cheeks. "Don't need small theater. Acted all the time. All women play roles. Even you," said Eleanora glaring at Alice, "you're pretending you're not broken inside by your husband's death. However, I'm a better actress than most of you. You should see me as a cheerleader." In a childlike voice she continued, "O'Dare, you need money for an investment? Here. You don't want to pay child support for your daughters? Here, I'll do it." Her voice changed again and became husky. "I played the role. Could have been bloody June Cleaver."

"You never actually acted in television?" asked Lena, her voice disappointed.

"No, *sweetie*, I never did." She clinked the cubes in the glass and took a swallow. "Plenty of girls came to Hollywood. Plenty went home. I was lucky. My uncle died."

"Why did O'Dare's first marriage break up?" asked Alice, working at bringing Eleanora back to their current situation.

Eleanora's lip snarled. "He never knew his father, yet he turned out just like him. Things get tough, they scram. O'Dare wanted Vanessa and his daughters to go away. Family cramped his dapper style." Eleanora took a drink. "I cut the deal with Vanessa. And what does O'Dare do? Finds a string of women. When the newness wears off—he's off. Don't know why he married Guthrie. Never wanted their child. I told him no more freeloading. He keeps his marriage together or he's out of my will. I thought when he saw the baby boy, he'd become responsible. Instead, he worked at making Cade's life miserable."

"Guthrie sent Cade to live with you during holidays and the summer. He had to like it here.

"He did. I took him places: amusement parks, the beach, parades, baseball games. Know what he liked best? Vineyards and plants."

"I imagine he's good company," said Alice.

"He is. Can you believe it? Cade never hated this vineyard until the three of them moved here. I never fell for O'Dare's line that he was sick. All the men in my family died before fifty, and I never believed my own son. Told O'Dare, 'Buddy, you're on your own.' I was just plain tired of being conned. He was all about needy bluster. You know? I was wrong." Eleanora wiped away tears with the flat of her hand before taking a swig and draining the glass. "Now someone is trying to kill my grandson."

"Who would want to do that?" asked Alice.

"I can't imagine. Someone who's a good shot by the looks of this house. Three of us on the porch and the shooter hits only Cade. Purposeful."

Alice's interpretation of the shooting wasn't the same as Eleanora's, but she kept her opinions to herself.

As the older woman reached for the bottle to fill her glass, it tipped away from her. Julian's quick hands caught it before much spilled. Lena rose and helped Eleanora out of the chair.

"Time for bed. You have a big day tomorrow. Time to prove yourself the ideal nurse. Feed the boy cookies. Boys like cookies." She flashed a smile at Julian who held up both hands and wiggled his fingers. "Cookies will stop his foolish talk of going off into the world and making it on his own."

"Where's Roddy?" moaned Eleanora. "Why didn't he show up at the hospital?"

"After you take her upstairs," whispered Alice, "do you feel too tired to talk?"

"Meet you in the kitchen," said Lena. "I need some of the ice cream I saw in the freezer."

With Lena's arm around Eleanora, the two women swayed up the stairs. Julian came to Alice's side.

"I don't like the way this is shaping up," said Julian. "We need a pow-wow before we see the police again."

"I don't believe the shooter was aiming at any of us," said Alice.

"Me either. Guy's a nuisance. Even Lena blindfolded could have shot granny. An easy target. But hitting the kid was an accident. Why's our shooter spreading terror? After all the murders we've snooped into, ain't no way noisy gunfire is scaring us."

"Nimble and Elka left before it happened. I don't think it's like the lawyer not to show up."

"Nah, he's a hop-to-it kind of guy."

"Wonder what the detective makes of this?" Alice's mind was off and running. She checked her white board list for possible connections. "Julian, what kind of mistake could Eleanora and Guthrie make that trumps Cade's vanishing? Why is Eleanora feeling guilty?"

"Maybe one that gets Guthrie murdered and Cade wounded? Could be a helluva mistake."

Chapter 33

Before the three sat, Audrey devoured her one scoop of vanilla ice cream served up in a stainless-steel bowl. The fur around her mouth wore a white, glistening beard of cream. With the bowl between her paws, she had that more-please expression. Alice, Lena, and Julian sat around the kitchen table, spooning creamy cherry Bordeaux ice cream into their mouths. Lena's eyes were closed, her cheeks hollowed and puffed out as her tongue savored the ice cream.

Julian said, "We should be in bed." He reached for the carton and scooped another helping.

"This is insanely good," said Lena. "The butterfat in this must be off the charts."

"People here get plenty of exercise," said Julian. "Don't have to hole up during Midwest winters and get fat."

Audrey whined, staring at Alice. "Sorry. I know you have a touchy tummy. No Bordeaux. Don't want whoop-whoop." She slipped her dog a treat from her pocket. Audrey rolled it around in her mouth before she spat it into her bowl.

"Better get to it," said Julian. "Where are we in the investigation?"

Alice summarized her conversation with Juliana. "Cade's tablet had a file named *Sunny*."

"The woman who lives in the vineyard?" asked Lena.

"Yes. When Audrey and I found Sunny, she told me Cade worried he might take after his father." Her mind took a stutter step. *The father who wasn't his father.* "He gave Sunny samples to match their DNA."

"Wait. She's homeless. How she gonna do that?" asked Julian.

"Long story. Once she worked for a science lab that tests animal DNA. She sometimes still works there if they get backed up with work orders."

Julian looked as if he were about to ask questions about animal DNA, but held up his hand. "Never mind." He shoveled a tablespoon of ice cream into his mouth.

"So?" asked Lena.

"Cade's healthy."

"Glupp?" said Julian, working the cherries over his tongue. Alice knew he was asking for more details.

"Here's the elephant in the room that no one in the family is talking about. Cade is not O'Dare's son," said Alice, her voice soft. "O'Dare is listed on his birth certificate, but he isn't the biological father. On his tablet, Cade kept a copy of his birth certificate and his parents' marriage license. He was born in the seventh month."

"Alice, we know that doesn't mean anything," said Lena.

"At birth he was an eight pound, nine-ounce baby."

"Oh. Still it's possible."

Julian swallowed hard. "Playing around if O'Dare's not the daddy."

"Guthrie mentioned she was about to be engaged when O'Dare swept her off her feet. They had a rushed wedding in Vegas. Maybe at the time, she didn't realize she was already pregnant."

"Maybe not," said Lena using her spoon as a pointer, stabbing at the air. "It does explain, however, why she never left her husband. I bet she was after the old lady's money."

"*If* she knew Cade wasn't O'Dare's son. Maybe," said Alice.

"This will break Granny's heart," said Julian with a shake of his head. "Kid runs off. She's destroyed emotionally. And he's not even her grandson."

Alice had ideas about that—no, not ideas—inklings. "We all love people who aren't blood related."

"The shooter didn't mean to hit Cade. I'm sure of it," said Julian.

Alice nodded. "Cade paced the deck before the shooting started. He got in the way. All the noise was to scare Eleanora or her grandson."

"Didn't scare me," repeated Julian. "Remember me saying the guy was a bad shot?"

"I wasn't scared either," said Lena while licking her spoon. "What? Why the look?"

"Right," mumbled Julian. "The question is why shoot out the windows?"

"Something we don't know. If the gunman had killed Eleanora, who'd benefit?"

"Eleanora doesn't have a will or trust," said Lena looking pleased with herself as she twirled her spoon like a baton.

"How do you know she doesn't?" asked Julian.

"I asked her," said Lena. "When we were getting ready for the show at the Hungry Fool, I asked her what it's like never to worry about money. Turns out she worries in a different way. When O'Dare died, that killed her old will and trust. He was the only one named. Her lawyer is after her to make a new one, but she didn't because for all of her pretended certainty, she didn't know what happened to Cade. Her plan is for him to inherit when he turns thirty because, well, he's young and inexperienced. Between now and then, the lawyer will probably be in charge and dole out money as he sees fit."

Both Alice and Julian pushed their empty bowls away and sat back. Alice was stunned. "Wow."

"What's wrong?" asked Lena.

Julian leaned toward her. "For one thing, the lawyer's disappeared." Julian faced Alice. "Is her lawyer a victim or a bad guy?"

"It's a puzzle," said Alice. "Okay, let's think about it. If the lawyer's the bad guy, all he has to do is wait for Eleanora to sign the trust forms, then he has ten years of access to her money. If he's a victim, who else is there who can possibly claim the inheritance? Only Eleanora's granddaughters. Can they inherit if the court has given them their portion of the inheritance at the time of the divorce? I'm too tired to puzzle this out."

"Never had enough money to understand a trust," said Julian. "My daughter doesn't want my collection of concert posters from the seventies. Nor my collection of belt buckles. Anyway, I'm tired like you."

"Me, too," said Lena.

"Audrey's collapsed on the floor. Look. Her dog treat is stuck under her lip," said Julian.

"Tomorrow, then," said Lena, "after we have a good sleep. I hope the police know something new and don't fix on Cade as the murderer."

"But, so glad they're keeping an eye on him," said Alice. "Knowing a guy named Noose is out there makes me nervous."

"I bet the shooter is someone we don't suspect, like Eleanora's husband," said Lena. "Oh, don't give me that look. He could've come back after all these years. Eleanora said it herself. The guy's a rat. If he found out about Eleanora's money, he'd want to eliminate Cade because he's competition. Besides, at his age, that would explain the shooter's unsteady gun."

Alice rolled her eyes and grabbed Audrey's leash. "Night, night." The two proceeded to the door as Lena and Julian continued the discussion.

"You're way off base. Sometimes I wonder if you have a screw loose. You're talking like there are two separate shooters. Do you see a guy in his eighties teaming up with Xavier? Do you see him sprinting away from the house?"

Lena shrugged. "Don't know, but I bet he can pull a trigger."

Chapter 34

Time: Friday, 2:09 a.m.

Alice fell into bed a little after two in the morning. Audrey, who could sleep anywhere, preferred the softness of a bed with covers she rumpled into a pillow. She let Alice know this new schedule of haphazard sleep was not to her liking and grumbled as she collapsed far from Alice's foot.

As she lay in bed, slipping between sleep and wakefulness, Alice remembered life-giving whipped cream. Her children, Jess and Peter, had brought home an abandoned wet puppy, much too young to be away from its mother. Although they tempted the dog with food and water, the puppy was too lethargic to eat. He kept his eyes closed. In desperation, Alice dipped her finger into whipped cream and dotted the dog's lip. A tiny pink tongue slipped out and swiped the white dot into its mouth. More dots followed until the puppy's eyes opened.

Jess found a doll bottle and soon the dog decided on life. Alice's husband, Baer, named him Jake. "It's all Jake, as my old man used to say."

Jake was their first Swiss Mountain dog. Two others followed.

Alice opened her eyes to Audrey's head hanging over her. "I'm okay. Dreaming, that's all. But I do need to find some whipped cream for Cade."

Audrey gave a snort and jumped out of bed to stare solidly at the door. That's when Alice heard a small knock. The clock read 5:16.

"Who's there?" called Alice.

"Mom, it's me."

Alice opened the door to Jess, who hurried into the cottage. "I worked last night at the clinic and didn't want to wake the family yet. Drew's mother rises as soon as I park in the driveway. At least Drew and the kids are used to me working nights but not Baba Okazaki. Did I wake you?"

"Yes, but it's okay," said Alice. We had something of a big day yesterday. Got to bed later than usual."

"What happened?"

"You first," said Alice opening her big, round eyes even wider to chase away sleep. "Coffee? I'm afraid all I have is instant."

"That's fine." Jess sat at the small kitchen table, her fingers laced in front of her.

Audrey checked out the two women before she found Alice's shoe and took it back to the bed.

"What brings you here?" Alice took down cups and filled them with water.

Jess sat quietly for a moment. "I went to see O'Dare's two daughters to his first wife."

Alice stood frozen, cups of water in her hands. She managed to press the open button with her little finger. "Why did you go see them?"

"Because . . . because Guthrie . . . I couldn't stand not knowing if they were indeed horrible people and wanted Guthrie dead to get Eleanora's money. Why are you grinning?"

"No reason. What did you learn?" Alice put the cups in the microwave and carefully kept her face turned away from her daughter as she pressed *start*.

"Mom, the daughters are nice people. Sierra, the older daughter, has two children. Cute girls. Sierra's married to an orthodontist. Their house looks like a mini-village for princesses. The other Huff daughter edits documentary films. I expected not to like them, but their lives are normal and full. I asked them about Eleanora and why they never visited. Sierra said they obeyed the agreement made between Eleanora and Vanessa, their mother. Mom, I swear, you are still grinning."

"Maybe a little. Please continue." Alice removed the cups from the microwave and stirred in the coffee powder all the while biting her lip.

"When they were little, they lived at the vineyard and have fond memories of how much fun Eleanora was. According to Sage, Eleanora had a closet of fancy clothes and wigs. Both daughters remember playing dress-up with her. She even allowed them to finger paint pictures with makeup." Jess shook her head. "I can't see them being involved in Guthrie's murder."

"Probably Guthrie was unhappy when she spoke of them to you. I felt sorry for Guthrie the night we talked because she was so focused and intense with her suspicion that her husband killed her son. At least Vanessa sought a divorce when the marriage wasn't working."

"Anyway, I wanted you to know they were shocked when they heard about Guthrie's murder, and I believe them." Jess took a sip of coffee and sat back in her chair. "Sage said there was another woman, before Guthrie, who was pregnant with O'Dare's child."

"Does she know a name?"

"No. Believe me, I asked."

"How did you find the daughters?"

"Internet." Jess's head dropped. "Sometimes at the mental health clinic we have to do background searches on patients. Over the months of knowing Guthrie, I picked up enough details to research phone numbers and addresses." Looking up at her mother, Jess said, "Okay, enough. Explain. What do you find so *funny?*"

"You're right. This is serious, but I can't help it. Snooping is seductive, isn't it?" Alice lowered her chin and pinched her bottom lip to keep from smiling. The grin came anyway.

Jess looked stunned. Her elbows went to the table, her hands to her forehead.

"Oh, God," she said. "I'm turning into my mother. Wait until I tell Drew."

"You can't help it. Naturally, you have my curiosity and your father's helpful nature. Even your job helping people in crisis contributes. Yep, you turned out a natural-born snooper."

"I guess now I'm part of the posse."

"I don't remember telling you I had a posse. That's Lena's word. Where did you hear it?"

"I don't know. I think Juliana said it in teasing. Said she plans to call her friends a posse, but she's looking for a cool name for them."

"Of course, Juliana. She's becoming a wonderful researcher."

"She wants to set up her own newspaper online. Fill it with investigative reporting. She has this idea Uncle Billy should work for her."

Alice put her hand over her daughter's. "Thanks for being part of my intelligence unit. The information about the estranged daughters helps."

"I worry about you and the situations you find. You know we'd work out something if you wanted to move to California?"

"We talked about this before. I won't say no. The vineyards are beautiful and the weather perfect. Someday I'll knock at your door for a permanent futon in the dining room, but not yet."

Jess shook her head. "I'm sorry about that. Drew said after all that happened with Dad, it was a cruel thing to do to you. But we wanted you at the house, and we had made commitments to exchange students and—"

Alice took Jess's hand. "I know. If you remember, it was my choice."

Jess's shoulders sagged. "I'm not sure if I'll worry more this summer with Henry living with you or less because you won't be alone. How long did it take for you to become battle-hardened after Peter and I left home?"

"Hasn't happened yet. As for this summer, you'll worry more, of course," Alice beamed at Jess. "It's okay."

"You're probably right," said Jess. "Now what about you? How was your day yesterday?'

Alice filled in the story, downplaying the danger as much as possible, but Jess paled. The two women hugged.

"I can't help it," said Jess. "I worry about you. Remember Sunday."

"Twelve-thirty. Come Hell or high water."

Chapter 35

Time: Friday, 5:51 a.m.

Alice listened at the door for Jess to drive toward the road before she took Audrey on an hour-long walk into town. With each step, she heard Jess's warning, *Don't let murder make you late for Henry's graduation.* Feeling renewed and energized by more play at the dog park and the morning walk in cool air, Alice let go of her annoyance at searching for her shoe which she found hidden in Audrey's rumpled blanket.

"Looks like it's time for breakfast," said Alice, and Audrey stood eager and obedient at the door of the cottage.

On the north porch, the table was set for the three guests, a fresh bowl of water for Audrey nearby. Alice took a moment to breathe in the perfume of flowers. From this side of the house, the broken-glass destruction from the shooting was in another world. Audrey closed her eyes and twitched her nose before plunging her face into the water as if bobbing for apples.

"Elka's here a little early today," said Alice. She looked at her watch again. "Audrey, you know everything I know about what's going on. I wish you could talk." Water slopped on the porch as the hound's mouth rose from her bowl and dripped water.

Julian was the first through the door. His hair beneath his orange bandana was damp, his chin smooth. He wore jeans and a long-sleeved brown shirt. As he approached the table, his step faltered. His shadow created by the morning sun appeared craggy, with one shoulder higher than the other.

"It's supposed to be warm today," said Alice.

"Haven't done laundry. Only clean shirt I got." Julian walked to the railing on the porch and gazed out at the vineyards. "Beautiful place. Too bad about a crazy person shooting up the house."

Lena came through the door carrying a basket of jammy rolls and whispering over her shoulder to Elka.

Facing Julian and Alice, Lena said, "Morning. I just told Elka we'll be quiet. Don't want to awaken Eleanora. Terrible day yesterday. Not my singing, of course." She gave a warning stare at Julian. "When Cade came home, I had such hopes. Alice how did you sleep? We slept like logs, didn't we Honeycake?"

Julian frowned.

Elka followed Lena outside, balancing three plates of eggs and bacon. "Be out with coffee and dog's breakfast next."

"May we help?" asked Alice.

"No." Elka moved back to the door. "Last night you clean glass."

After the forensic team had left, Lena buzzed through the clean-up of glass by pushing Alice aside and saying, "Good for me to work out this tension."

The three guests draped their napkins as Audrey's nose explored the smell of bacon. Breakfast became a silent affair, the excuse being not to awaken Eleanora. With the last bite of a roll, Alice saw purple movement near one of the outbuildings.

"Excuse me," she said, and took hold of Audrey's leash. "Come on girl."

"What do you see?" asked Lena. "Are we in danger again?"

"No. Just checking on something," said Alice.

As she walked around the corner of the utility garage, she found Sunny dressed as usual in her long purple coat, her long gray dreadlocks tied at the back of her neck, stocking hat on her head. She looked tired.

"Do you remember anything more about Cade?" asked Alice.

"Not about Cade. Is he all right?"

"He's still in the hospital. We haven't heard anything new, but we expect him home today."

"Is that why Eleanora left early this morning?" asked Sunny.

"I don't know what you mean? She left?"

"Before dawn. I saw her in one of the John Deere carts. They drove toward the road. Another driver sat in a car with the motor running and waited for them."

"Who was with her?" asked Alice.

"I don't know." Sunny lowered her head. "I couldn't sleep. I saw your light on. Eleanora came out of the house. At first, I thought she might leave something in the cooler, but she left."

"Was she with a man or a woman?"

"I think a woman. Eleanora threw this on the ground when she got out of the cart near the car." Sunny held out an earring of yellow beaded strands. "Do you think she wanted me to have it or should I take it to the library. Maybe she found it and wants to put it in the Lost and Found. It's pretty."

"Oh, Sunny." Alice threw her arms around the homeless woman. "This earring tells me so much. May I keep it for a couple hours?" Alice removed a plastic bag from her pocket and slipped the earring inside. "I'll return it to you. And yes, yes, Eleanora wants you to have it." said Alice. "Thank you, Sunny."

Alice took off at a dead run back to the porch. Audrey loped alongside.

"We have to check on Eleanora right now," called Alice. "She may not be in her room. She left early this morning."

Both Lena and Julian stood and headed for the door. Elka saw them rush for the stairs and followed. Bursting into Eleanora's room, they all saw it was empty. Bedcovers were thrown back. Her nightgown, crumpled at the bottom of the bed. Even her purse sat on the dresser, the cell phone next to it.

Alice turned to Elka. "Is there anything like a plastic bag in this room or bathroom?"

"No. I get one." In a flash Elka disappeared.

"What's going on?" asked Lena.

"Looks like she received a call and left," said Alice.

"Maybe it was from the hospital?" said Julian. "Maybe the kid took a turn for the worst."

"Maybe," said Alice, "but you said the wound wasn't that serious." From her pocket she revealed the earring. "Look familiar?"

"Rayne," said Lena. "I don't have a good feeling."

"Me either," said Julian.

"We need to call the police," said Alice. "Here's what I want you to do. Julian, please call the hospital. They won't tell you anything about Cade's condition, but you should be able to talk to him on the phone. Ask if Eleanora and Rayne have been there."

"Why wouldn't she leave a note to tell us where she went?" asked Lena. "At least she could say Rayne called."

They searched the tops of furniture for anything she may have left behind.

"Wouldn't leave message in room," said Elka as she came through the door with the plastic bag. "In office."

Alice pressed her hand against the panel and the door popped open. They all peeked through the doorway. On her desk was a note. *In case I'm late in coming home, I'm up the hill.*

"So, she's okay?" asked Lena.

"At least she didn't feel threatened until she got outside. Then she threw the earring when she saw Sunny," said Alice. "Can't be okay. And look. There's blood on the earring as if she ripped it from Rayne's ear."

"What does *up the hill* mean?" asked Julian of Elka.

"Hill," said Elka as she pointed to the back of the house. She held out her arm and with the other hand chopped at each word, giving Julian a visual display. "House, vineyard, river, other vineyard, hill. Up the hill."

"She drove in a car up the hill?" said Alice. "I'll take my car. Elka, what's up there?"

"Cabins for people who like birds, like to walk."

"Alice, take Audrey and go," said Lena.

"No." said Elka. "Mr. Nimble say dirt road bad. Month ago wash out with snow water coming down from the mountains to hills. Wait for police."

In frustration of not having gloves, Alice used the plastic bag to scoop up Eleanora's nightgown by first turning the plastic bag inside out, capturing the gown, and smooshing the bag around it. "At least we'll be ready."

All four were back downstairs with Julian calling the hospital and Alice, the police. Lena answered the knock at the door to find Nimble on the porch.

"Do you know anything about the cart left at the end of the drive-way?" he asked.

"Eleanora drove off," said Lena. "Alice called the police. We found a note stating she's up the hill."

Nimble's hands went to his hips, his eyebrows drawing closer together.

"I don't know what more to tell the police," said Alice. "I don't have specifics. They're sending an officer. I feel so helpless."

"You said Eleanora drove off?" asked Nimble.

Alice explained the disappearance of Eleanora.

"If someone has taken her by car, they'll have to take the paved road on the east side of the hill. It will take them at least two hours to approach any of the cabins because they need to first drive south, skirt around the hill, and then back north. Our western slope is shorter but dirt-packed and too steep for a car. I can't imagine kidnapping someone and going to a house on the eastern side. Too many houses close together. Our western side of the hill, pretty much dangerous and isolated. Better location for hiding out. However, I don't see Eleanora hiking to a remote area. My best guess, they have to be topside, on the ridge, accessible by car and hidden from neighbors."

"What do you suggest we do?" asked Alice.

"Our dirt road next to this block of grapes is faster. Only way up, however, is by hiking. We'll take the John Deere cart part way."

Alice and Audrey raced to retrieve her backpack. When she came back, Alice commandeered a cart.

"Whoa!" said Nimble. "What's going on?"

"You said it yourself. Dirt road takes less time. It will take the police hours to drive up there, but they don't know exactly where to go. I've got a dog. We're ready."

With a projectile explanation, Alice explained her information and worry, holding out the earring as proof.

"Audrey and I've got this."

"Don't think so. I know these hills better than anyone, and I'm driving. Besides, in the passenger seat, your dog could tip out."

Alice relented and moved over to the passenger seat. Reluctantly she pushed an unhappy Audrey to the wagon-size flatbed behind her. "It's okay girl. Think of it as a baby pickup."

Nimble floored the peddle, and they took off with a jolt of a golf cart, much less than the lightning speed Alice wanted.

The hard, flat road paralleled the vineyards. The cart rumbled over a narrow stone bridge, almost wide enough for a car. Here the river was a trickle. A small cemetery with leaning pock-marked stones sat next to a tree line of evergreens. As the cart began the climb, the incline became steep, turns hairpin, stones spit from struggling tires, and boulders peeking through the dirt rocked the cart.

"We won't be able to continue with the cart for long. It isn't a mountain goat."

When the cart dangerously tipped, Alice reached back to steady Audrey. Nimble advised they hoof it.

"This is where the spring melt washed out the road. We're down to a heavily rutted path. Be careful. Hang onto your dog. We don't need either of you sliding down a hundred feet on your backside."

Nimble took point, scanning the tree line for tucked-away cabins. Alice and Audrey followed for another mile before the incline significantly increased.

"I see a few cabins. Remind me how people get up here?"

"Generally, they hike. I'm ruling these cabins out. No way for Eleanora to walk here. We need to go higher to where the road widens. You gonna make it?"

"Audrey and I will try." Alice found the steep trail had her sucking air after ten yards. Her feet slipped. "Toto, we're certainly not in Kansas, anymore," she said, attempting a joke.

Taking a moment to calm her heart by kneeling and nuzzling with Audrey, she asked, "Nimble, are you Cade's biological father?"

He turned and when he spoke his voice was high pitched. "No. Where'd you get that? No. Why would you think that?"

"Sorry. Guthrie told me she was dating someone before she ran off to marry O'Dare."

"And you're thinking that was me?"

"She was attractive, you're attractive, about the same age. You've gone out of your way to be nice to Cade. And Rayne thought you looked familiar."

"I gave him two books about wine. That doesn't make me his father. I don't know what to add about Rayne."

"You gave me wine lessons to prepare me as his advocate with the family. Nimble, why do that unless you knew he'd be home soon? Cade called you to give him a lift from Mitten to the vineyard, but the walk is easy-peasy for someone who is twenty. My guess is you picked him up from wherever he's been hiding and drove him home."

"Okay, I helped the kid leave and helped him come back. He was in a bad way. The family's screwed up, and he needed a chance to work hard. See how real people live. But I'm *not* his father. I was married to Jean for five years before we divorced. We never had children. Tried fostering some who got a raw deal. I got to see how kids first get scared then permanently angry. If Cade were mine, you think I'd let O'Dare make him feel like dirt?"

"My mistake," said Alice. "Sorry. I had the wrong impression."

Once they resumed the climb, Alice kept her head down, minding the irregular surface. In her sixties, she didn't want the indignity of landing on her face, pitching down a slope, or hearing her bones break.

Deep into the forest of trees, high on the hill, more desolate cabins appeared as the slope lessened. At each cabin, Nimble cautioned Alice to stay back by raising his hand before he cut through trees, only to find the structure empty. Alice took the moment to check her phone. No bars of service.

"Now that we're up here, shall I try Audrey?" asked Alice.

Once she gave Audrey the scent of the nightgown in the plastic bag, the hound's nose searched the ground and then lifted into the air as if confused. For another mile as they passed sparse cabins, Audrey showed no interest. Alice and Nimble grumbled they should have remembered water. Cords of slobber thickened around the dog's mouth. Audrey needed a drink.

Then, Audrey gave a tug and began to move faster, her nose in the air.

"She's caught something."

The cabin wasn't far and set back from the paved road.

"I don't see a car," said Alice.

Nimble held up his hand, crept among the trees and back again.

"The black car's on the other side of the cabin, and I spotted a Harley."

What to do? Alice mentally kicked herself. She had been in a similar situation before with no cell access to call for help. She crunched through leaves to peep at the bike.

A gun cocked. A determined young man stood behind them with his handgun raised. Alice estimated he was sixteen or seventeen, height about five-six and shockingly familiar looking.

"Your dog bite?" he asked.

"No. She's very gentle. Are you Xavier's friend?"

"Brother. Half-brother," he corrected.

"What's your name?" asked Alice.

"Austin. Austin Eyestone."

"Not Nettle?"

Austin's face tightened, and he raised the gun a little higher. "Nah, Nettle was . . . one of Ma's guys . . . before."

His arms were heavily tattooed, his head shaved on the sides, a plume of black hair like a rooster's tail hung over his eyes. Alice was about to ask him about the gold lettering on the motorcycle, spelling out *Noose*.

Austin's eyes followed Alice's gaze. "The bike belonged to Xav. It's mine now. Ma said the woman at the vineyard killed Xav. That true?"

In her softest voice Alice asked, "You weren't there when it happened?"

"No. I wish I was."

Alice wondered what more he thought he could do. Guthrie was dead.

Taking a breath, Alice assessed if it were possible to talk this boy down. His rigidity made him dangerous. *Of course.* Alice felt stupid. If she hadn't been tired all the time from sleeping irregular hours, maybe she would have tied the police story together: the boy who hung out at the bar waiting for Xavier, the boy with an angry tattooed mother and school projects due before graduation. Rayne had two sons, and if this one didn't accompany Xavier to the vineyard, who did? *Rayne. She killed her own sister.*

"What happens now?" asked Alice.

"We talk to Ma."

Austin gestured with the gun for them to walk to the cabin.

"Is this your mother's cabin?" asked Alice.

"My dad's," answered the kid. "They're divorced."

Rayne opened the door. "He's not afraid to shoot any of you."

Here in the cabin, Alice thought Rayne wild-eyed and clearly out of her depth as she held a revolver. Her hands shook.

Ignoring the gun and Rayne whose mascara smeared around her eyes, Alice walked past her and noticed one earlobe had dried blood on it as if someone ripped out an earring.

Pretend this is Limekiln and you just walked into the Methodist Church office, and Bev is typing the program for Sunday, thought Alice. She took a deep breath and forced a smile.

"Whew! That's a climb. May I have some water for my dog?" asked Alice as politely as she could. She felt Nimble and the boy standing behind her. "And I could use some too. My throat is so dry." She gave a little cough for effect.

Rayne seemed jarred by the simple question. "NO. Maybe. Later. Sit over there."

She gestured to a wooden chair next to Eleanora, who looked more peeved than frightened. Her hair was messy, and the knees of her pants appeared to have dirt from a fall as did the elbow of her sweater. Her hands were tied in front of her with ragged twine, wrists red.

Across from them sat Eleanora's lawyer with his hands tied behind him, a piece of duct tape across his mouth. He wore jeans and a pull-over, loafers, no socks. Alice guessed Rayne had snagged him first which explained why Roddy Merritt never arrived to welcome Cade home.

"You, floor," said Rayne to Nimble. He sat, grabbing his knees with his arms.

"Where's the rope?" asked Rayne.

"We used all we had," said Austin. Pointing to Alice with his gun, he added, "She asked me what happens now."

"Did you call the cops?" Rayne glared at Alice.

Wary of not selling the lie and hoping not to give too much information, Alice turned to Nimble. "Did you call them?'

"No, why would I?" answered Nimble. "We were out walking. Besides, I got no bars up here." He patted his phone.

"How did you find us?" asked Rayne.

"Kinda stumbled on you. Audrey's a bloodhound and that means she needs lots of exercise. Nimble was gracious enough to show us a new path for our walk. Audrey is a very curious girl. Can we all have water now?"

Audrey rose and stood next to the sink. Rayne nodded. "Only the dog."

Alice found a large bowl and filled it with water. Audrey submerged her face and water slushed over the edge.

Merritt rolled his eyes. Rayne pulled her lips inside her mouth, slow to decide what to do next. Alice kept low next to her dog and checked out the cabin filled with wooden furniture, very typical of a fishing cabin in the Midwest.

"We can't hang around here, Ma. You said we'd be in and out."

"Where you think you and me are going to move two men, two old ladies, and a dog?"

"I texted Dad. I told him we might need help."

"You what?" Rayne paled.

"I texted Dad when you were driving the old lady up the road. He knows how to make a person—you know."

"I told you, your father can't know we're up here." Agitation made Rayne pace the room while watching Merritt, Alice, and Nimble. Alice tried to catch Nimble's eye. First, he tipped his head to look out the window at the sky and then the floor behind the lawyer.

When he turned back to the room, he said, "Hey, I'm only an outsider. Anyone care to explain what's going on?"

Alice tried to follow Nimble's gaze, but her angle was wrong.

"Eleanora, are you all right?" asked Alice.

"Shut up. Everyone shut up," yelled Rayne.

"Nuts!" said Eleanora, "Rayne, honey, I have to pee."

"Shut up!" shouted Rayne.

"Is there a bathroom?" asked Alice.

"Of course, there's a bathroom." Rayne looked at her son and then at Eleanora. "I have to think."

"I still have to pee," said Eleanora.

Alice felt the younger woman's frustration and fear, saw her breathing become heavy. She had started something too big for her to handle. Probably one simple kidnapping of a lawyer followed by another simple kidnapping of an older woman. But now Austin complicated the situation by bringing in two more people, and a mean ex-husband was on his way. In the name of cleaning up a mess, what would Rayne decide? If Nimble made a move, perhaps toward Austin, Alice knew she'd need to take on Rayne. But after the steep climb, her leg muscles wobbled. Also, Rayne was at least twenty years younger. Both kidnappers had guns pointed in their direction. Both fidgeted. Probably no plan.

Oh, Baer, how do I stop this?

Chapter 36

Time: Friday, sun high in the sky

"I said I have to pee," said Eleanora.

Rayne whipped around as if to deliver a smart-ass comment, but said, "Sign the papers, and I'll show you the bathroom."

Eleanora made a face and shot a glance in Merritt's direction. His head tilted, eyebrows raised.

Alice didn't decipher their communication, but Audrey stood and made an insistent gargle sound in her throat and had that urgent look in her eyes.

"We shouldn't have mentioned the p word in front of Audrey. It's been a hard climb for her," said Alice. "Things loosen up. Rayne, may I?"

Rayne's frustration ramped up even more, her voice brittle. "Okay, but don't try anything. I swear, I'll shoot you in the back if I have to."

Alice rapidly moved to the door. "I know. What possible value could our lives have?" Then in passing Rayne, she added, "You shot your sister, right?"

Alice's harsh question silenced the room of speech and halted small movement. Breathing hard, her face flushing, Rayne stood at the door with the gun pointed at the taller woman.

"You run, you're dead."

"I know."

This was Alice's chance to look for a weapon. Audrey put their lives in jeopardy by pushing boundaries to explore trees for the perfect squat-down. Wanting to make this moment count, Alice evaluated rotted branches on the ground. A handful of dirt? The surprise of a tossed pine cone in the face?

All the while, Rayne stood in the doorway with her gun raised, her knuckles white.

Audrey rammed her head into thick weeds and underbrush, then wrenched it back, wearing a hairnet of spider webs.

"Audrey, you don't know what kind of spiders are in there." With her bare hand Alice swiped the sticky webs away. Audrey found the right spot for a private moment. A black spider skittered beneath a leaf and disappeared, leaving no chance for it to become Alice's weapon.

Faint strains of a motorcycle's growl came from below as it struggled up the killer incline. Alice knew sounds bounced off hills, particularly from a raspy Harley. She had nowhere to run for help. If she was right, Austin's dad traveled in their direction. She decided to take Audrey back inside the cabin without a pine cone or spider to hurl at Rayne.

"Oh, for pity's sake, Rayne. Give it a rest," said Eleanora with contempt. "The dog had to go. Remember I too need a ladies' room. Do I go to the bathroom, or do I step outside?"

Rayne's lip curled as she reluctantly agreed but kept Eleanora's hands tied. She checked out the bathroom and allowed Eleanora to enter.

When the older woman returned to the chair by the table, she asked, "Rayne, what exactly do you want?"

"Respect," said Rayne a little too quickly. "You're going to sign those trust papers."

"Lots of luck with that," said Eleanora.

"I brought Merritt up here because it's time for you to sign." To

Alice, Rayne's words sounded rehearsed, as if she practiced in front of a bathroom mirror to sound confident and in control. "You're giving everything to Cade." Rayne's anger was palpable.

"Cade? You snatched me to do that? I'm going to do that anyway," said Eleanora. "All of this is pointless."

"But, since O'Dare's death, you haven't, have you? Now you will," said Rayne. Bracing her feet shoulder width apart, she used both hands to aim the gun.

Follow the money nagged at Alice. *If Eleanora dies, Cade would inherit, but what is Rayne's role?*

Eleanora glanced at the barren room. Alice flinched when the older woman's voice lifted with contempt. "I don't see any papers."

"Where are the papers?" asked Alice, hoping she sounded encouraging.

Rayne retrieved a briefcase from a wood box next to the fireplace and removed a crisp stack of printed pages. With one hand she flipped pages marked with Post-it flags reading *sign-it and date* tape. Rayne continued to rattle on about inheritance details, like Cade fully inheriting at thirty. Eleanora and Alice looked at each other aware.

Merritt dropped the twine bindings behind him, removed the duct tape from his own mouth, and rolled his shoulders. "Jig's up, darlin'. They're not buying your act. You were supposed to untie me first, force me to open the briefcase, and allow me to tell my woeful tale. I was on my way to the vineyard to greet Cade and present Eleanora with the trust papers when you forced me into your car." He stood and cracked his neck with stretching. Turning to Rayne he said, "You don't understand, do you?" Rayne shook her head. "When were you to have the time to read the trust document. How were you supposed to know Eleanora wants Cade to inherit at thirty?"

Rayne spun around as if under attack. "You told me."

"Roddy?" asked Eleanora.

"Long story. Just sign the papers, Eleanora. Give the money to Cade. It's what you want."

"She might be wondering if that will get her murdered," said Alice. "Or Cade."

"Shut up," yelled Rayne.

"I was wondering that," said Eleanora with her chin raised. "I think I'd like to hear the full story, the long story." She twisted her shoulders in Merritt's direction.

"Look, you were going to give the money to Cade." Gone was his usual funeral-speak tone, replaced by boredom. "Eleanora, how many times in the last several months have we talked about this?"

"Sign the money over to a grandson no one can find? Where was the sense in that? What was I to think?" Eleanora's eyes grew large as she twisted toward Alice. "Who would take care of the money if Cade weren't found?"

"Merritt," answered Alice.

Eleanora turned her head and fidgeted as if she wanted to cross her restrained arms. "I'm not signing until I know what's going on."

"As the outsider here," said Nimble raising his hand, "I'd like to know that too.

"Cade's my nephew," said Rayne. With a sideways glance at Merritt, she straightened. "Austin and I are Cade's only relatives. We have every right to look out for him, and he should have a will naming us if anything unfortunate happens to him."

Eleanora's face paled. Merritt put a stick of gum in his mouth and chewed with frustration.

"Eleanora, Rayne has kept her part of the bargain all these years even after you stopped O'Dare from marrying her," said Merritt. "Xavier was Rayne's son and your grandson." Again, the room stilled. "You know O'Dare dated her before his divorce from Vanessa was finalized. When Dad was your lawyer, he advised O'Dare to keep Xavier's birth a secret. He didn't want to give you another reason to deplete the trust. You hoped O'Dare would learn responsibility if he saw his first family receiving a huge slice of his inheritance, but he never did.

Given his proclivity for women, Dad was protecting you—with your loose permission, of course."

"I was the reason he met Guthrie," said Rayne. "I introduced him to my family. She stole him."

"Xavier was my grandson?" Eleanora's bravado was gone.

Alice felt sorry for everyone. Rayne had a son to O'Dare and Guthrie had not. But Cade stood to inherit the Whipkey fortune while Rayne kept her son's identity hidden from Eleanora. No wonder Xavier grew into fury.

"Did Xavier know O'Dare was his father?" asked Alice.

"Didn't tell him until the family moved to Mitten. O'Dare was sick. Xavier had a right to know who is father was."

"What happened the night Guthrie and Xavier died?" asked Alice feeling troubled.

Merritt raised his eyebrows, signaling to Rayne that she had the floor. Alice held Audrey tighter. Listening to confessions while stuck in an isolated cabin in the woods with two people ready to shoot and a lone motorcyclist coming up the road—never good. But she hoped one cobweb of sticky truth would lead to another.

"I went to see Guthrie," said Rayne. "Nothing was supposed to happen. I told Xav to leave the tire iron behind, but he thought we needed it to scare her into telling Eleanora that he was the older grandson. He had told me how he threatened Cade . . . and Guthrie and Eleanora. Xav said his threats worked. It scared Cade enough that he ran off." A sadness brushed her face before anger took over. "Xavier had a right to O'Dare's estate. For years Cade lived with wealth. It was Xav's turn to inherit." She shot a look at the lawyer. "Roddy stopped sending our payments. We needed that money."

"He was sending you my money?" asked Eleanora.

"Following Dad's plan after you told him to clean up O'Dare's messes."

"Xavier wasn't anyone's mess." Rayne fired up. "You said the payments had to shrink because of processing the paperwork after O'Dare's death."

"So, when I asked you to stop payment on all debts, you already had diminished payments to Rayne?" Eleanora sat taller indignant. Merritt nodded. "Accounts show money went out. Where'd the missing money go if not to Rayne?"

"Sounds to me like you fed Rayne legal bullshit," said Nimble.

"Eleanora, I was looking after your interest. An estate is complicated."

"Everything is in my name. What was so complicated?"

"I only wanted our share. Xavier was O'Dare's son," said Rayne. "He promised me Xavier was in his will. I knew you wouldn't listen to me, but Guthrie knew who Xavier was. I asked her to tell Eleanora."

"Oh man," said Nimble, shaking his head. "Even I know that long-live-the-new-prince speech would make Guthrie crazy even if Xavier was her nephew."

"Rayne, exactly what happened the last time you saw Guthrie?" asked Alice. "Why did you arrive so late at night?"

"I had to wait until Xavier got off work. When we got to the house, Guthrie was drunk, and you're right, crazy. She didn't want Xavier to get anything. Said I wasn't allowed to tell Eleanora about Xav. Pulled a gun on me. Me? Her own sister?"

"She had the revolver ready?" asked Alice more as a statement than question.

"She did."

"Why did she shoot? Did she know about Xav's threats to Cade's life?"

"Look, he didn't mean to hurt anybody. When he spoke to Cade, he was just blowing off steam. You know—older brother to younger brother."

Alice wondered if Rayne really didn't know about the significance of Cade's birth. "Rayne, online he threatened to kill Cade if he didn't disappear. He even threatened Guthrie and Eleanora with a beating two weeks ago if Cade came back."

"Xav would never do that."

"He didn't mean it," said Austin. "It was a joke online. He never would have run anyone down with his bike. Honest."

Eleanora gasped.

"Guthrie was the crazy one," yelled Rayne. "She told us to get out. Insulted me. Me! *I* was supposed to marry O'Dare, not her. Xavier was the firstborn son, not Cade. Xavier told Guthrie Cade wasn't coming back, ever. Said he met with Cade and warned him to get out of his way." Rayne's head fell forward. "But she may have thought Xavier did more than just warn Cade." Rayne swallowed hard, her eyebrows tightening into an angry face, words spilling out. "He wanted his share, that's all. All these years we lived on the crumbs I begged from O'Dare."

"Your string of gents didn't pay the bills?" asked Eleanora.

A scream ripped through the cabin. "Don't push me you old cow. All of this death is on you." Rayne's chin came up defiant as if ready to shoot.

Hoping her voice was soft enough, Alice said, "Guthrie shot Xavier, and he ran out of the house. You struggled to take the gun away," said Alice. "I'm guessing she fought back, and you shot her three times."

"She wouldn't *stop*. She kept fighting. I wanted to follow my son, but she wouldn't stop."

"Rayne, you are a lousy negotiator." Merritt clapped his hands.

"What do you mean?" Rayne wiped away tears from her face with the flat of her hand.

"You admitted murder in front of witnesses."

"Then we get rid of the witnesses," said Austin. Alice thought she saw his hand shake, but his eyes were calculating punishment. Rayne flinched as she looked at her son.

"How did you see this working out?" asked Alice of Rayne. "What was your original plan? After all, Rayne, you may have shot Guthrie, but she brought the gun into the argument. And Austin hasn't really been part of a crime. Right?"

"Not part of a crime?" asked Eleanora. "He's probably the snot that fired at the house and wounded Cade."

Alice wondered if Eleanora was right. Austin was about the right height and the shooter sprinted like a kid.

"Can we all cool our jets?" shouted Nimble. "Nobody is shooting any-body." The quiet man's yelling served to scold the tension in the room.

"Rayne, is it true Austin played no part in the house shooting?" Alice looked at Rayne who sucked in her lips.

"No part. I only wanted to scare Eleanora. Make her feel vulnerable, think about dying, so she'd sign the papers. Hitting Cade was an acci-dent. He walked into *my* line of fire." Rayne's look to Austin was severe.

"One more thing," said Alice, "who first mentioned to you that Eleanora should sign the estate over to Cade?"

Silence followed as Rayne's eyelids lifted in Merritt's direction.

"I can tell you that," said Eleanora. "He did. Merritt began skimming money from my trust as soon as he took over from his father four years ago. I stupidly gave him my power of attorney. I never said anything because, at first, it was a little, and I respected his father too much to accuse his son."

"Eleanora, it was for petty expenses to take care of O'Dare's obliga-tions. Why log in every nickel?"

"I keep track of my money in binders, Roddy. But you know that." Eleanora glared at her lawyer.

"Okay," said Nimble holding up his hand, "for the outsider here, Rayne's been getting money from Eleanora's estate for years, engineered by Daddy Merritt. Son Roddy's been stealing money from Eleanora for at least four years. Then O'Dare dies, and Roddy gets greedy. He cuts off Rayne? That about right?"

"That's right," said Eleanora.

"So why does this guy," his thumb pointed to Merritt, "go with the plan that names Cade the heir?" asked Nimble. "I don't get it."

"Because with Cade named as the heir, Roddy keeps control of the cash," answered Eleanora. "Cade's interested in an education, and he believes I trust my lawyer. If I should die, Roddy would still be in control."

"You hoped to see Xavier named as the heir, didn't you?" asked Alice, making eye contact with Austin's mother. "How does having Cade as the heir help you now?"

Eleanora leaned toward Rayne. "It doesn't help her unless the plan now is to kill him after I sign the papers. She is his aunt and has a claim on his estate."

"Sounds like a smart plan," sneered Merritt.

"Only one problem, Rayne," Eleanora tilted her head in Merritt's direction, "He's a thief. What makes you think he'd ever turn the money over to you?"

"You were *stealing* from her?" asked Rayne. "You're planning to cut me out?"

"Rayne," said Alice. "He used you to kidnap Eleanora. Once she signed the papers, Merritt would have wound you up until you shot her. You'd go to jail for the rest of your life. And I think he could string out the legal settlement of the estate for years. Money goes to his pocket. He never meant to share with anyone. But now, the sticky problem is what to do with Nimble and me. He can't allow us to contradict his story. Will he tell the police you shot all of us? What about Austin? He's a witness too."

Rayne moved closer to her son. "Wait," said Austin. "Ma, what do we do?"

No answer followed. A heavy, blasting growl rattled the cabin.

Austin said, "It's Dad. He'll take out this asshole. Mom, it's Dad."

"Good." Rayne pointed the gun directly at Merritt. "Gaius Eyestone will take care of you. All of you. And Eleanora, Gaius will see to it you sign those papers this time, giving *me* the estate."

Talking stopped as the roar of the engine cut out, but more motorcycles droned in the distance. Both Rayne and Austin looked pleased.

When the door opened, the cabin filled with the acrid smell of exhaust. A tall man with a shaved head and a full beard walked in, a wall of a man dressed in black, heavily tattooed, dripping chains. Alice slipped low to the floor and wrapped Audrey tightly in her arms as the hound's tail whipped with pleasure. The dog wanted to greet the big man. Alice feared what he might do if Audrey's nose hit his crotch. Gaius looked around the room and stunned Alice with his first question.

"Austin, you get that school project done like you said?"

"Most of it."

"The answer is, 'No, sir.'" He walked to his son and took the gun. "No reason for this to come to the attention of the cops. Rayne, I told you in the divorce, not to set foot in my cabin." He looked down at Alice. "Austin do any harm here?"

"He pointed his gun at me," answered Eleanora.

"Then your answer's 'No, sir,'" said the big man. More motorcycles revved engines outside the cabin. "Get your bike, Austin. We're leaving."

"But—" said Austin.

Alice thought the son struggled with torn loyalties.

"What about me?" asked Rayne. "Gaius, none of this is my fault. It's her fault." She pointed to Merritt. "And his fault. Will you listen?"

"I said Austin and me are leaving." His voice was cold. "Anyone asks, we're riding through. The men outside will verify that. You?" His voice announced the verdict. "On your own."

Father and son walked out the door. Tears formed in Rayne's eyes. Alice could almost feel sorry for Rayne as all the bikers rode off.

"It's over," said Alice rising from the floor. "This has been unfortunate, but it doesn't have to go any further. Put the gun down. Let us go."

Rayne's shoulders sagged. "No. I want what is *mine*. Why was I never good enough for O'Dare? Why did you hate me?" Eleanora looked away with nothing to say. "Why did Guthrie have to take everything from me?"

Eleanora's face softened. "He'd have made you as miserable as he made Guthrie. I coddled O'Dare too much as a child because he was my son, but I knew what he was. Charming but empty. He always had the commitment of a feather in the wind. He believed he was entitled, and therefore, wanted to live without consequences. I stupidly protected him."

They heard a chorus of Harley-Davidsons approaching, pistons firing unevenly in the distinct growl. Merritt grabbed Rayne's gun and held it on the three women and Nimble.

"Gaius is coming back," said Rayne. "Just wait." She stood like a sentry. Alice's stomach knotted.

"Don't even think about getting out of this," said Eleanora to Merritt. "I have proof of what you did."

"You think you do, but I know a battery of lawyers and accountants to prove your homemade ledgers with sticky yellow Post-it notes are wrong. Oh, and look. I seem to have the gun. So good luck."

Alice pictured that first day of the police investigation with Merritt spending hours in the house. She guessed he searched Eleanora's office. Perhaps he removed evidence or perhaps he dropped notes to the floor not bothering to hide his intrusion. Let her wonder what was missing.

"Did you reload the gun after the shooting at the house?" demanded Alice of Rayne.

"Gaius took that gun." Guilt crept into her tone.

"Mr. Merritt, if the gun you're holding is the one that shot Guthrie, the bullets are for target practice." Alice stood at an angle, reasoning that if he shot, there was less of a chance he'd hit something vital. In her fist, she gripped Audrey's harness, wedging her thigh in front of the dog's face. "One shot for Xavier. Rayne took three shots to put down her sister. That means only two shots are left." She hoped she was correct. Her knowledge of revolvers came from watching cowboy films as a child.

"I figure a bullet still makes a hole," said Merritt, but his grip loosened on the gun.

Nimble stood facing Merritt and held out his hand. "I'll take the gun. You said it yourself. Eleanora can't hurt you. No reason to make a stand before Gaius's bikers enter."

Merritt held his position long enough for two men to walk into the room.

"Mrs. Tricklebank, sorry for our delay," said Steve, owner of the Hungry Fool. "We left the bar as soon as we received Lena's call. She said you needed a posse." His big grin triggered Audrey's tail to wag as she leaned toward him. "None of us have ever been in a posse."

Nimble took control of the gun in Merritt's hand and with his elbow popped the lawyer below his ribs, causing him to double over.

"A call from Lena?" asked Alice. She felt confused. *Why'd Lena call the Hungry Fool?* "Are you sure?"

"Of course, it was ME!" said Lena as she swept into the cabin and threw her arms around Alice. "I called because I had the business card Steve gave me in case I wanted a job, and when Julian called the police again, we stumbled around explaining where you went. And the detective insisted on checking with the hospital first because he thought Cade was a suspect in his mother's murder. AND, that nice policewoman said they needed special vehicles if they wanted to go up Hill Road. I think she called the state police. SO, with all the delays, I called Steve. They have a ton of special vehicles. Motorcycles! See my wild hunches do pay off."

Alice clutched her best friend a little harder in another hug, relishing the blessing of Lena's grab-bag problem solving. Lena was all wind-whipped blonde curls and pink ruffles, the fabric revealing her soft midriff rolls. *At least*, thought Alice, *she had the good sense to wear blue jeans for riding the back of a motorcycle.*

"Bunch of us were at the bar," said the older tall guy who'd stared at Alice while she was at the Hungry Fool for Lena's show. "Gaius is a Saturday regular. Never comes into the Fool during the week, but he'd just heard about Xavier and had questions. He knew his son sometimes hangs out in the parking lot, waiting for his half-brother to get off work. He received a text from his kid and hightailed it out, railing about his ex-wife, Xavier, and Austin."

"About then, I called, Steve," said Lena.

The bar owner grinned and picked up the story.

"And Shango here mentioned Gaius had a cabin." His grin grew impossibly bigger. "Whole bar saddled up in case you needed help. No one wanted to be left out of a rumble. 'Course everyone outside is older than dirt," said Steve. "We knew we needed to make noise, come in hot if we were taking on Gaius's crew. The cops are three minutes behind us."

Shango edged closer to Alice. In a soft voice, he whispered, "I don't got a lot of words. My nephew told me what you and your dog did. This one's payback for helping to find Kiley."

Alice nodded once and held her dog's leash tighter, remembering Audrey and the lost girl who wanted the bunnies to come to dinner.

Nimble put the only gun in the room in his pocket and untied Eleanora. Rayne sat at the table, weeping. The lawyer with no socks leaned the back of his head against the wall.

Slinking into the cabin with his hands in his pockets was Julian. The retired truck driver didn't look pleased with the drama of riding a motorcycle up the hill. The bandana covering his thinning hair was askew.

"See, Love Muffin, I saved the day," said Lena. She poked her head out the door and waved like the Queen of England. Lena then cocked her hip, and with a suggestive stance, knocked on the door three times. All the engines revved three times in ear-splitting growls that shook the cabin.

Before helping Eleanora into the car for the long ride down the east side of the hill, Alice asked, "I wondered why you didn't name Cade as your heir right after your son died. Did Sunny tell you what she knew?"

The older woman gave a sad smile. "Hours after she told Cade. In her own way, Sunny is a good friend. I should have confronted my grandson right away, put all this family doubt to rest, but I never imagined he'd take it this hard or that Xavier had threatened terrible things. I thought it better to let things be. I knew Xavier was Rayne's child, but didn't know he was O'Dare's. We all have too many dangerous secrets."

Chapter 37

Time: Saturday, 4:47 p.m.

"We aren't done yet," said Eleanora as she watched the police car and Detective Galati drive down the vineyard's winding driveway to the road. "The police have Rayne in custody for murder and kidnapping. They finally acknowledge that Cade has no connection to his mother's murder." She turned away from the windows to stare at her grandson. "Why did you leave me?"

Alice, Lena, and Julian watched Eleanora force the confrontation with the truth.

"I'm sorry, Nana. I needed to be on my own. You know, vineyard work." His left hand went to his right arm in a sling as his nostrils flared. He didn't make eye contact although he stood tall and defiant.

"That's only partially true," challenged Eleanora. "You don't want to mention the DNA test?"

Wham! Thought Alice. *Time for the nitty-gritty.*

Cade's face paled as his lips compressed. His eyes met hers. A sideward glance seemed to say he measured whether to run. "Nana—"

"You've been my grandson for twenty years. Getting out of it isn't so easy, Mister. Who taught you to juggle?"

"You did." His voice was soft like a guilty child's.

"Would you know how to count cards or win at black jack if it weren't for me?"

"No." A tiny smile formed on his lips.

"Have you forgotten backyard practice learning the classic Danny Thomas Spit-Take?" She faced the others in the room. "The boy sprays spit with the best of them. Perfect reaction timing. That comes with all those hours we watched taped television shows from the 1950s. Who taught you to identify grapes?"

Cade's eyes widened with surprise. "Nana, Nimble did that."

"Keeping you on your toes. Testing if you're listening. Cade, this is your home. Whether you like it or not, I've always been your grand-mother. Everyone here will tell you we love others even if we don't share their blood. Family is greater than simple ties. It's years of choice. I *choose* you, Cade Huff, as my grandson."

Cade's eyes closed, and his face wrinkled. For a moment, he strug-gled with what to say. Audrey walked next to him, positioning her head under his hand. He looked down at the dog, moved his fingers into her fur, and said in a small voice, "Nana, I didn't want to disap-point you."

"Well, this has taught me a lesson," said Eleanora to the group, her voice becoming loud. "Next week my grandson and I meet with a *new* lawyer to draft new paperwork for what to do with this life-destroying Whipkey money we're saddled with."

"Nana, I don't want it. Really."

"Good, because you're not inheriting it. I'm setting up a founda-tion. Cade, when you turn thirty, you'll be one of two administrators for the funds and receive a salary. Until then, I've asked someone who has my confidence to help me guard against vultures who want the loot."

Lena's mouth opened as her eyes grew bigger. She grabbed Alice's hand.

"No, Lena, I'm not thinking of you or Alice," said Eleanora.

"Despite me being kidnapped and threatened with death in the cabin, I barely know you two. No, I'm asking Elka to monitor and help me distribute money to charities until Cade takes over. My bones are not as young as they used to be, but I want to play with children again. See my great-granddaughters. You, my grandson, will receive the title to this house and the vineyard."

"You mean now?"

"Of course, now. Things are going to change. You like making wine? Now you've got a vineyard." Eleanora's chin came down with finality.

Cade's body visibly relaxed, but a sly smile crossed his lips. "If I get the house, where are you going to live, Nana?"

"Cheeky! My own grandmother would say, 'This boy's plain cheeky.' Wonder where you get that attitude?"

"From you, Nana." Cade's cheeks rose with a huge smile as he stepped forward to give his grandmother an enveloping hug.

"You got that right," said Eleanora. "You betcha."

Eleanora let out a howl of a laugh, which set off Audrey, whose head tilted back, throat opened, and baritone baying filled the room.

"Come on," said Eleanora. "Everyone, grab some water. To the backyard. We're all practicing a spit-take. Got an idea this one here's got talent." The back of Eleanora's hand swatted Julian's chest.

He rolled his eyes as he sought out Lena. Alice thought she heard him say "Lordy."

Chapter 38

After dinner Alice and Lena sat on the front porch and watched the setting sun gild trees and grape leaves. Audrey lay belly down, eyes closed. Julian, a beer drinker, joined Nimble at the table on the side of the house and puzzled through a wine lesson.

"I like tidy endings," said Lena. "So many of our cases end with things undone."

"Like what?"

"Cade has no one to tell him about his biological father."

"He may learn about him if he chooses. Guthrie told me she gave a picture to her parents of the young man she almost married. In his own time, Cade may contact his other grandparents."

"Good. He has a path. Then, I wish Eleanora had coughed up more information about her past," said Lena. "Her spongy explanations bothered me. Also, I couldn't find any record that she ever married. Julian's taken to calling her *the dowager empress*."

"Time to let the mystery go. We all have secrets. And I think she's right. Everybody wears a mask."

"Not me!"

"Of course, not you. Especially not you." Alice grinned and raised one eyebrow.

"I handle kerfuffles and snafus differently than most people," said Lena.

Lena turned her attention to the sunset, Alice, to her dog's ears.

Here we are in a beautiful setting, with colors and geometrical lines tamping down anxiety. Or masking future dread . . . like being on time for Henry's graduation, thought Alice. *Wonder if Breakiron made it to Mitten's Knack and Kraut? A shame if her family missed it.*

"I'm tired, but I don't think I can sleep tonight," said Lena.

"Me either. Out here on the porch, things feel different," said Alice.

"How?"

Alice pushed up the sleeves of her pull-over. "When Baer died, I didn't want my children feeling burdened. You and I have friends who take advantage of their children. I didn't want mine to think they needed to hover. You know, *whatever will we do with Mom?* Even though we're in our sixties, I don't feel old. What about you?"

"Me either," said Lena. "Wise through experience, that's me, but certainly not old."

"Jess asked me if I want to move in with them."

"Not for another fifteen or twenty years, I hope. What is she thinking? You and I have many murders yet to solve. We'll include Julian, of course."

Alice smiled at her best friend, not wanting to see her own future filled with dead people. "Lena, what I'm getting at is . . . what I have to admit . . . I miss my children and grandchildren. I know my life will go on as before in Limekiln, but now the Midwest seems lonelier. Does this make sense?"

"You'll have Henry this summer. And us for a while. I meant to tell you, Julian and I are leaving together this summer to visit his daughter and my sons. The ol' stinker and I have finally set a date for the wedding. Before Halloween." With a glint in her eye and a proud smile, Lena added, "Wearing white hasn't exactly proved successful for my first four marriages. Will I look good in a black pointy hat?"

"You'll have flair. If not white, how about a nice Halloween apricot?"

"Apricot? Too tame. I want fiery sparkles, maybe on a dark burnt sienna background. Just a reminder, you're wearing a dress." Lena's voice was merry. "Matrons of honor usually do."

"You're visualizing something poufy?"

"Yards of chiffon? Spiky, platform heels making you six-foot-six. Think of the drama," teased Lena.

"I'm thinking Audrey will cause me to fall on my face if I do."

"At least tell me you're glamming up for Henry's graduation."

Alice felt a chill curl around her spine. Be *there on-time.* "I bought a new pair of flats. Patent leather."

"Whoop-de-do! You're becoming a wild woman, Alice Tricklebank," said Lena, her tone snide.

Alice's thoughts of the future washed over her listening. Burnished golds darkened in the vineyards, and purple shadows increased. The two women watched the streaks of color blend and deepen.

"It's glorious," said Lena.

"Our very own crayon box."

"Alice," Lena said, her voice softening. "When I came into the hilltop cabin, why did you have Audrey entrapped in your arms? Did you think she might attack?"

"Not attack. Rayne's ex-husband was huge and scary. I was afraid of what he might do to Audrey if her nose became too curious."

"Good move. Not everyone likes slobber."

"I worry for her. Audrey has a particular attraction to big men." Alice paused because she didn't want to share her notion that Audrey had a spiritual connection to Baer. Instead, she said, "I think when Audrey was still a puppy there was a big man who was kind to her. Now when she sees someone big, she wants to reclaim that love."

"She knows we're talking about her."

Audrey's head was off the floor, tongue lolling out the side of her mouth in a classic ha-ha-ha face.

"Tomorrow Julian and I will leave at the crack of dawn for Disneyland. I've never been, and Julian has promised roller-coaster rides, although he hates them."

"Henry's graduation is tomorrow. I've been watching the clock since we arrived. Tick, tick, tick. Jess wants me there at twelve-thirty on the dot. In a couple of days, we leave for home. I told you Eleanora gave me her Lincoln?"

"Big boat of a car."

"Old enough to cause some fear of finishing the trip, but big enough to hold Audrey's stuff and Henry's."

"I know I can be silly, but Alice, I worry about you," said Lena as she squeezed her friend's hand. "Where is your stuff in this life?"

"I have Audrey. We live in Limekiln. Everything is good. Now if I can convince Juliana to take down the website she created *and* if I can be at graduation on time, all is clear sailing."

"You deserve an uncomplicated day."

"It will begin at 12:30 p.m. tomorrow." Alice glanced at her watch.

They squeezed each other's hand and watched the sun disappear into stripes of purple.

Chapter 39

Time: Sunday, 9:32 a.m.

"Audrey, where are the keys?" Alice's heart pounded. "Sweetie, not today. Today is Henry's graduation. Keys!"

No demand moved Audrey to retrieve the keys from a hiding place. Alice went to her small purse and dumped the contents. No keys. She repeated the action with the backpack, opening all the zippered compartments. She remembered putting the keys on the table. Moving flat placemats and checking under the table didn't produce the overlooked keys.

"Please, Audrey. Keys?"

Audrey went belly down and crossed her paws. Her tongue hung out of her mouth as if she were laughing. *Ha-ha-ha.*

"Okay, I acknowledge you're the best nose in the world, and I promise never to forget your favorite toy. Please? Find."

The hound continued to look at her owner with loving eyes, then jumped off the bed and dragged the deflated kiddie pool Alice had packed to the center of the room. Her eyes were filled with expectation.

"Oh, sweetie, we don't have time for bopping ice cubes in the pool." At home, Audrey enjoyed several minutes bouncing cubes with a tentative paw before rolling into the icy water.

"We have a long drive. That's why I want to leave early." Alice was now a madwoman, pulling covers from the bed and shaking them, lifting pillows, giving each a plump chop to see if keys dropped to the floor. Bathroom tub and behind the bathroom door—no. Closet—nope. Under furniture—nada. Picturing Audrey's paws on the kitchen sink, Alice removed the stopper and probed the drain. "Yuck. All that and no keys."

With loving, innocent eyes, the bloodhound swiped away a cord of slobber by licking her own nose.

"Audrey! I need the keys." Alice was in tears. "Please don't make me leave you alone."

The hound sat and watched Alice's every move. In desperation, Alice grabbed a paper towel and left the dog in the cottage as she ran to the rental car and rubbed the steering column near the ignition. Running back, she found Audrey barking so hard her front feet left the floor.

"Shhh. It's okay. I'm back. Shhh." She wrapped her arms around Audrey. "Shhh. I'm sorry. I know you don't like to be alone. Please, Audrey, find!" She pushed the paper towel to Audrey's nose and imagined her dog said, *Oh, that.*

The hound swaggered toward the window and stood on her hind legs, bracing herself against the wall before barking. Practically tearing curtains from the rod, Alice whipped the fabric aside. On the sill—keys!

Alice grabbed her dog and backpack of supplies and ran to the rental car. Audrey stopped dead for a quick squat-down. Alice's heart began to beat faster, and she felt a pain in her throat. After the dog was ready to move, Elka came out of the house, and Audrey again stopped. *She's probably expecting a treat*, thought Alice.

"Mrs. Alice, you should be on road half hour ago. You late. Is Sunday. Much traffic." She slipped a treat to the dog. It only took a moment for Audrey to crunch the treat and swallow, but Alice heard a clock ticking.

"Can't stop to explain. Wish me luck."

Audrey took her time jumping into the passenger seat, and Alice fumbled with hooking the tether to the dog's harness.

"You are so smart-looking," she said, hoping the throbbing pulse in her neck wasn't visible. Audrey was outfitted for Henry's ceremonial day. Breakiron had given the hound a new police-issued harness with thick, padded leather straps. Galati had even presented the dog with an honorary badge from the county. "Audrey," said Alice admiring her dog. "You're a bad-ass."

Driving down the twisting driveway and feeling sweaty, Alice checked her own attire. In her mind she heard Lena say, "Are these the only colors you own? Black slacks, a gray top and jacket? Really?"

"Gray matches my hair," said Alice aloud to Audrey. "The jacket has four pockets for dog treats and folded paper toweling." Audrey's eyes seemed to approve.

Turning the car onto the road, Alice ran her hand through her tangled, short curls. "Here, we go."

Almost instantly as she joined the highway south, the traffic clogged. A car was pulled over for a ticket, and naturally, today of all days, people needed to slow down to watch the man's discomfort as he tapped the steering wheel with his fingertips.

"You think that guy was speeding?" Alice's voice was tight with fear. "I don't even want to think what Jess will do if we don't make it. She might rescind her permission for Henry to visit this summer. Oh, Audrey. What will I do?"

Cars continued to creep along. Trucks rumbled in idle. Motorcycles wove through traffic. The car grew warm. Audrey, restless.

Alice checked the clock. She estimated she was still an hour out. The clock blinked 10:45 a.m.

"We don't have to be seated until twelve-thirty. We still have plenty of time."

When traffic halted, Alice texted Jess, who texted back. *Where are you?* Alice had no chance to reply. Cars moved, and her foot became heavier. Cut left. Cut right. Audrey barked at being jostled. A cord of slobber stuck to the dash.

"Sorry, sweetie." Her eye caught 11:23. "At least now we're making time."

Her phone pinged as the traffic slowed. Construction cut a lane. Jess wrote: *Walking from the parking lot into the stadium with Baba and Jiji. At least they woke early this morning. Where are you? Jiji has his camera. We were hoping for family pictures.*

"Can't answer that yet," said Alice aloud, aware of Jess's implied zing of criticism. The other grandparents efficiently got up early, wisely left the house early, were ready for photographs early. Alice swallowed her fear.

Finally, Alice left the highway at twelve-ten. When she drove past the football field set up like a stadium, she saw barricades blocking the entrance of the parking lot. Alice swept down a side street, in a panic for parking. Several blocks away, she found a spot. Gathering her backpack and Audrey, she took off at a dead run. Audrey loped beside her, but by the time Alice arrived at the gate, feeling hot and sweaty, the entrance was locked. Her watch read 12:35. Music played on the field.

Alice called to a short guy in a suit, standing by the bleachers. After a quick explanation and an urgent plea, he said, "Well . . . I don't know."

"The music has started. Please. I have to see my grandson graduate."

"I'll have to talk to . . . Um. I believe he's already on the stage."

"Please!" Her heart was hammering. She had already missed pictures. Jess would never forgive her if she missed the ceremony. And Henry's disappointment—too crushing for words. Alice felt dizzy and sick.

A police officer came forward. "I'll handle this." The little man in a suit gratefully relinquished authority.

"Come with me," said the officer as he opened the gate and firmly took Alice's elbow.

Alice blabbered details about her grandson, no ticket for her, Henry's fib about epilepsy, owning a bloodhound with separation anxiety, and being caught up in a murder, kidnapping, and a scary motorcycle guy. "Oh, and California traffic."

The officer stopped. "A murder?"

"Two," Alice corrected shyly. "Please, can I just stand in the back and watch my grandson?"

He gave her a superior grin. "No."

The police officer escorted her behind the length of the bleachers, and there at the end of the bleachers was a firetruck and an ambulance aligned with the stage.

"Alice," said the officer, "Detective Galati called the department and asked us to give you the best seat in the house." With that he directed her toward the firetruck. "You're up there in the driver's seat. The dog can join you. Travis will give your dog a boost."

A paramedic came forward, picked up the hundred-pound dog with ease, and hoisted her onto the passenger seat. All the paramedics and firefighters grinned as Alice climbed into the driver's seat of the truck.

Alice felt confused. How had Galati known she needed help? It took a moment to remember Elka's concern. "She probably bullied him into helping," whispered Alice feeling immense gratitude.

The graduation ceremony had begun with the entrance of the graduates. Alice thought to protest this gift, but the seat had the best view, and Henry's height and beard made him stand out among all the others also gowned in blue.

Tears collected in her eyes as she watched the ceremony. She looked forward to spending a whole summer of building memories.

"Henry William Okazaki."

As Henry walked across the stage, head high, he collected his diploma with dignity and shook hands with the principal. Grandpa Jiji knelt with his camera to record this memory.

"Hit the horn," came a voice. "Not in keeping with regulations, but you want him to know you're here."

When Henry walked toward the stairs to descend, Alice blasted the firetruck horn. Her grandson looked up, startled, and became the ten-year-old Alice remembered. Holding up his diploma in victory, he jumped the last three steps from the stage and kicked his heels together, just the way Grandpa Baer had taught him.

"Baer, I want an easy trip back in that old Lincoln," whispered Alice. "Your grandson is coming home for the summer, so no dead bodies. Can you please make that happen?"

Audrey looked at Alice quizzically and sneezed, sending dog snot splat against the window of the firetruck.

"I know what you're thinking," said Alice, running her hand over Audrey's velvety ears. "Fat chance. But a grandma can dream."

Acknowledgments

This was a rich year for friendships both old and new. Thank you!

Bloodhound owners, handlers, and trainers. Thank you, Cindy for allowing me to go on a walk with Merle. Thanks, Pat for phone questions and sharing stories. Thank you, Aldo and Bloodhounds West Northern Chapter for Bonckers Newsletter. So many stories and lovely pictures of magnificent dogs.

Ed at Regusci Winery, for answering my questions about bloodhounds romping through vineyards and for sharing personal experiences. Rombauer Winery for clarifying the role of owls. Marilyn at the Inn at Occidental who gave information about California small towns.

Rachel, my editor, who worked through the holidays to ready the mystery for corrections.

Long-time friends Nancy, Barb, Carolyn, Peg, Carol, Rich, Karen, Dave, Diane, Joyce, Paul, Linda, and Charlotte, for encouragement, support, and suggestions over coffee.

Thank you, Tom, for spit-take lessons.

The Barrington Writers Workshop members who ask spot-on questions, offer suggestions, and encourage my efforts.

Chicago Writers Association for posting publicity suggestions and offering support.

And always Al who shuttles me to book fairs, takes pictures, reads copy, rereads copy, and understands that messy stacks of paper lying about the house are probably important to me. I'm sure he scratches his head at my bursts of writing during the middle of the night or sudden need to do research. Yes, we went to an RV show. A bump on his head from a low door didn't deter him from offering suggestions for Alice and her posse.

Even with readers, editors, and helpful emails from friends, errors always seem to elbow their way into the mystery. All these nuisances are mine. Such a bother.

CPSIA information can be obtained
at www.ICGtesting.com
Printed in the USA
LVOW13*0517290518
578704LV00002B/10/P